The House *on*
Rockaway
Beach

The House on Rockaway Beach

EMMA BURSTALL

HEAD of ZEUS

An Aria Book

First published in the UK in 2022 by Head of Zeus
This paperback first published in 2023 by Head of Zeus,
part of Bloomsbury Publishing Plc

9 7 5 3 1 2 4 6 8

A catalogue record for this book is available from
the British Library.

ISBN (PB): 9781786698919
ISBN (E): 9781786698896

Typeset by Divaddict Publishing Solutions

Printed and bound in Great Britain by
CPI Group (UK) Ltd, Croydon CR0 4YY

Head of Zeus Ltd
5–8 Hardwick Street
London EC1R 4RG
WWW.HEADOFZEUS.COM

To Mike Gray, fly fisherman extraordinaire

'The cure for anything is salt water: sweat, tears, or the sea.'

Isak Dinesen

Prologue

In her dreams, she'd often return to Rockaway. She'd find herself walking along the wide, open beach with the warm sand beneath her feet, watching the Atlantic waves crash and roll.

Or she'd be back in her grandmother's quaint old house, testing the wooden floorboards to see which ones creaked, or hiding in the lookout tower, where she felt like a seagull, alone and free.

Sophie knew every nook and cranny of the place, every strange quirk, like the pantry door that wouldn't quite shut, and the hollow benches beneath the windows with lids that opened, so you could conceal your precious things inside. She could even smell her grandmother's cherry pie, baking in the oven.

Sometimes, while asleep, she'd fall downstairs or tumble off the swing bench in the porch and hurt herself.

'Pampy,' she'd shout, for that was the silly name they called her grandmother, and Pampy would come running.

She gave the best hugs. 'There's no shortage of cuddles in this house,' she'd say in her soft American accent, pressing Sophie to her bosom. And as if like magic, the hurt would go away.

Sophie never wanted to wake up and when she did, she'd cry. Rockaway was far away and she hadn't been for so long. It seemed to have existed in another life.

She wished she could stop having these dreams because they made her sad, but they kept on coming back, night after night, each one seemingly more vivid than the last.

It was almost as if they were trying to tell her something.

One

Sophie glanced at her sister, sitting beside her in the back of the taxi, and wondered why they'd always disliked each other.

The fact they hadn't met since their mother's funeral five years ago, and hardly at all for the twenty-odd years before that, didn't seem to matter. Time melted away and though Celia had undoubtedly aged since their last meeting, she still had the same wide, high forehead that made her look babyish and haughty at the same time, the small, upturned nose everyone except Sophie deemed cute, and the narrow mouth with its V-shaped bow and tucked in edges that curled into a simpering little smile.

Sophie crossed her arms over her chest and looked away quickly, while Celia's small chin remained raised, her eyes resting firmly on the road ahead.

There must have been occasions, Sophie thought, gazing out of the window once more, when as little ones they'd 'played nicely together', but she honestly couldn't recall any.

3

Her most abiding memories were of nasty scraps when they'd scratch, pinch and pull each other's hair. Celia would end up sobbing, even if she had the lesser injuries, and Sophie would try to calm her down before their parents heard.

Later, as teenagers, they'd take it in turns to steal each other's clothes and make-up. The rows were ferocious. No matter who started the argument, however, Sophie always seemed to get the blame. Why? The corners of her eyes stung and she bit her lip to stop tears coming.

The sisters had hardly exchanged more than three words since they'd met, as arranged, by the Arrivals barrier at John F. Kennedy airport in New York City. Now, as they whizzed along Belt Parkway, a formidable, six-lane highway circling the boroughs of Brooklyn and Queens, Celia cleared her throat and asked after Layla, Sophie's twenty-one-year-old daughter.

Celia was just making small talk; she wasn't really interested in her niece and hadn't seen Layla since she was a child of eleven with sticky-out front teeth, long since straightened, and ginger hair, currently dyed pink. They probably wouldn't even recognise each other now.

'She's fine,' Sophie replied, still staring out of the window. She wasn't going to pander to her sister. 'Really well.'

'Good,' said Celia, before falling silent again.

Soon they were heading down Flatbush Avenue prior to crossing the giant, steel bridge connecting mainland Queens to the Rockaway peninsula. This was a thin strip of land rimmed by golden beaches, with long fingers stretching far out into the roaring Atlantic Ocean.

Once they left the bridge and entered the peninsula itself, the scenery changed from a broad, multi-lane highway, where the car was most definitely king, to much narrower avenues with cycle lanes and sidewalks and timber-clad houses of different shapes and sizes.

Tanned folk in colourful shorts and T-shirts were out and about, walking their dogs or chatting lazily on street corners. There was a laid-back, seaside feel and even in the air-conditioned car, Sophie could sense herself breathe more easily, as if the very atmosphere were lighter here.

Her head turned this way and that as she stared eagerly at the green parkland on one side and then the homes, with their patches of small front garden, on the other. For a few minutes, she almost forgot about Celia. The place felt familiar yet strange, too, as if she'd known it in a different life.

She supposed it *was* different then, seen through her child's eyes when she still fizzed with wonder and excitement. Now, with her middle-aged vision, she noticed not just the bright colours of people's clothes and the blue sky overhead, but also the weeds sprouting through pavestones and the odd broken fence and overflowing garbage bin.

Had the place always had its grungy side? She supposed so, but back then she'd thought it quite perfect.

The vibe changed again as the taxi rounded the corner into a wide, tree-lined street flanked by grand, detached houses with front porches, pillars and fancy gable roofs. Sophie wound down the window and stuck out her head, wanting to take it all in.

'Be careful, lady,' barked the driver in a New York

accent. He hadn't smiled once on the journey. 'You could get yourself killed.'

There was no danger of that, but she drew back in just a little to appease him.

They were in a cul-de-sac. At the very end, a grey concrete sea wall, with an opening in the middle, protected residents from the beach and the ocean.

Here, Sophie could detect no hint of dirt or decay. Lawns were deep green and carefully trimmed, while garden borders were filled with thick seagrass, lusty-looking Montauk daisies and blousy pink, purple or blue hydrangeas.

Sprinklers made a comforting tsk-tsk sound as they squirted out bobbled jets of crystal clear water, and American flags hung proudly on poles outside front doors, or suspended from attic windows.

On every driveway, swanky cars glittered in the sunshine: a shiny Cadillac here, a convertible Porsche or Chevrolet there, and sometimes a humdrum Honda, probably belonging to a child or housekeeper.

A grassy island in the middle of the road divided the traffic, but there was none today. In fact hardly anyone was about, just a few workmen in back-to-front baseball caps and dirty white vests clinging to their bodies with sweat. They were mixing concrete on the pavement and dumping it in buckets, ready to carry it through an open side gate into the backyard.

When they were about two-thirds of the way along the road, Sophie let out a whoop; she couldn't help it.

'It's there! Look! Piping Plover House! Oh my God! It's exactly as I remember it!'

Leaning out further, with her elbows resting on the window ledge, she spotted a tall, imposing house at the very end of the left-hand row. It was set just a few metres back from the sea wall, beyond which were the golden beach and glinting ocean.

The house was painted dove grey, with white gables and window frames. It also had a grassy garden sloping down to meet the scorched pavement.

While all the other homes were smart and well cared for, however, the paintwork on Piping Plover House was cracked and peeling and the grass had grown so high it was like a meadow, a haven for butterflies and bees.

What's more, perched rather unsteadily on the main roof was a peculiar rectangular brick tower. Listing slightly to one side, it had windows running all the way round and appeared to have been cobbled together some time after the main construction.

On the very top was an unusual weathervane – a large, plump bird with long thin legs and a stout bill. Its paint had worn off and the metal had rusted to an orangey grey.

'The lookout!' Sophie shrieked again, pointing to the wonky tower. 'With the piping plover on top!'

Celia merely grunted.

Sophie's skin prickled with irritation and before she could stop herself, she swung round to face her sister.

'Aren't you even a little bit pleased to see it? You *must* be.'

Celia pursed her lips and shrugged.

'God, you're a misery,' said Sophie, her eyes narrowing. 'Nothing's changed.'

Her body tensed, as if anticipating a punch, but Celia wouldn't stoop to such levels now. Instead, she gave one of her smug little smiles.

'Wait and see,' she said, smoothing down the front of her pale pink cotton shirt. 'It's going to be horrendous inside. You won't be so enthusiastic when you realise how much work we've got to do.'

Sophie could feel her excitement dribble away and her shoulders sagged. A lump formed in her throat and she swallowed, wanting to cry. She wouldn't, though. Not now. Not in front of Celia.

The car came to a halt right outside the house and the sisters were hit by a wall of heat which made their lungs hurt. Sophie pushed some strands of thick yellowy-red hair off her forehead and clambered out, noticing how the flight had made her bare ankles swell. She could feel the sweat starting to prickle in her armpits and on the back of her neck.

Thrusting a hand into her tan hemp bag, she pulled out her red purse and was about to pay the taxi driver when Celia stopped her.

'I'll split it with you,' she said, producing her own purse and delving inside for some notes.

Her brown eyes met Sophie's, pale and blue-grey, like seawater.

'We'll split *everything* down the middle. Then there'll be no room for misunderstandings.'

Sophie flinched. It was sensible, of course, but even so, she couldn't help feeling offended. Perhaps Celia, with her fat bank balance, suspected her poorer older sister might try to take advantage.

But when Sophie turned towards the house once more, her excitement returned. The place seemed to be beckoning her in, its darkened windows hinting at hidden mysteries.

Her heart started to pitter-patter as she carried her suitcase, as if it weighed nothing, up the flight of splintered wooden stairs towards the front door. She could hear Celia close behind, making heavy work of bumping her bag up each step, pausing every now and again to draw breath. You'd think she'd got rocks in there instead of clothes.

Once on the timber porch, Sophie scanned around and felt the blood whoosh to her pale cheeks.

'The swing! I can't believe it's still there!'

Plonking down her suitcase, she hurried towards the wooden chair at the other end of the porch. Just big enough for two, it was suspended from the ceiling by lengths of thick, fraying rope.

It was a bright, hot day at the end of July and there was no wind, so the chair was quite still, just waiting, it seemed, for someone to set it in motion.

The cushions had long since gone, but this didn't bother Sophie. She settled onto the hard, slatted seat and pushed herself off.

Leaning back, she closed her eyes for a few minutes and allowed herself to savour the delicious swaying sensation she remembered so well from childhood.

A warm breeze brushed against her cheeks and ruffled her hair. She pushed again, harder this time, and it seemed as if she might take off at any minute and fly up, up into the clouds to join the swooping seagulls.

'Come on, let's go in.'

Celia's thin, reedy voice dragged Sophie back to the present. Reluctantly, she stopped the swing while her sister rootled in her smart white leather handbag and fished out a key.

Together they walked towards the front door, which was painted royal blue, although the paint was cracked and peeling.

Celia slotted the key into the brass lock, which had acquired a greenish tinge through age, and the door swung open, taking with it a section of rotten wood, which fell to the ground. Anyone could have come along and shoved their way in; the place wasn't exactly secure.

'Poo!' said Celia, stepping inside. 'Disgusting. I knew it.'

But Sophie scarcely heard. As soon as she entered the front room, it was as if the years folded together like a concertina and she was a little girl again, gazing in awe at the dark brown wood-panelled walls, which seemed to stretch up for miles before meeting the ceiling.

The floor was wood, too, and on the right, a heavy wooden staircase with thick, ornately carved banisters led to the first floor.

To the left was a big brick fireplace. It was empty, but the blackened flue suggested it had once been much in use.

The faded, floral curtains were partially closed, but through slim gaps you could spy the glass panes behind, smeared with such thick, salty sea spray you could hardly see through.

Beneath each window was a built-in bench seat. The cushions were made of the same shabby fabric as the curtains and frilly pelmets. They must once have been white with little pink flowers, but had now turned yellow. Most of the colour had leeched out of the pink, too, and there were rips, with bits of stuffing poking out.

Sophie was too busy surveying the room to notice, however. She was taking in the squashy beige sofa she'd used both as a trampoline and a place on which to snuggle up and fall sleep.

The old wooden rocker was still there, too, with the ceramic crucifix on the wall behind, and she could still picture her grandmother on the chair, inviting one or other of her small granddaughters to climb on her comfortable knees, sometimes both at the same time.

Beneath the battered white piano was the square wicker basket, filled with moth-eaten blankets which they'd covered their legs with on chilly nights. And above Sophie's head was the funny bamboo lampshade, shaped like a teardrop, which she'd imagined was a bird's nest.

A coating of dust covered all the surfaces and spiders' webs dangled from the ceiling corners. Sophie quite liked them but Celia shuddered.

'We can't stay here,' she said firmly. 'We'll have to find a hotel.'

Sophie frowned. She knew the kind of place her sister meant: somewhere costly, preferably with a spa.

'We'll be all right here,' she insisted. 'We can clean the bedrooms and I've packed fresh sheets for us both.'

Celia's brow wrinkled like fingertips after a long bath.

'It'll be much better,' Sophie persisted. 'We'll be able to start work first thing in the morning.'

'OK. But we've got to clear out the whole lot in two weeks. After that, I'm off. If we haven't finished, you're on your own.'

Sophie stepped across the room to pull back some dusty curtains. Afternoon light entered the room and now she could clearly see the intricate, framed sampler hanging on the wall.

There were plenty of other pictures and photographs dotted around – many with a religious theme – but this one seemed to act like a magnet, drawing her in.

It was a surprisingly accurate representation of Piping Plover House in a previous era, when it was as neat and well maintained as its neighbours. The picture was surrounded by a decorative border, and Sophie could still recall her grandmother, Pampy, taking it down to show her.

Pampy had designed and embroidered the sampler herself and you could just about make out her real name – Orla O'Brien – and the date – September 1966 – in small, neat stitches in the corner.

'She loved this place so much,' Sophie said with a sigh, noticing the weather vane, oh so carefully embroidered in white, grey and orange; the picture-postcard front garden with its low, clipped hedges and freshly mown lawn, and the doll-like flowerpots filled with pink and blue blooms.

'No wonder we adored it here,' she went on, spotting the funny little white cat, poking its head around the corner of the house, and the upright mailbox, painted in the colours of the American flag. 'It was so different from what we were used to, wasn't it? It always seemed magical.'

There was silence for a moment, then Celia turned round, her brown eyes blazing.

'You've got no idea, have you?' she said, icily.

'What?' Sophie didn't understand.

Celia's mouth started to pucker in an odd sort of way, as if someone were gathering in the waistband of a skirt.

'I despised this house and everything in it,' she said in a low voice that was almost a whisper. The room was very quiet but with the front door still open, you could just about hear the distant sound of waves, slapping against the shore.

'Sometimes I think I even despised Pampy, too.'

Two

Sophie stared at her sister for a few moments, half expecting her to say she'd got in a muddle and the words had come out wrong.

But she didn't. Instead, she pulled back her shoulders and raised her chin, to prove that though she might be small in height, she was a force to be reckoned with.

As if Sophie needed reminding.

'You don't mean it, do you?' she asked at last. 'You didn't really despise Pampy – you loved her. I did too. So did everyone – except Mum, that is.'

Sophie knew she sounded childish and whiny but the truth was, she felt like a child whose safe little world was under threat. Pampy had always been her hero, almost a saint, in fact. She was kind and generous, patient to a fault; she wouldn't say anything mean about anyone. Sophie needed to cling to this image, no matter what. It had been the one constant in her topsy-turvy life.

Celia's lips parted, as if she were about to comment, but she must have thought better of it and closed them again.

'I shouldn't have said that,' she said finally, refusing to meet Sophie's gaze. 'It was stupid of me. Forget it.'

Before Sophie could probe any further, Celia had put down her bag and was striding towards a closed door at the back of the room, her smart white leather sandals slapping on the wooden floor.

Sophie watched her sister turn the metal doorknob, which Pampy had decorated in oil paint with little red tulips and dark green leaves.

In an instant, Sophie was struck by a wave of nostalgia so powerful she had to stop for a minute and take a few deep breaths to steady herself.

They were in the kitchen, a big, light, square room, scarcely changed since the fifties. It had pale pink walls and mint green tiles, once fashionable but now looking quaint and worn, and there was a door on the left leading to the garden.

Facing them was a rectangular window overlooking the lawn with a dusty yellow roller blind above. Beneath the window was a stained white porcelain sink and draining board, with ill-fitting melamine cupboards that were painted pale pink like the walls.

Someone had scribbled in coloured crayons on the cupboard doors: a funny, stick woman in a triangle-shaped dress; a dog – or was it a horse? – with a body like a fat sausage and four twig legs.

Sophie might have done them herself; she wasn't sure.

Pampy wouldn't have minded, though; she must have liked the drawings or she'd have painted them over.

An old-fashioned table, covered in cracked yellow Formica, stood near the wall, and around it were four black and white vinyl chairs. Sophie remembered swinging her stubby legs underneath the table as she ate her breakfast cereal – Rice Krispies, probably from home.

Above the table hung a picture in a cutesy driftwood frame. It had been there for as long as Sophie could remember.

'There's no place like home...' it said, within a border surrounded by drawings of ladybirds, buttercups and bees, 'except Pampy's.'

As far as Sophie was concerned, her real home *was* Piping Plover House. It was where she'd felt happiest and most secure, after all.

To the right of the sink, attached to the wall, was a wooden rack, which had been used to stack crockery. Pampy never had a dishwasher; she thought it was a waste of money and besides, she said, washing and drying up together after a meal was companionable.

She had a great number of tea towels stacked neatly in a drawer, all decorated differently with squirrels and rabbits, flowers, birds, trees and drawings of places that Pampy had visited. When it had been Sophie's turn to dry, she'd been allowed to pick whichever one she wanted.

'The pantry!' she said suddenly, more to herself than Celia, who was opening drawers and cupboards. 'I wonder if it's still there.'

Spinning round, Sophie was delighted to spot two

partially closed doors, side by side, just as she remembered. The first led to the small, dark, windowless larder, which used to send thrilling shivers up and down her spine.

Once inside, she stopped for a moment, closed her eyes and sniffed, remembering the distinct aroma of sweaty Cheddar, Monterey Jack and warm, slowly rotting vegetables.

All four walls were lined with floor-to-ceiling shelves on which Pampy had stored her home-made chutney, marmalade and jam, as well as bread, ham and so on. She had a fridge, but used it mainly just for drinks, insisting chilled food didn't taste as good.

Some tins of fruit and suchlike remained on the shelves, and a few sticky-looking jars of chutney, no doubt way out of date. And there was a distinct whiff of mouse pee. For all Sophie knew, a whole family of rodents might be watching her now from their nasty little nest behind the skirting board.

'I was terrified of this place.' Celia's voice made Sophie jump. 'I dreaded it when Pampy asked me to fetch something.'

'Me too. D'you remember the legs of ham that smelled like farts?'

Celia made a snorting noise, which was almost a laugh, but her amusement quickly faded.

'We'll have to hire a huge skip – maybe two. There's so much junk. I hate to think what the bedrooms are like.'

Junk? To Sophie it was treasure. How could two sisters, who had shared so many of the same experiences, have such different perspectives?

Celia left the pantry first and Sophie closed the door

behind them. She was thinking that someone – a neighbour perhaps – must have disposed of any fresh food after Pampy died, otherwise the whole house would have reeked.

While Celia went to explore elsewhere, Sophie opened the second door, to a small utility room, housing a white washing machine and tumble drier. They looked so old and rusty, though, it was doubtful they still worked.

An ironing board with a ripped pale blue cover was propped against the wall. Beside it, a cracked grey plastic linen basket was still piled with clothes, needing to be pressed.

It was eerie to think how long the clothes had been there, waiting for Pampy. Sophie picked an item from the top and smiled. It was a cotton apron patterned with red cherries and decorated with frills around the bib and front pocket; Pampy had been a sucker for hokey sentimentality.

Pressing the fabric to her nose, Sophie hoped to be transported back to childhood, but the cloth smelled like stagnant water, so she quickly folded the apron again and replaced it on the pile.

There was a great deal more to see, but Celia was keen to prepare her bed for the night. The sisters managed to find two buckets, a ragged mop, a pile of folded up cloths, some ancient cleaning fluid and a vintage vacuum cleaner, complete with zip-up dust bag. They lugged the lot upstairs.

One by one, they opened the doors to the four bedrooms leading off the wide, airy landing. Celia quickly chose the biggest, at the front of the house, insisting she needed to be close to the bathroom, which was right alongside.

Sophie was about to object until she spotted an opportunity for point scoring and leaped on that instead.

'Do you have a problem?' she asked fake-innocently, her eyes wide with sisterly concern. It was naughty, of course, but she couldn't resist. 'With your bladder, I mean? Or, um, your bowels? Needing to be so near the loo...' She cleared her throat.

There was a pause while the normally cool-as-a-cucumber Celia flushed red.

'Certainly not! I just don't like having to grope around in the dark when I need a pee.'

She was properly riled. Sophie bit the insides of her cheeks to prevent a grin. She was being immature, of course, but then so was Celia. It seemed they'd both reverted to childhood; it hadn't taken long.

Now she'd ruffled her sister's feathers, Sophie wasn't so bothered which room she slept in and chose a smallish one at the back of the house, overlooking the garden.

Everything in here smelled damp and musty, so she ripped off the faded purple quilt, the rough sheets and pillowcases covered in pilling, and threw them on the landing, ready to be dumped.

The purplish curtains and pelmet across the leaded window were thick with dust, so she took them down, too. She'd rather string a clean sheet across the pane as a makeshift blind.

After that, she vacuumed the grubby cream carpet, scrubbed the shell-shaped headboard, upholstered in faded pink velveteen, and dusted the surfaces of the teak bedside table and chest of drawers.

Out went the yellow lampshade, with grime between each pleat, and the speckled brown and white rug. A fan of mid-twentieth-century artefacts might want it, but she sure as hell didn't.

As she wiped the now bare light bulb, she found herself pondering why it was she'd never found any of the furniture or furnishings here strange or ugly, yet they were pretty old even then. But of course she'd thought just about everything to do with Pampy was wonderful. If she'd claimed she could spin straw into gold, Sophie would have believed her.

Once the bedroom was habitable, she went to find Celia again, who was sitting on the steps of the porch with her back to the house, talking on the phone.

'It's hideous,' she heard Celia say. She was hunched over her knees and her back looked ridiculously narrow, like a child's. 'Even worse than I imagined. Everything's filthy, I can hardly bear to sit down.

'I can't see anyone wanting to buy it,' she went on. 'Maybe a builder. If I were them I'd knock it down and start all over again.'

Sophie felt the blood rush to her temples. From the way Celia was speaking, she might just as well have thrown down Pampy's photograph and trampled on it, along with Sophie's most cherished memories.

'No,' Celia said firmly. 'Thanks, but you'd hate it here. Honestly, I'd rather you kept an eye on Rory.'

Ah, so she was talking to her husband, Neil. The couple had two sons, Rory, aged about nineteen, and Rupert, about twenty-two – Sophie couldn't remember exactly.

'Is he?' Celia went on, 'Excellent. I was worried he'd

fritter away his whole summer. You know what he's like. It'll be really good for his Spanish...'

Typical Celia, thought Sophie. Rory would be on holiday from university now, probably wanting to loaf about like his peers. But Celia wouldn't stand for that. She'd have signed him up for a foreign language course or found him an internship with a top-notch Spanish firm. Achievement was her maxim; the word 'fun' didn't enter her vocabulary.

Sophie might have felt sorry for her nephew except the last time she'd seen him and his brother, they'd struck her as entitled little brats. No wonder her daughter Layla didn't want anything to do with them.

Celia put down her phone and rootled in the white handbag at her side. Out came a set of keys, a comb, a make-up bag and various pens, which she plonked in an untidy heap on the floor.

Then she pulled out a slim white pack of cigarettes and a box rattling with matches.

Celia smoking? Sophie was surprised. She'd never seen her sister with a cigarette, not once; she'd always been far too sensible and health-conscious.

Feeling like a voyeur, Sophie pretended to cough and Celia turned abruptly.

'Oh, it's you!' she said, sitting up straight, her eyes wide. She looked like a kid caught with her mitts in the biscuit jar.

'I didn't know you—' Sophie started to say, but Celia interrupted.

'I don't normally. Just when I'm... Neil doesn't like it.'

'I bet he doesn't.' Sophie was about to add something passive-aggressive because Neil had always disapproved of her. However, an unexpected change in Celia's demeanour made her stop short.

Her normally straight back and shoulders were bowed and she looked less confident than usual; beleaguered, even.

Sophie couldn't ever remember having seen her sister like this. She was The Great Celia – the fabulous family doctor, the perfect parent, marathon runner and style icon, to boot. Nothing defeated her.

'You should stub that out.' Sophie nodded at the fag end, which was in danger of burning Celia's fingers. She seemed surprised, as if she hadn't noticed.

'Oh! I need an ashtray.'

Casting her eyes around half-heartedly, she proceeded to grind the cigarette stub into the floor, then she pushed the remains through a gap in the wooden decking onto the sandy ground beneath.

Their parents would have been appalled, especially their father. Laughter gurgled in Sophie's stomach and spurted up into her throat in sharp little spasms. Fearing she might explode, she asked if she could join Celia on the step.

By the time Sophie sat down, her laughter had subsided and for a while, the two women remained side by side in silence. Sophie would have been content not to speak at all, just to savour this rare moment of harmony, but Celia had something on her mind.

'Would you still keep it if you could?' For once, her thin, reedy voice was soft. She tipped her head back to indicate the house.

'Oh yes,' Sophie replied, continuing to stare straight ahead.

'But why?' said Celia. 'I genuinely don't understand. The beach is lovely but there are nice ones closer to home. Rockaway's quite shabby in parts and the house needs masses of work. It'd cost a fortune to do up.'

Sophie paused for a moment. 'We must have different standards,' she said finally. 'I love Rockaway; I don't think it's shabby. And the house means a lot to me.'

'It's a dump!'

'I disagree. Anyway, it's part of our history. I'd like Layla to be able to come here – and her children and grandchildren. Your kids, too, if only you'd let them. I'm sure they'd fall in love with it as well.'

She glanced at Celia, hoping for a nod, or even just a glimmer of acknowledgement, but her expression didn't change.

'I've got this idea of turning it into a summer retreat for writers and artists,' Sophie persisted, picking at the seam of her white T-shirt. 'I'd have yoga classes and maybe painting and cookery. I've always wanted to do something like that...'

'Dream on.' The sharpness in Celia's voice had returned and she sat up straight, her chin jutting. 'I can't wait to get it off my hands. I can't imagine why Pampy left it to us; we hadn't seen her for years.'

This was painful territory but there was no turning back, not if Sophie were to have the slightest chance of achieving her goal; she hadn't quite given up hope yet.

'That was Mum's fault,' she said with a frown. 'It had nothing to do with us. Pampy adored us.'

Celia gave Sophie a strange look, impossible to interpret.

'Won't you reconsider – please?' Sophie's mouth felt dry and scratchy; she loathed having to ask her sister for anything. 'You know I'd buy you out if I could. We could put it on Airbnb,' she wheedled, trying not to sound desperate. 'We could charge quite a lot if we did it up properly. I'd take care of the administration; you wouldn't have to be involved at all.'

Money mattered a great deal to Celia; surely this might sway her? But she shook her head and rose.

'I won't change my mind,' she said, 'so you might as well forget it. My boys are going to want their own places soon. They can have my share of the sale for deposits.'

Sophie thought of her two spoilt nephews and felt a burning in her chest and throat, as if she'd eaten too much chilli. Celia and Neil could easily give their sons cash for deposits without flogging this place; they could probably buy them a whole house each.

'You selfish cow.' The words shot from her mouth before she could stop them and when she rose, the shadow of her five foot eight inch frame threatened to swallow up her shorter sister.

But Celia hadn't been intimidated by Sophie as a child, and certainly wasn't now.

'You're the selfish one,' she said with deadly calm. 'Stop trying to bully me into something I don't want.'

Her eyes narrowed to thin slits and Sophie could sense the tension in her sister's muscles. Her own were stretched taut, too, like the strings of a tennis racquet.

'You'll regret it.' Not quite trusting herself, she took a step back. She hadn't felt this angry for years. 'I feel sorry for you, actually. You're one of those sad fuckers who know the price of everything and the value of nothing. I'd really hate to be you.'

If Celia were offended, she wasn't going to show it. 'Thanks,' she said, with a sarcastic little smile. 'I knew I should have got someone to come here instead of me. I was stupid to think we could do it together. I won't make the same mistake again.'

She still hadn't raised her voice; she hadn't needed to. Sophie had imagined her sister could no longer rattle her, she'd thought her skin had grown too thick, but Celia had managed it somehow; she always did.

Assuming the conversation was over, Sophie made to move; there was a lump in her throat again and she feared she might cry, but Celia hadn't finished yet.

'You know…' she continued, 'you never did understand the first thing about me. You've always gone around with your eyes half shut.'

Sophie swallowed; what did she mean?

'You're a fool,' Celia went on coolly. 'Always have been, always will be. You can't even see what's staring you right in the face.'

Three

Celia was standing very upright, legs astride, hands on hips. She wanted to appear dominant and in control. It was obvious from Sophie's expression that she'd succeeded.

The sense of power and superiority made her feel quite giddy. As a child, she'd always enjoyed getting one over on her big sister, and nothing had changed.

Sophie was still older, taller and physically stronger, and Celia had still managed to reduce her almost to tears. It was immensely satisfying.

Trembling with rage and upset, Sophie turned her back and started to march down the porch steps. Meanwhile, Celia returned to the house, mission accomplished.

The other good news, as far as she was concerned, was that, thanks to her triumph, she was now entitled to a tasty reward. She was ravenous, having eaten nothing all day but a packet of pretzels and a small pot of fruit on the plane. At last, she could allow herself to consume the hummus and falafel salad she'd bought at Heathrow airport and tucked away in her bag.

Success meant food, while failure required self-punishment and denial. Celia had stuck to this routine since her early teens and it had served her very well. She still only weighed seven and a half stone and could think of no reason to alter her philosophy, even though life was uncomfortable at times. Pain and struggle made you stronger, and in her experience few got to the top without enduring a fair amount of both.

Taking the plastic container of salad out of her handbag, she examined the list of ingredients before placing it on the kitchen table.

Four hundred and sixty-five calories was quite a lot for one meal, but the oily dressing came in a separate pot and she didn't have to use it all.

She tipped the food onto a plate, which she found in a cupboard, and nibbled on a piece of carrot while she went upstairs to change into black leggings and an orange crop top.

Experience had taught her that as long as she did twenty stomach crunches and ten press-ups before each evening meal, she wouldn't suffer guilt pangs afterwards. If she felt full, she'd have a brisk walk as well.

Standing in front of the full-length cheval mirror in a corner of the bedroom, she admired her lean arms, running her fingers along the firm, flexed biceps and giving them a prod.

In profile, she could see the outline of her hard, round buttocks, and the pleasing mounds of her hamstrings. They represented a good deal of work, many hours of squats and resistance training. She was proud of them.

Her stomach wouldn't stop rumbling, though, so she completed the exercises as quickly as possible. Then she headed back to the kitchen, where she drank a full glass of water to fill her up a bit, before settling down to consume her meal.

As she dipped a slice of crunchy red pepper into the hummus, she found herself wondering what it would be like not to have such a strict regime. She couldn't remember when she'd last eaten ice cream or chocolate, or potatoes or even a whole slice of bread.

Sometimes, in cafés or restaurants, she'd watch, amazed, while other women tucked into pudding or biscuits and cheese, but she rarely felt envious. In fact, more often than not, she'd find herself pitying the diners, because they were usually on the podgy side. Thin women, like her, didn't tend to do dessert. Fact.

A shadow passed over her. Who was she trying to kid? Sometimes she felt trapped in a prison of her making, with no way out. No one knew how mean she could be to herself, not even Neil.

He'd have been shocked to hear her inner critic, haranguing her on the porch earlier when she was with Sophie: *'Why did you eat that whole bag of pretzels, Celia? You were sitting on your fat arse for hours on the plane, weren't you? You didn't need them. You're not allowed any food, now. Hah! Serves you right for being a greedy guzzler.'*

At that moment, her hunger had really started to bite and

she'd reached for her cigarettes. Only because Neil wasn't around, though.

He couldn't stand the smell of fags, let alone what they did to your body. He was such a purist. There again, so was she, except when she was so famished she'd do almost anything to kill her appetite.

It was a strange merry-go-round she'd climbed onto, but at least from the outside, her life looked pretty bloody perfect. Seeing the admiration and jealousy in others' eyes made it all worthwhile.

She thrived on admiration; her father had taught her to want it and she'd worked her socks off to get it. She wasn't about to turn her back on it now. Besides, if it suddenly stopped, what would be left of her? She couldn't look up to herself.

She tried to eat slowly but the food still seemed to disappear in a flash, leaving her by no means satisfied. She'd have nothing more now till breakfast, so distraction was the only thing for it.

Picking up her phone, she strolled into the front room and dialled Rupert's number. He didn't like her to call him at work, so she invented an excuse.

'Hello, just a quick one. Did you remember to pick up your jacket?' She'd bought it for him for his birthday from a shop in Jermyn Street. It was very expensive. 'They should have done the alterations by now.'

'Yes. Got it.' He sounded annoyed.

'Excellent. I hope they did a good job. Make sure you're completely happy. Do take it back if you're not.'

'I *am* happy.'

'Great. I'm glad. How's work?'

'Busy.'

'I'm sure. And Eleanor?'

She was his girlfriend of two years. They were talking about moving in together.

'She's fine. Look, Mum, now's not a good time. Sorry. Can we speak tomorrow morning?'

'I'll be in bed. I'm in Rockaway, remember? It's five hours behind.'

'Oh yes, I'd forgotten.'

There was a pause. She hoped he'd ask about her flight, the house, when she was coming home and his aunt, Sophie, but he was desperate to hang up.

'All right then,' Celia said with a sigh. 'I'd better let you go. Speak soon.'

'Bye.'

'Bye, my darling.'

She remained on the sofa for a while, staring into space, her legs curled up beneath her. Rupert was a good son. He'd had his stroppy moments as a teenager, but he'd always worked hard at school. She was insanely proud of his First from Oxford University and loved to tell people about his graduate job at JP Morgan.

He was already on a handsome salary and would no doubt rise quickly through the ranks. She'd bet he'd have made his fortune by the time he was forty.

She'd put a lot of effort into both her boys and thus far, Rupert had accomplished everything she'd wanted for him. Now, though, she had an uneasy sense he believed her mothering role was over. He didn't want her advice any more and it frightened her. Anything could happen if she were no longer in charge.

Take Eleanor. She was nice enough, smart and very pretty. But she came from a broken home and her parents weren't exactly from the top drawer either.

Rupert had travelled far more widely than her and he'd had a much more privileged upbringing. The cracks might start to show if they married and had children. It was no use Celia pointing this out, though; she'd only make him angry.

As for Rory, well, she had to keep a close eye on him, too. Unlike his brother, he had a lazy streak as well as a tendency to push the boundaries. At least she still had some authority over him. All the while she paid his university bills and gave him his monthly allowance, he knew he had to toe the line to a certain extent. This was some comfort.

Her thoughts drifted back to Sophie. What would she be doing now? Pounding the streets after their argument? Or was she in her bedroom upstairs, punching her pillow? Honestly, she was her own worst enemy. She'd never listened to a word their parents said. She had only herself to blame for being poor.

If she'd worked at school, gone to university and picked more suitable friends and boyfriends, she'd have found herself a successful husband and a good job. Then she could have bought Celia out, hung on to this stupid house and there'd have been no disagreement.

Celia sniffed. Some people were impossible. Snapping out of her daydream, her eyes fell on her white gold engagement ring, with a very large, round, sparkly diamond in the centre. It was from Liberty in Regent Street and she and Neil had chosen it together; she wouldn't have trusted him to pick it on his own.

Stretching out her hand, she admired it on her slim finger, where it sat neatly, just above the matching wedding ring.

It probably wouldn't fit on Sophie's little toe, let alone her wedding finger. She really was quite large. You wouldn't call her fat, though. She was tall and big boned, with broad, swimmer's shoulders and long legs. If she dressed well, used better hair products, wore some make-up and lost a few pounds, she'd be very attractive. The trouble was, she didn't seem remotely bothered about her appearance.

In actual fact, it might be rather nice not to worry constantly about your image, but winners, like Celia, had to look good. It was all part of their brand.

Her boys knew this, too; she'd made sure of it. She'd always cooked healthy meals for them, with lots of protein and vegetables. And she'd insisted on plenty of fresh air and exercise. None of this lounging around watching telly or playing on their phones, which other children seemed to do these days.

If she'd caught her sons loafing when they were younger, she'd made them go for a bike ride or to play tennis.

Neither of them was overweight and they both dressed smartly, especially Rupert. Rory could be a bit of a slob around the house, in tracksuit bottoms and scruffy old T-shirts, but he scrubbed up well when he needed to.

Celia sighed. He wasn't very good at keeping in touch. Even worse than Rupert, in fact. She probably wouldn't hear from her youngest son all the while she was away, unless he wanted something, of course. She'd ring and leave texts as usual, knowing he wouldn't respond. He said he rarely looked at his messages, but he answered them quickly enough when they were from friends.

Walking over to the window, she searched for Sophie and frowned. There was no sign of her. If she were out, hopefully she wouldn't leave it too late. She might be infuriating, but Celia wouldn't want her to come to any harm. They were sisters, after all, and Celia supposed she did care about her a little.

Upstairs, she undressed and put on her white towelling robe. She was weary after her journey and would have a shower and go to bed.

Feeling in the pocket of her gown, she found a small box of tablets: her sleeping pills. She tried not to take one too often, but felt perfectly justified tonight.

She popped one in her mouth and swallowed it down with some water. It would take about half an hour to work, then she could look forward to seven or eight hours of uninterrupted sleep. Bliss.

She wouldn't be disturbed by Sophie. Nor would she be plagued by gnawing hunger pangs. Sometimes, the stomach cramps got so painful, she'd lie awake all night, praying for breakfast time.

It wasn't easy being Celia, she thought, climbing under the white sheet and switching off the light. But she wasn't about to give up the struggle any time soon. She'd rather be herself, with her thin bod and fat bank balance, than poor old loser Sophie, any day.

★ ★ ★

Sophie was so angry and upset, she wanted to get as far away from Celia as possible. It was quite obvious she had all the power and there was nothing Sophie could do. Without her sister's cooperation, the house would have to be sold. Someone would come along, rip it apart and change everything, probably even its name. Of Pampy and their long, hot, happy summers together, there'd be no trace.

Sophie hadn't quite reached the bottom of the porch steps, however, when a loud scream made her stop in her tracks.

'Aiiiiii! Nino! Come back here this minute, you sonofabitch!'

Before she could locate the source of the racket, a gangly, dark-haired youth, aged about thirteen or fourteen, sped past her towards the beach, clutching a bottle of something in his right hand. His breath was coming in short, sharp bursts and his arms were pumping furiously.

Soon after came a plump, middle-aged woman in a pale pink shirt tucked into a pair of white Bermuda shorts. She had short reddish-purple hair, a red face and she was puffing loudly and running as fast as she could, but there was no way she'd ever catch the boy up; he was far too quick and nimble. Undeterred, she continued chasing him through the gap in the sea wall while Sophie stared after them.

They briefly disappeared from view, then the boy re-emerged on top of a towering sand dune, which ran all along the beach in both directions, as far as the eye could see. Sophie had read somewhere that it had been built as protection from storms following Hurricane Sandy.

The boy paused momentarily on the summit to look

over his shoulder. When he clocked the woman, starting to struggle up the side of the dune after him, he hared off to the right in the direction of a large breakwater.

Without thinking, Sophie took a few steps backwards up the porch steps for a better view. She wondered if the woman would throw in the towel at this point and head for home, but she was clearly made of sterner stuff.

Bending forwards with head and shoulders bowed, arms and legs splayed, feet at a quarter to three and backside in the air, she continued the ascent.

Thanks to the commotion, Sophie had temporarily forgotten about Celia. She remembered now, though, and her stomach lurched. A quick glance over her shoulder established that her sister had slunk inside. Relieved, Sophie continued on down the steps and turned left, following the same route as the boy and his pursuer. The sea, she thought, would surely calm her nerves, and it was the perfect time of day – much cooler now the sun was preparing to set.

As soon as she passed through the gap in the sea wall, the ground turned mostly to sand and she bent down to take off her socks and shoes.

Someone – the angry woman, probably – had dropped some plastic flip-flops by the entrance and Sophie placed her white trainers alongside. Well-worn and distinctly grubby, she reckoned no one in their right mind would want to steal them.

Her mind started to wander and she closed her eyes, breathing in deeply to allow the salty sea air to penetrate way down into her lungs. It occurred to her this was the first time she'd felt able to relax all day, or certainly since meeting up with Celia at the airport.

With any luck, she'd be asleep by the time Sophie got back, or at least in her bedroom with the door firmly shut; Sophie certainly had no intention of returning any time soon. She'd rather walk from one length of the peninsula to another than risk further confrontation tonight.

She'd been intending to turn left and climb the dune further along, so as to avoid bumping into the angry woman. A grumbling voice, however, warned that it was too late. The small lady was half sliding, half stomping towards her, muttering angrily to herself.

'Ay, *porca miseria*,' she chuntered. '*Gesù! Che cazzo di casino!*'

The woman was so lost in her own world she didn't immediately spot Sophie standing at the bottom of the dune, staring up at her. Then her dark, narrowed eyes met Sophie's pale, blue-grey ones.

'Holy shit!' she said again, this time in English, and Sophie instinctively froze.

'What the…?' the stranger continued, before checking herself. 'Excuse me. I didn't see you there…'

To Sophie's surprise, the woman's frown softened, her eyes widened and her face broke into a wide, impish grin.

'I try to curse in Italian so people won't understand,' she said, in a strong New York accent. 'I didn't realise anyone was listening…'

'It's fine,' Sophie replied, amused. 'I've heard a lot worse.'

The woman smiled again. 'Well that's a relief! You new round here?'

Sophie nodded.

'I didn't think I'd seen you before. I'm Gianna,' the woman went on, 'but everyone calls me Gigi. I live at number thirty. I've got two boys and a girl...' Her dark brows came together again.

'My boy, Nino, just stole my husband's whisky. He'll be so mad if he finds out.' She clicked her tongue. 'Nino's fourteen years old and he's gotten into bad habits already. He used to be a good boy, no trouble at all, but this summer – ever since school finished – he's turned into a wild thing. I don't know what's come over him...'

She let out a sigh and shrugged, as if to say, *What can you do?* Then she smiled impishly once more. 'Kids! You can't live with them, can't live without 'em. You got any?'

'Yes,' said Sophie. 'Just one – a daughter.'

'Ah.' Gigi shook her head ominously. 'You'd think girls would be easier but they're real *sneaky*. My daughter, Mariella, she's sixteen. She looks like butter wouldn't melt in your mouth, but man! The things she gets up to behind my back!'

Now Gigi was no longer red in the face and growling, Sophie noticed she was actually really rather pretty, with olive skin, high cheekbones and round brown eyes, carefully made up with brownish gold eye shadow and black mascara. A pair of big gold earrings peeked through her hair.

'Where are you from, if you don't mind my asking?' she said next, and when Sophie explained she and her sister had inherited Piping Plover House, she seemed intrigued.

'I knew your grandmother a little,' she said, stepping

alongside so that they could hear one another more easily. 'When we moved here ten years ago, she was already quite frail and didn't go out much. But I chatted to her over the fence when she was in her front garden. She was a beautiful lady – so polite and well-spoken. I always asked if she needed anything – groceries and stuff – but she never did. I didn't know she had children and grandchildren; she didn't seem to have many visitors.'

This made Sophie sad. A shiver of guilt ran through her, though if Pampy had wanted her help or even just her company, she'd only have had to pick up the phone or write a letter – but for whatever reason, she never did.

It was almost a year since she'd died. Sophie only found out when she received a letter from her grandmother's lawyer, outlining the will. It seemed Pampy had developed pancreatic cancer and the end had been mercifully quick.

Sophie's father, Paul, had been dead fourteen years and her mother, Teresa, or Terry, five years. It was lonely being an orphan, even an adult one, and it had sometimes crossed Sophie's mind to try and get in touch with Pampy, now that both parents were gone. Unfortunately, though, she'd dallied and dithered, fearing another rejection, then all of a sudden, it was too late anyway.

'What are you going to do with the house?' Gigi asked next. She didn't seem in any hurry to leave. When Sophie said she wanted to keep the place but her sister was determined to sell, Gigi made a sympathetic noise.

'That's a shame. It's one of the nicest houses in the street, I've always thought so – and the location's perfect.'

Sophie asked what Gigi did for a living. It turned out

she ran a small delicatessen-cum-café a few blocks away in Belle Harbor, close to the main shops. It was called Gigi's.

Gigi explained that she made most of the food herself – fresh lasagne, slices of pizza and pasta dishes to eat in or take out; panini and focaccia with a choice of salami, prosciutto, thinly sliced pancetta or buffalo mozzarella; melt-in-the-mouth cannoli stuffed with pistachio nuts and ricotta; chilled calamari with lemon and parsley; gelato, ice cream of every imaginable flavour, and tiramisu. Just hearing about it made Sophie feel hungry and she promised to visit the shop soon.

'Anytime,' said Gigi. 'It's always busy at lunchtime but the afternoon's usually quieter. If you come around half ten you'll meet my regulars. There's a group come in for coffee and pastries every single day of the week. They're a friendly lot. We get the occasional lowlife, but not often. I guess you find them anywhere.'

'I'll drop by tomorrow,' Sophie promised, starting to move away. 'I look forward to trying some of your ice cream!'

It was almost 8 p.m. and the fiery tangerine sun was sinking like a giant sceptre below the horizon. Vibrant red and purple clouds spread their feathery tendrils across the blue-violet sky. The ocean, as if in tribute, had transformed itself into a sheet of cobalt blue glass, mirroring the display above in all its glory.

Meanwhile, the sand, becoming cooler by the minute, had turned into a long, winding stripe of burnished copper, as if it wanted to remind you of the division between earth and heaven.

Scores of tiny piping plover birds were dancing along the edge of the water, silhouetted against the fiery sky. Sophie recognised them by their distinctive movements: run, stop, peck and repeat. They were foraging for sea worms, tiny molluscs and crustaceans and never seemed to stand still for a minute.

The sight brought back memories of similar strolls that she used to take with Pampy when she was a child. As night fell, just before it was time to lock the doors, close the curtains and settle down for the evening, Pampy would suggest a walk, usually while Sophie's mother was putting Celia to bed and Grandpa Donal was out or away.

In fact, now Sophie thought about it, he was often absent during their visits. He'd be there for a day or two, then disappear off on some holiday or other.

He liked walking and carpentry, though Sophie never saw any of his work. Pampy always said he needed time on his own and to be honest, Sophie was glad, for she never felt comfortable in his presence.

On quiet evenings, Pampy and Sophie would walk, hand in hand, down to the water's edge and watch the Rockaway sunset in all its ostentatious glory.

'My!' Pampy would say, in a soft, almost other-worldly voice that sent tingles up and down Sophie's spine. 'Doesn't it make you feel small?'

Pampy was so gentle and loving back then, always checking to make sure Sophie was warm enough, asking her about her school and friends and praising her for even the smallest achievement.

Somehow, she always managed to make Sophie feel

extra special, as if she were her very favourite. Sophie was pretty sure this couldn't really be true, because everyone else seemed to think she was big, clumsy, badly behaved and gingery, to boot.

Pampy called Sophie's hair 'Titian', and said she had lovely, delicate skin, like porcelain. 'Pale complexions are much prettier,' she'd insist. 'I can't think why young girls lie out in the sun for hours on end to get a tan. They go all leathery and wrinkled!'

By now, the sun was nothing more than a sliver of light above the inky water, like a segment of orange. Sophie waited in anticipation for it to dip below the horizon. When the last glimmer disappeared, she continued to stare at the blackness for quite some time and found herself sighing in awe and sadness.

She'd always found nightfall both beautiful and melancholy, a bit like her memories of Rockaway – and Pampy.

Four

After a while she resumed her walk, watching the lights turning on in the windows of the houses that ran all along the length of the beach.

The tide was quite high so that the breakwaters, positioned at regular intervals along the shore, were largely submerged, with only their stumpy, barnacled tops visible. She paused several times to pick up a shell or a pebble, enjoying the faintly salty, fishy smell and the feel of bumps and ridges or rounded smoothness between her fingers.

She shivered, feeling lonely all of a sudden, and pulled the phone from her pocket.

A short message from Layla, wishing her luck on the trip, lifted her spirits. Layla knew the score; she was well aware her mother had been dreading seeing Celia.

I'll call tomoz, Sophie texted. *Luv ya xx*.

The only other message was from Sophie's ex-partner, Richard, asking if he could pop round to pick up some books he'd left behind months ago when he moved out.

Frowning, she clicked off the screen and replaced the phone in her pocket.

She must have walked about a mile and a half by now, which was quite hard work on the sand, and her legs were beginning to get tired. It was difficult to believe that only this morning she'd been on the plane from London; she felt as if she'd been away for days already.

It was a relief when, before long, an area of bright lights came into view and she picked up the distant sound of rock music.

Now, she could see a giant white gazebo high up on the boardwalk ahead. It was open to the sides and shaped like a pagoda with two small domes. Inside, on a raised platform, a live band was playing to what appeared to be a sizeable crowd.

There were four of them – three young men, two with electric guitars and one on the keyboard, and one very tall, athletic, long-legged woman with blue hair, in a silver sequinned dress.

'She's good.'

Surprised, Sophie turned round to see who had spoken. A man was leaning casually against the barrier, with one foot resting on the railing. He was wearing flip-flops, a dark T-shirt and baggy, carpenter-style shorts with big, bulging pockets.

'She's amazing,' Sophie agreed, following his gaze. 'I love her voice.'

'I'm Joe, by the way,' said her companion, and he reached out to shake her hand.

'Sophie,' said Sophie coolly, offering her hand in return.

He gripped it tight and pumped so hard that she was taken aback again.

'Are you English?' he asked, when he finally let her hand go. 'You sound like Mary Poppins!'

Catching his eye by mistake, she detected undisguised amusement.

'I'm from south-west London,' she replied primly, realising she did sound exactly like Mary Poppins.

'Bingo!' said Joe. 'I knew it before you opened your mouth! London's great,' he went on, 'but I prefer Derbyshire. The Dales are beautiful. I'm a country boy at heart.'

Sophie was surprised again. She hadn't had him down as a globetrotter and besides, most Americans confined themselves to UK tourist spots like Canterbury or Bath, rather than the English countryside.

'Excuse me,' she said, feeling self-conscious about her voice for the first time. She straightened up and made to move. 'I need to get something to eat.'

He settled back against the barrier, resting his arms along the top railing.

'I can recommend the fish tacos – if you like fish, that is,' he said drily, not bothering to turn his head. 'Bon appetit.'

'Pico salsa?' asked the woman at the tacos stall, ladling a mound of red cabbage into a soft tortilla already groaning with crispy cod, cold veggies and sour cream.

'Please, and a Coke,' said Sophie, wondering how on earth she'd manage to eat it. It was going to be messy, for sure.

She strolled past a wooden cocktail bar selling frozen piña coladas, margaritas and other drinks with peculiar names like Juicy Lucy, Voodoo and A Short Trip to Hell.

Someone had painted ocean scenes with a difference on the front and sides of the shack: a giant blue octopus playing the drums, a mermaid with purple hair and a harp, and a gold starfish clutching a ukulele.

A little further on was a concrete bench overlooking the beach, but this was occupied by a group of boisterous teenage boys who seemed to have no intention of moving. Feeling quite weak, tired and very thirsty all of a sudden, Sophie decided to abandon her fruitless search for a chair and plonk on the ground instead.

There was a bit of space near the concrete bench and she settled down gratefully, leaning back against the railings and crossing her legs. She opened the Coke first and took several big swigs; nothing to her had ever tasted so good.

It was only after six or seven forkfuls of her fish tacos that she began to slow down and become more aware of the four teenage boys on the bench next to her. She couldn't see their faces properly but could hear them perfectly well, and what she'd assumed was laughter now sounded more like an argument.

'Give it here!' the youngest boy said and the large boy, who was closest to Sophie with his back turned, mimicked him in a silly baby voice.

The youngest boy repeated himself. 'It's my dad's,' he added, with a slight catch in his throat. 'I need to give it back.'

He lunged forwards and the large boy jumped up, holding

aloft an almost empty whisky bottle, so it was out of reach. There was a noisy struggle and after a few moments, he passed it quickly to his mate, who hurled it over the railings onto the beach.

Sophie had shrunk into the shadows, hoping not to be noticed, but didn't like the mocking tones of the older boys' voices. She felt sorry for the younger lad and what's more, the longer she looked at him, the more convinced she became that he was Gigi's son, Nino, who'd run past Piping Plover House earlier in the evening. She gobbled down the last of her taco, and decided to intervene.

'Excuse me,' she said, standing up tall and adopting her most authoritative voice, 'that bottle belongs to Nino. Let go of him at once or I'll call the police.'

The boys, surprised, swung around. Nino stared at Sophie, his mouth hanging open.

'H-how do you know my name?' he said at last. 'Have I seen you before?'

Sophie stepped forwards into the light, so she was in full view of his tormenters. 'I'll explain later,' she told him. 'Quick, go and get the bottle. If it's broken, they'll have to buy you a new one.'

Without another word, Nino darted off to find the nearest steps down to the beach. Meanwhile, Sophie, pretending not to be scared, stood tall, with her hands on her hips, while the other boys eyed her up menacingly. She was secretly hoping Nino would hurry. She didn't fancy taking on these lads in a physical fight; she wouldn't stand a chance.

Luckily, Nino soon returned, triumphantly waving the bottle, covered in sand.

'It's not broken,' he cried, grinning at Sophie. Then he looked at the others and narrowed his eyes. 'No thanks to you.'

Sophie tensed, half expecting the bigger boys to snatch it again or worse, try to give Nino a beating. Thankfully, however, they seemed to have lost their appetites for both boozing and bullying.

The bigger boy stuck his hands in his pockets and signalled to his mates that it was time to go, then one by one they slunk off, cracking jokes and laughing as they went.

Nino was busy wiping the sand off the bottle with the bottom of his T-shirt.

'Let's walk home together,' Sophie said. 'I'm Sophie, by the way. I'm staying just up the road from you. I saw you running past earlier and met your mother. We had a nice chat.'

Nino stared at his feet and frowned. 'She's going to be so mad at me, and if she tells my dad…'

'Then what?' asked Sophie gently. 'What will he do?'

'Ground me, probably for weeks.'

He kicked disconsolately at some gravel with the toe of a dirty white sneaker. 'And make me do lousy jobs like cleaning the cars and stuff.'

'Why did you do it, if you knew he'd go ballistic?'

Nino shrugged. 'It was stupid. Jake invited me along. He told me to bring booze, so I did. I said they couldn't drink a lot – just a few sips – or my dad would notice, but they ignored me. If you hadn't shown up they would've finished the bottle.'

'Is Jake the boy who was here?'

Nino nodded.

'He's bad news. I should keep away from him. How full was it before?' She nodded at the bottle, which had hardly any booze left in it.

'Almost up to the top.'

She made a face. 'Oh dear. Will your dad be home now?'

'Nah. He's working nights all week.'

'Good.'

Nino raised his eyebrows. 'What do you mean? He'll find out the minute he gets back.'

Sophie took a deep breath. 'Not necessarily. Look, I'll buy you another bottle. You can top this one up—'

'Would you do that? Really?' Nino's eyes suddenly sparkled with hope.

Sophie nodded. 'On one condition – that you apologise to Gigi and promise not to steal your dad's booze again. Agreed?'

She paused, allowing time for her words to sink in. She'd learned from raising her own daughter that teenagers hated being told what to do. They needed to feel they had a choice.

Nino swallowed several times and grimaced, as if he had a sore throat.

'OK,' he replied at last, his head bowed, before giving Sophie a sly look through surprisingly long black lashes. 'Mum won't remember about the booze if I put it back tonight.'

'Deal or no deal?' she went on. 'It's totally up to you.'

Nino's bottom lip pouted and all of a sudden, he looked about five years old.

'Deal,' he muttered, kicking again at the gravel under his feet.

'Great,' said Sophie, extending a hand, which he took. 'Let's shake on it.'

Soon, they were turning right up a small dark alley that led from the beach. They were still a block away from home, but Nino explained it was quicker to get to the liquor store by this route. Plus, they were less likely to bump into anyone he knew.

He was walking very fast now, anxious to make it to the store before closing time, and Sophie had trouble keeping up. Her feet were still bare, and she cursed herself for leaving her trainers behind. It would serve her right if she trod on some glass or stubbed her toe on a paving stone.

'Isn't there somewhere that stays open later?' she asked, pausing for a moment under a street lamp to catch her breath, but Nino said no.

'We'll just about make it – if we run.' And with that, he broke into a sprint, leaving her lagging behind.

'Wait for me!' she cried, imagining him arriving at the shop just in time, only to be thrown out because he was underage. But he didn't hear.

The only thing for it was to run, too, which was something she hadn't done for a very long time.

Her heart was racing, her feet stung and her legs screamed in protest, but she didn't slow down until she reached a long parade of shops. Most were in darkness but about halfway along, one store was lit up and she spotted Nino hovering in the doorway.

Now she knew where she was going, she relaxed to a

jog, gulping in as much air as she could on the move. The atmosphere was still thick and heavy and she could feel sweat trickling down her neck and prickling in her armpits.

Despite her discomfort, however, she was surprised to feel a small and unexpected shiver of pleasure. Not only had she managed to sprint barefoot and further than she'd imagined possible, but here she was, at nearly eleven o'clock at night, helping a strange teenage boy out of a scrape.

The inside of the shop was cramped and poky. Shelves laden with cans and bottles lined every wall.

A heavily tattooed man in a white vest stood behind the counter. He had a small, pointy beard and his black afro hair was pulled into a squashy top knot, like a powder puff. He was rapping his knuckles on the wooden counter in time to the music, blaring out from a tinny speaker nearby.

'We're closed,' he drawled, eyeing Sophie up and down. He lazily rolled a ball of gum around his mouth a few times before chewing.

Sophie felt the heat rise up through her body to her cheeks.

'No you're not. The door's wide open!'

The man rested his elbows on the counter and leaned forwards, showing off his beefy shoulders and brawny biceps to their full advantage. She realised he was older than he looked; little wrinkles ran from the corners of his eyes and his hair was flecked with grey.

'We close at eleven – says so on the window.'

'Well, it's only a few seconds past,' Sophie replied huffily.

'Don't make no difference,' he said, shrugging his hefty shoulders. 'Rules are rules. I can't serve anyone after eleven o'clock.'

'That's absurd!' She turned to Nino for support, but he had slunk off, embarrassed, to the far end of the shop and was pretending to study a wine label.

'I just want a little bottle of whisky,' she said more softly. 'It's to pay someone back and it's really important. Pleeeease?'

The man hesitated, his big hand wrapped around a bunch of keys sitting on the shelf.

'My young friend here did a silly thing,' she went on, wheedling. 'He stole a bottle of whisky from his dad. He was only going to try a sip, but his friends got hold of it and now it's almost empty. His dad'll kill him if he finds out. We've got to replace it before he gets home from the night shift.'

To her surprise, the man threw back his head and laughed.

'Why didn't you say? My old man used to beat me for stealing his liquor, and I've still got the strap marks on my butt to prove it.'

He fiddled with the belt on his jeans and for one wild moment Sophie feared he was about to show her the evidence. Instead, however, he came out from behind the bar, strode over to one of the top shelves and took down a bottle like the one Nino was holding.

'Here,' he said. 'Go put this in your daddy's cabinet right away. And don't be so foolish again, young man. Next time Mommy might not be so inclined to help you out – and who in the world would blame her?'

'Oh, I'm not his mother,' Sophie said quickly, reaching into her handbag for her credit card. 'I'm just a friend.'

'Is that so? Then you're lucky to have such a very kind friend.'

Nino nodded. 'I know.'

When the man handed the liquor to Sophie in a brown paper bag, she thanked him profusely.

'Glad to help,' he said cheerfully, following them to the door with his set of keys. 'Just don't let on you got served after eleven p.m. or I'll be in big trouble myself.'

Sophie promised that she wouldn't.

'I'm Terrell, by the way,' he went on, putting the key in the lock. 'You'll probably see me around. I'm a lifeguard. Most days I'm on the beach. I just work here from time to time to help out a friend.'

Assuming that he'd finished, Sophie started to move away but he stopped her.

'Do you like the beach?'

'Oh yes, I love it.'

Terrell seemed pleased.

'Great! That's great,' he replied, taking his big hands off the key in the lock and rubbing them together. 'I'll see you on the beach, then.'

'He's really into you.' Nino was giggling as they started walking down the street.

'Shh!' Sophie hoped that Terrell hadn't heard. 'Don't be silly.'

Secretly, though, she couldn't help feeling a little flattered.

It was with some trepidation that she walked back to Piping Plover House, praying Celia would be asleep, or at least in her room.

The porch light had been left on but inside was silent and dark.

The damp, musty smell was still there, but once she put on the overhead light, the place seemed less forbidding. Memories of cosy evenings on the sofa with Pampy came floating back. She barely even noticed the dust and cobwebs as she settled happily on Pampy's rocking chair and swayed to and fro. Its creaking noise made her feel drowsy, and she found herself reaching for one of the old blankets in the wicker basket beneath the piano and closing her eyes.

Her breathing slowed and she started to enter that delicious, hazy space between wakefulness and sleep when you find yourself in a world of strange, dreamlike visions and unfamiliar sounds and sensations.

She tried to rouse herself, thinking she should go upstairs to bed, but the pull of slumber was as determined and relentless as the tide.

All of a sudden, something cold brushed against her cheek and she felt a weight, like a hand, settle lightly on her shoulder. At the same time, a faint but unmistakable scent filled her nostrils. It was the aroma of oranges and lemons mixed with something floral – jasmine, perhaps, or rose. It was the cologne Pampy always wore.

Sophie gasped and her eyelids sprang open. She was quite sure that Pampy was standing right behind her, bending over, her hand on Sophie's shoulder, her face up close.

'What...?' She swung around, her heart pumping furiously. She half expected to see the ghostly figure of her grandmother and wasn't sure whether she'd smile or scream. But the scent vanished as quickly as it had come and there was nothing there at all.

Five

The heat! Sophie had quite forgotten about the sticky, heavy heat that seemed to settle on you like a second skin.

Pampy, of course, had never installed air conditioning; she said it wasn't necessary by the sea. Instead she had big wooden ceiling fans with old-fashioned, pull down switches. They whirled the stagnant air around, creating a bit of a breeze, but the constant rattle irritated Sophie, so she had to turn hers off.

All through the night she woke every hour or so, slick with sweat and gasping for water. She found that reversing her pillow and wriggling across the bed to find a cooler patch provided some relief. Then she lay awake with her eyes closed, listening to the distant swish of the ocean, until exhaustion tipped her over the edge and back once more into a fitful slumber.

It wasn't until dawn that she finally dropped into the sort of deep, dreamless sleep almost no amount of noise can disturb. When she opened her eyes again, it was a surprise to see shafts of bright sun piercing the gaps in her makeshift curtains, lighting up the grubby cream carpet.

On reaching for her phone, she was dismayed to discover that it was past ten o'clock and a feeling of dread, like a stone, settled in the pit of her stomach.

All of a sudden she was a teenager again, waiting for her father, Paul, to barge uninvited into her room. Like most of her friends, she'd wanted to laze in bed at weekends, sometimes until 11 a.m. or later. This enraged her father, who'd shout at her to get up, using big words like 'slatternly' and 'indolent', as if he'd spent hours scouring the dictionary for the perfect insult. Celia, of course, rarely slept in and was usually up in time for breakfast, even during the holidays.

Sophie thought her father totally unreasonable – and told him so. Her defiance aggravated him even more and they'd row ferociously, but he was bigger, louder and more powerful than her. She'd end up bursting into tears and storming out of the house, only to have to return some hours later with her tail between her legs, because she had nowhere else to go.

Nothing but an abject apology would satisfy him, then would come the humiliating dressing-down and painful punishment, like having her favourite clothes confiscated, or not being allowed to see her friends.

She could still remember sitting alone in her room after being grounded, counting the days until she was eighteen and old enough to leave home for good. Her sole ambition was to get a job – any job – that paid enough for her to be able to rent her own place and never have to set eyes on her father again.

Although she hadn't spent a night in Celia's company for many years, Sophie was certain her sister would still be an early riser. She was her daddy's daughter, after all. This morning, she'd probably already run five miles along the beach, showered, dressed and answered all her emails.

A loud crash downstairs brought Sophie back to the present and she jumped up and pulled a light white cotton robe from the open suitcase beside her bed.

Peeking behind the sheet, which she'd strung over the window, she could see there was no one in the backyard. Pampy's flowery borders had long since died and were filled with straggly weeds, which had turned brown in the sun.

The lawn, too, was a yellowish brown, and parts of the old wooden fence were collapsing. By contrast, the garden backing onto theirs was lush and green.

However, when Sophie opened the window wide and leaned out, she could just about see the glittering ocean to her right, with white horses galloping gaily across the waves.

The sand was as golden as the sun itself and there wasn't a single cloud in the bright blue sky. How could she possibly feel gloomy on a day like this?

She padded in bare feet across the carpet before twisting the doorknob and tentatively stepping onto the landing. Pausing for a moment to listen again, she could hear no more crashes.

Bracing herself, Sophie took a deep breath and walked downstairs, running her fingers along the dents and scratches in the dark wooden handrail, which she found strangely comforting.

There was no one in the sitting room, but the dusty curtains were no longer closed and the windows, covered in milky salt spray, had been thrown open.

Now, Sophie could hear someone moving about in the kitchen and when she opened the door, a delicious scent of fresh coffee filled her nostrils. Her mouth watered and her stomach rumbled, reminding her it was hours since her last meal on the boardwalk.

'Oh, hi,' she said.

Celia had her back turned and was crouching on the ground, taking things out of one of the cupboards below the sink. On hearing Sophie's voice, she swivelled round.

'I got you a coffee,' she said, pointing to a white cardboard cup with a plastic lid on the melamine table. 'And a bagel with cream cheese.'

Her tone wasn't exactly friendly, but it wasn't spiky either and what's more, she'd even bought breakfast, which was totally unexpected. A peace offering, surely? Sophie's spirits rose a little.

'Thanks,' she said, walking towards the coffee cup and picking it up. 'How did you get to the shops? I didn't think there was anything nearby.'

'Taxi.' Celia sniffed. 'I've been up for ages.'

There was a superior edge to her voice, which made Sophie's hackles rise, but she managed not to retaliate. Instead, she took a sip of her drink, which was hot and strong, just as she liked it.

As the warm liquid trickled down, a sense of well-being

spread through her body. She grabbed the white paper bag, and pulled out half of the plain bagel. The bread was thick, chewy and slightly salty and sweet at the same time.

'I'm sorry about last night.' Sophie's mouth was full so she could only mumble. 'I said some horrible things. I didn't mean them.'

'We were both out of order.'

Celia was surrounded now by an assortment of cleaning materials – crusty old bottles of bleach, tins of shoe polish, a red plastic bucket and dry, wrinkled rags.

'I've hired a car. We can pick it up after midday. We'll need it to take stuff to the charity shops. There's a skip arriving in a few days.'

'Wow!' Sophie was genuinely impressed; for once, she was grateful for her sister's extreme efficiency.

'We need cardboard boxes and bin bags,' Celia went on, rising now and tipping the remains of one bottle down the sink. 'Most of these are dead. I can't think why Pampy kept them. I wonder what happens with recycling here. We'll have to find out.'

Watching how long it was taking Celia to clear out just one cupboard reminded Sophie of the huge task in hand. Now she knew for sure she'd lost the battle over Piping Plover House, she might as well get stuck in herself.

'I'll make a start on the living room,' she announced. 'I'll put everything in piles. We can decide what to do with them later.'

She hurried upstairs to splash her face with cold water before getting dressed in some old denim shorts and a faded yellow T-shirt.

Then, without looking in the mirror, she pulled her hair up into a loose bun and slipped her bare feet into her plastic flip-flops, reminding herself to fetch her grubby trainers from the entrance to the beach, where she'd left them last night.

Until the skip arrived, there was a limit to what she could achieve so she decided to start going through the various books, papers and magazines lying around, checking there was nothing of value – sentimental or otherwise – before plonking them on a 'CHUCK' pile in the corner.

It was strange flicking through the dusty women's magazines, some dating way back to the seventies and eighties, and imagining Pampy doing the same.

Some of the pages had been earmarked and Sophie wondered if her grandmother had ever made the crocheted hat or cooked the 'Easy-Peasy Lasagne'.

A quick Internet search established that she might be able to donate some of the books and magazines to local libraries, nursing homes, doctors' surgeries or women's shelters, and she jotted down a list of phone numbers to call later.

The moth-eaten cushions went on another pile destined for the recycling bank, along with a worn rug and the dusty blankets from under the piano.

She chose to keep Pampy's sampler of the house, but didn't want the other pictures – a flowery print in a wooden frame and a bland seaside landscape, which could have been of anywhere.

There were three faded photographs in tarnished silver frames on the mantelpiece. They were covered in dust, and she used a corner of one of the cushions to clean them off before examining them properly.

One was of Pampy and her husband, Donal, standing on the church steps after their wedding. It was in black and white and Pampy looked slim and elegant in a full-length gown with a tightly fitted bodice, a wide A-line skirt and lacy sleeves. Her longish dark hair had been loosely curled and she was hanging on Donal's arm, her veil thrown back, smiling widely as she gazed up at him.

Dressed in a morning suit with a pale waistcoat and dark tie, he stood very upright and unsmiling, as if wanting to remind guests that marriage was a serious matter, not an excuse for frivolity.

This chimed with what Sophie remembered. Her grandmother had never spoken ill of him behind his back, but Sophie certainly had the impression he was very much the head of the family and his word went.

Her mother had gone much further. She used to say he was a religious fanatic, who tried to impose his own, rigid version of Roman Catholicism on those around him. When he was out, the house was filled with music and laughter. The moment he returned, however, the music would go off, the laughter would cease and everyone would scurry about, trying to look useful.

Sophie always thought Donal was like her own father. She never could fathom why Pampy or her mother had agreed to marry either of them.

The second photo was of Sophie and Celia when they were little. They were sitting side by side on the swing bench on the front porch in pastel sundresses and white sandals, eating ice creams.

The third was one of Sophie's old school photos. Aged about eleven, she was dressed in uniform – a white shirt under a royal blue sweater with a small yellow logo on the front. Her face was still round and girlish and her nose covered in freckles. She'd always hated those freckles and still tried to cover them up with foundation when she went somewhere special.

Back then, her loose, shoulder-length hair was very obviously reddish and slightly wavy. It was only later that it faded, helped along by the blonde highlights that the hairdresser put in.

She had a small smile but shyness lurked behind her pale, blue-grey eyes. It was a head and shoulders shot but instead of sitting upright, she was hunching inwards, her arms tightly by her side. She looked self-conscious and a bit wary, as if she wasn't sure whom, if anyone, she could trust.

Sophie rarely liked photos of herself and this one had been no exception. She recalled trying to persuade her mother not to buy it because she thought it made her look fat.

She didn't realise Pampy and her grandfather had received a copy and she would certainly have vetoed it if she'd known. However, her heart now rather went out to this younger, more vulnerable version of herself.

She was touched Pampy had kept the photo in such a prominent place all these years, and also rather pleased there wasn't an individual one of Celia, too.

It confirmed what Sophie had always wanted to believe

– that she *did* have a special place in Pampy's heart. Whatever it was that had caused the fallout with Sophie's mother must have been quite spectacular.

By midday, Sophie had already made good progress. All her grandmother's music, which had sat for years gathering dust on top of the piano, was to be donated or recycled. She'd taken down the dirty curtains, folded them up and put them in a big pile, along with the cushions and threadbare rugs.

Most of the books in the little wooden bookcase against the back wall were terribly worn, so they went on the rubbish pile.

By now, Sophie's hands were filthy and the dust was making her sneeze. When she strolled next door to wash her hands and drink some water, she found Celia hadn't been idle, either.

Countless old kitchen items had been removed from cupboards and were on the floor in distinct heaps. Sophie did a quick scan. There was nothing much she wanted: just a few bits of china, perhaps, to remind her of her grandmother.

'Shall we go and pick up the car?' she asked.

Celia nodded. 'We'll have to get a taxi. I don't think it's in walking distance.'

The blue Toyota waiting for them on the garage forecourt was underwhelming, but it had plenty of space in the back. On the way home, they drove through a street lined with local shops and found a parking space outside a grocery store. There was a tempting display of fruit and fresh vegetables spilling onto the pavement: giant golden peaches, black and green grapes, dark red strawberries, glossy green avocadoes and mounds of leafy broccoli.

Next door to the grocery store was a smart-looking nail salon. It was clearly very busy and successful. Further back, Sophie could see rows of ceramic foot spa basins and ladies lounging on reclining chairs, leafing through magazines. It looked delightful and she decided to treat herself to a pedicure before she went home.

She was so busy admiring the scene, she quite forgot the main reason for being here and was now reminded by Celia.

Inside the grocery store was dark and cool. The narrow aisles were crammed with organic muesli, wholegrain pasta, spelt bread – and the chilled section had a tempting array of fresh meats and cheeses.

Everything seemed quite expensive, though, so they just bought black bin bags, milk, bread and a few other essentials, plus some grapes and apples, which they couldn't resist, and several bottles of lager.

When they went to pay, the smiley, middle-aged woman behind the till asked Sophie where they were from.

'I heard we had visitors from the UK,' she said, packing the shopping into a large, crackly brown paper bag and passing it to Sophie. 'Word gets round fast!'

Sophie stepped out into the burning heat once more with a smile on her face. It soon faded, however, when Celia practically wrenched the shopping from her arms, shoved it in the back of the car and banged the door shut.

'They're so bloody nosy,' she snapped. 'What business is it of theirs where we live?'

She was wearing pristine white plimsolls and a

close-fitting blue and white checked blouse, rolled up at the sleeves and tucked into a denim miniskirt. She looked fit, trim and annoyingly attractive.

Sophie wanted to make a catty remark about how wearing tight clothes in a humid climate was bound to make you grumpy. She managed not to, though.

'I don't mind the questions,' she said instead. 'I think it's rather nice they show an interest.'

Celia scowled. 'I hate fake-friendly people. They make my skin crawl.'

'Miserable old cow,' Sophie muttered under her breath. Luckily, Celia was clambering into the driving seat and didn't hear.

Sophie was about to hop in beside her when she spotted a big sign on a wooden board above a café on the opposite side of the street. It said 'GIGI'S' in curly yellow letters.

'Let's grab some lunch there,' she suggested, pointing to the shop. 'I met the woman who runs it last night. She's a neighbour of ours. She seems lovely.'

'She's not our neighbour,' Celia said nastily. 'We don't live here.' But Sophie was already crossing the road, narrowly avoiding an elderly man on a rusty old beach bike with upright handlebars.

There were a few round wooden tables and chairs on the pavement outside Gigi's, beneath a jaunty grey and white striped awning. The café was, as Gigi mentioned, extremely busy, with people queuing at the glass counter for coffee and food, while those who had already been served sat on benches around long wooden tables.

Menus were chalked on blackboards on the walls, along

with the prices, and Sophie's mouth watered at the thought of home-made ravioli stuffed with burrata, gorgonzola and walnut salad, sandwiches filled with almost anything you wanted – fresh focaccia, crusty panini or flatbread, sweet Italian sausage, prosciutto, arugula, eggplant, cheese.

As Gigi promised, there were also numerous varieties of gelato, or Italian ice cream, including hazelnut, pistachio, almond, cinnamon, cherry, peach and lemon.

A scent of herbs, meats and cheeses filled the air, laughter was coming from the tables and there was the constant bubble and hiss of coffee being brewed and milk frothed. Every now and again the staff, in white aprons and hats, would call for something from the kitchen and a new person would appear, bearing a giant carton of milk or a tray of hot pizza slices.

At first, Sophie didn't spot Gigi at the far end of the counter by the pastries and cakes. She, too, was in a white uniform, and she'd tucked away her distinctive hair.

When their eyes met, Gigi's face lit up in a huge smile.

'*Cara mia*,' she cried, squeezing out of a small gap at the side of the counter and hurrying towards Sophie. 'My dear friend, I owe you a great big thank you.'

For a moment, Sophie couldn't think what she meant, then she remembered Nino and the whisky. Before she could say anything, however, Gigi was throwing her arms wide and wrapping Sophie in a tight embrace.

Sophie glanced back at Celia, staring at them with huge open eyes, and had to stifle a laugh. Uptight as hell, if Celia hated strangers asking questions, then such public displays of affection must surely be her worst nightmare.

The other customers were agog, clearly itching to find out what all the fuss was about, and it was worth their wait. When at last Gigi released Sophie from her grip, after planting powdery kisses on both cheeks, she stepped back with a flourish, cleared her throat and proceeded to recount the whole story of last night, liberally embellishing as she went along.

'Luckily my friend Sophie was there, we bumped into each other on the beach. Turns out she lives a few doors down from me – fancy that! It was once her grandmother's place and now it belongs to her two beautiful granddaughters.'

Sophie winced. She could imagine Celia's fury and didn't catch her eye. Half the Rockaway community seemed to be here and it wouldn't be long before everyone would know about the sisters' inheritance. They'd probably be stopping them in the street to ask what they planned to do with Piping Plover House.

Now Gigi was holding aloft a large white cardboard box.

'Here, have this,' she said, passing it to Sophie.

The lid wasn't properly closed and Sophie was delighted to see a delicious-looking assortment of filled panini and dainty home-made cakes and biscuits.

'There's no need—' she started to say, but Gigi shook her head.

'It's my pleasure and besides, you must be hungry! You can have a little picnic on the beach!'

As soon as they were outside, Celia's scowl deepened.

'A picnic!' she said nastily. 'What does she think we are – a couple of kids?'

Sophie was about to say she rather liked picnics, when

a tall, well-built man crossed the street towards them and stopped them in their tracks.

'Mary Poppins!' he said to Sophie with a big grin.

He was wearing dark sunglasses and a canvas khaki hat with a wide brim, but the smile and swagger were unmistakable. It was Joe, from last night.

Casting round for the right words, Sophie blurted out the first sentence that came into her head.

'Why has your jacket got so many pockets?'

The greenish brown gilet over his white T-shirt was, indeed, covered in bulging pockets and a small pair of black scissors hung from a loop on his chest.

'It's for fishing, you idiot,' Celia muttered.

'You got it,' he said to Celia, still grinning. 'I need bait from the fish store up there.' He tipped his head in the general direction. 'I'm hoping to catch a nice big sea bass for my dinner.'

He removed his hat and ran a hand through his longish fair hair. He was handsome, with a tanned face and body, thick, muscular arms and legs and a strong, straight nose.

'And who might you be?' he asked Celia. 'I didn't realise there was another Mary Poppins in town.'

For some reason this made Sophie bristle, and she was even more annoyed by her sister's response.

'I'm Celia,' she said, flashing white teeth. Gone was the scowl and she flicked her dark hair girlishly. 'I love sea bass.'

'Yeah?' said Joe. 'Tell you what, if I catch two, I'll give you the other one.'

Celia dipped her head to one side, so she was looking up at him through her long lashes.

'Now there's an offer I can't refuse. We're staying on 146ᵗʰ Street. Here's my number. You've got no excuse not to call.'

Sophie was outraged. The hussy! She wanted to tell her sister off; she had a husband, for goodness' sake!

Joe must have noticed her indignation and seemed amused.

'Why, thank you, ma'am!' he said, before tucking Celia's number in a front pocket. Then he popped the hat back on his head and tipped the brim.

'Well I'll be on my way. Lovely to meet you two ladies. See you around.'

The sisters watched in silence as he sauntered off, whistling a jaunty tune. It was only once he was well out of hearing that Sophie allowed herself to vent.

'What a prat!' She glared at Celia, who was still gazing after Joe with a thoughtful look in her eyes. 'Did you hear me?' she snapped. 'I said he's a class A jerk. He thinks he's IT – and he's so not.'

This time, her words seemed to get through. Celia came out of her daydream, stood up straight and crossed her well-toned arms.

'I think he's rather nice,' she said softly. The corners of her mouth curled. 'And *very* fit.'

Six

Why did she do it? Why did she compete with Sophie in front of Joe and try to put her down? Celia disliked herself for it.

It was obvious there was a spark between those two, even if Sophie hadn't noticed, and what was the harm in that?

There was nothing to prevent Sophie from having a little summer fling, if she wanted one. She was unattached and probably deserved some romance after what she'd been through: money and work worries, a relationship break-up, problems with Layla, and so on.

Celia, on the other hand, had everything – a great job, rich husband, two clever sons and a massive fuck-off house in south-west London, not to mention the French villa.

Their lives could hardly be more different, one golden, the other distinctly tarnished. But even so, Celia had clocked the interest in Joe's eyes when he spoke to her sister and she hadn't liked it.

She was supposed to be the stunning one, the apple of her father's eye, his shining star.

It was mean of her, she knew, but she couldn't seem to help herself.

Back at Piping Plover House, neither of the sisters suggested having lunch together and Celia went straight to her room. She'd seen inside Gigi's box of goodies and didn't trust herself. With any luck, Sophie would scoff the lot, removing all temptation before Celia ventured down again.

Taking a notebook from a drawer, she sat on the end of her bed and proceeded to write down what she'd consumed so far today: two mugs of coffee with skimmed milk – 30 calories; small bowl of granola with skimmed milk – 230 cals; half cup of black grapes – 55 cals; five almonds – 35 cals. Total – 350 cals.

She smiled. Good. She'd just have a bit of fruit for lunch, and then reward herself with a reasonably big supper. This way, she'd easily keep to her one thousand five hundred calories a day allowance. If Sophie tucked into Gigi's rolls and pastries, she'd probably consume twice that in just one sitting.

Celia's thoughts turned to Joe again and her stomach fluttered. He was *hot*. Checking her face in the mirror, she noticed to her dismay that her complexion was rather dull and blotchy, so she decided to use a facemask.

She'd brought two with her from her favourite beauty salon. They were supposed to leave her skin looking 'firmer, tighter and fresher', and she was eager to see if they lived up to their promise.

Joe was about the same age as her, she reckoned.

Attractive men often preferred glamorous, younger women, so she'd need to put in some effort. She was confident she'd win him over, though; she'd soon have him eating out of her hand.

She'd never once been turned down by a guy she fancied, not that she'd ever followed it through once she was married. Adultery wasn't her thing, but there was nothing wrong with flirtation. It was great for the ego. Everyone needed a boost now and again.

After washing her face, she tied her hair in a tight ponytail and applied the mask, which was bright blue. It had to be left on for twenty minutes.

Celia would have an apple afterwards, and then crack on with some household tasks. She wondered what to wear for doing the chores. She'd have to look gorgeous, just in case Joe dropped by.

Strolling over to her wardrobe, she remembered one of her female patients, a gardener, looking a million dollars in some torn and faded denim dungarees and a stripy Breton top.

The patient had come straight from work to the surgery. Her hands were muddy, her cheeks rosy and her eyes sparkled. Most of her long fair hair had escaped from its plait and was trailing messily around her face.

Celia didn't have dungarees but her gaze fell on her khaki cargo pants, with big pockets and rolled up ankles. They were suitably rugged and would go well with her red and white stripy T-shirt. She was sorted.

Would Sophie really mind if she and Joe had a little dalliance – without the sex, of course? If so, it'd be Sophie's own fault. She seemed to have no clue earlier on that Joe was trying to chat her up. And she'd given him no reason to believe she was keen on him, either.

On reflection, Celia decided, she shouldn't feel the slightest bit guilty. In this life, if you wanted something, you had to go for it. Otherwise someone else would get there first.

She washed off the mask in the shower, shampooed her hair and moisturised her skin from top to toe. The cargo pants and T-shirt went really well together, and she was careful not to apply too much make-up, not wishing to appear overdone.

On the landing, she had a brief exchange with Sophie about their grandmother's ugly old sewing box, which Sophie wanted to keep. Celia, who loathed clutter, said she was welcome to it.

When she finally entered the kitchen, her appetite had mysteriously vanished, which was a bonus. Now, she'd skip lunch altogether and save calories.

Gigi's box of goodies was still on the table and when she looked inside, she was surprised to see quite a lot left. She closed the lid with a shudder, shoved the box in the fridge and quickly left the room, shutting the door firmly behind her.

While Celia was upstairs, Sophie took a plate of food for herself onto the porch. Sitting on the swing bench with the plate on her lap, she felt a sense of heaviness again. It was

Celia's presence weighing her down. This whole visit would be so much more enjoyable without her.

After last night and this morning, Sophie realised she was falling in love with Rockaway all over again. Even the name sounded romantic and thrilling. It was derived from 'Reckouwacky', a Canarsie Native American word. The Canarsie were the first people to live on the peninsula. She longed to explore the area and really get to know some of the locals and hear their stories.

Perhaps she should offer to clear the house herself and put it on the market, so Celia could go home; it was a thought, though she doubted her sister would agree. She'd hate to think of Sophie making decisions on her own almost as much as she loathed being here herself.

Sophie nibbled on the edge of a miniature bread roll, stuffed with mozzarella, fresh basil and rocket leaves. It was super fresh and smelled delicious, but she wasn't hungry any more and could hardly taste it.

The sun was at its most intense now, which didn't help, and although the porch was shady, the air felt thick and soupy, which made her sticky and uncomfortable all over.

She yearned to swim in the ocean, but resolved to tackle a couple more jobs before allowing herself another break. This wasn't a holiday, after all, though she wished it were.

Instead of finishing the front room, something made Sophie decide to go into her grandmother's bedroom, on the second floor.

Passing her room at the back of the house, she ascended

the wooden stairs leading to another wide landing, off which were three more closed doors.

The first opened into a bathroom, just as old-fashioned as the others, with a dusty cream carpet that had seen better days.

The rectangular tub was a dirty pink colour, like the pedestal washbasin, which had a crack in the bowl and a knob of dried out soap in a wooden holder on the ledge.

Pampy's toothbrush and paste were still in a white china mug inside a metal holder screwed to the wall, while her flowery quilted dressing gown hung on the back of the door.

Leaving the door ajar, Sophie peeked in the next room, which was full of junk: cardboard boxes, a broken chair, several suitcases, a rolled up carpet, some old curtains in a heap on the floor, a couple of wicker baskets and a rusty ironing board with a torn cover.

The single bed in the corner had a bare mattress with a dip in the middle. Broken springs? This must have been Pampy's dumping ground, where she plonked everything she couldn't quite bear to throw away because it 'might just come in'.

Her bedroom at the front was more or less as Sophie remembered from all those years ago, right down to the curtains in the big bow window overlooking the street, decorated with brightly coloured flowers and hummingbirds.

Those drapes must be over forty years old but they weren't torn or frayed, merely tired-looking.

It was a wide, high room, full of light, and although everything in it had seen better days, it retained a certain comfort and grandeur. Sophie had certainly thought it quite splendid as a child, imagining that the Queen slept somewhere exactly like it.

Back then, Pampy's door was always closed and you had to knock before entering. Waiting for an invitation was a tremendous thrill. It wasn't as if Pampy ever said no, but still, Sophie believed one day she just might, which added to the excitement.

Most mornings, as soon as she woke, she would tiptoe upstairs, tap lightly and listen for her grandmother's welcoming voice: 'Come on in!'

Peeking her head round the door, Sophie would usually find Pampy in bed, propped up against white pillows, her long, silvery hair streaming out around her like a waterfall.

She would smile, pat the space beside her and Sophie would dive under the warm covers, enjoying her grandmother's distinctive orangey-floral scent.

Everything about her fascinated Sophie then: the softness of her hair and skin, which felt so different from Sophie's own; the funny, criss-cross patterns of wrinkles on her neck, the way her gold wedding band was stuck so tight it would never come off, and the stories she would tell about her own childhood and that of Sophie's mother.

Now, though, there was no Pampy and the bed was covered with a faded fuchsia pink, yellow and turquoise bedspread, matching the curtains. An empty feeling lodged in Sophie's stomach which, even after all these years, she knew only her grandmother could fill.

On either side of the bed were two white, French-style side tables on which stood lamps with fancy shades, like pleated skirts with loopy frills around the bottom edge.

Built-in cupboards lined the right-hand wall while to the left was a small door, camouflaged by the same pale, striped wallpaper as the rest.

The entrance to the lookout tower! A little shiver of excitement ran up and down Sophie's spine. She used to call it Pampy's secret door, and was only allowed to open it and venture upstairs if her grandmother were with her.

The rules didn't apply any more, of course. Even so, Sophie found herself looking round furtively to check no one was watching before twisting the brass knob.

There was only a small flight of stairs up to the lookout room and they were so narrow her shoulders brushed the walls as she ascended.

She remembered Pampy telling her that, for years, she'd wanted a 'room in the sky' where she could watch the stars, but it was a long time before her husband would agree.

The builder they chose hadn't tried to construct something to blend in with the other properties in the street, or even with Piping Plover House itself. Planning rules must have been lax in those days.

Still, Pampy loved her secret hideaway and often went up there to 'star-bathe', as she called it, sitting in her chair or lying on cushions on her back to soak up the beauty of the night sky.

The wooden floor creaked when Sophie entered and she stood for a moment, surveying her surroundings. Big windows on every side let in masses of light and when she looked to her left, she could see the ocean.

Pampy's dainty armchair, with a loose, white linen cover, was facing the sea, and beside it was her old-fashioned telescope. A blue and white striped hessian rug lay on the floor and there was a low bookcase filled with paperbacks against one wall.

The temperature was almost unbearably hot and Sophie tried to open the windows, but they were locked. Casting around for a key, she noticed Pampy's little wooden sewing box on the other side of the armchair.

It was a funny-looking item, rectangular in shape, with a wooden handle, four stumpy legs and wooden struts on both sides. Sophie could remember playing with the box when she was little, enthralled by its many drawers, which opened and closed using a clever folding system.

She would spend ages sorting through the special tin, containing buttons of every size and shape, and turning the darning mushroom and giant wooden crochet hooks into imaginary people.

She couldn't wait to find out if they were still in there, but decided to take the box downstairs, where it was cooler. It wasn't heavy to carry and the handle felt smooth and warm.

At first, she attempted to slide off the two lids on top and when this didn't work, she tried lifting instead. Straight away, out popped two drawers on either side, which expanded at opposite ends like a concertina. Only the large drawer at the bottom didn't move.

The mechanism had seemed like magic to the young Sophie.

To her delight, the blue and red tin of buttons was still there, with the words 'Time for Tea!' on the side and a picture of a smiling lady with fluffy blonde hair and a scarlet headband on the lid. The smiling lady was holding a white cup to her lips, as if she were about to take a sip.

Sophie traced her finger around the smooth, curly black letters. She must have examined the picture countless times because she could even recall the lines of steam, drawn in black, and the row of white pearls around the woman's slender neck.

Alongside the tin were assorted packets of needles, some bent-handled tailor's shears, pinking scissors with jagged edges, a silver thimble, a fabric measuring tape and heaps of silver and gold safety pins.

The compartments beneath contained balls of coloured wool and cotton reels, along with bits of silky ribbon and leftover lace. There were also various zips, some new, others clearly unpicked from discarded clothes and kept for emergencies, plus metal poppers, hook and eye fastenings and squares of different types of fabric, presumably for patches.

Honestly, if you had an emergency wardrobe malfunction, like a tear, a drooping hem or a missing button, Pampy would have been the one to ask. Sophie was impressed.

Finally, in the bottom drawer, she discovered a bright pink silk pincushion. A little gasp escaped from her lips and she took it out almost reverentially.

Shaped like a tennis ball on top, it was supported by six plump little men who looked like Japanese sumo wrestlers with pale round faces, small black eyes and absurd black ponytails, sticking up at right angles from the crowns of their shaven heads.

Each little man wore a different-coloured top – emerald

green, peacock blue, yellow, orange, ruby red and purple. They had once enchanted Sophie, who had given them all names and tried to plait their hair.

She'd always wished she could detach them from their base and play with them individually, but here they were, still hanging on bravely, joined together for eternity whether they liked it or not.

The silk on top of the cushion was tatty now and punctured with holes. As Sophie stroked the soft cheeks of the little men, it felt strange to think she'd done the exact same thing some forty years before. It was almost as if the last few decades had never happened, and she was back to being the little girl who had found such wonder in small things.

After replacing the pincushion, she took out the wooden darning mushroom, pitted with deep scratches made by the needles Pampy had used to mend woollen socks or jumpers. She couldn't find any crochet hooks, but discovered a pair of short, fat wooden knitting needles, which she was sure she'd used to knit the multicoloured scarf that she'd given her father one Christmas.

A shadow crossed her mind. The summer before, Pampy had shown her how to cast on and off and Sophie had spent most evenings working away on that scarf. She must have been about eight years old.

She'd been excited to watch her father open the parcel on Christmas Day, carefully peeling off the sticky tape and refolding the paper so it could be used again. He'd said thank you, of course, but had hardly looked at it, commenting only on the holey bit where she'd dropped a stitch.

How she'd longed for him to ask how many hours it had taken to finish, to compliment her on her skill, on all the different colours she'd chosen and the lovely tassels Pampy had helped her attach to the ends!

Instead, he'd shoved the present to one side and opened Celia's, a story that she'd written and illustrated herself. This, he'd read aloud, taking time to praise her choice of vocabulary and admire her vivid illustrations.

Sophie replaced the knitting needles with a shudder and was about to close the box when something else caught her eye. In the bottom drawer, lying on its side, was a small, plain, rectangular cardboard container with the words '12 x White Tailor's Fabric Marking Chalks' written on the lid.

It was such an ordinary-looking item that at first, Sophie wasn't going to bother to investigate. Besides, she was feeling unsettled about the scarf and eager to put the sewing box away. Out of the corner of an eye, however, she spotted something protruding from the edge of the lid: a triangle of folded paper. Thinking it was probably just a bit of lining, she picked up the container and tugged gently on the paper, but it wouldn't come out.

The container rattled when she shook it – there was definitely something in there – so Sophie resolved to open it after all. Inside were several bits of grey-white chalk, which Pampy must have used for marking fabric.

Now, Sophie could see the triangle of paper was attached to a bigger piece and, on closer inspection, it appeared to have been carefully folded and slipped under the chalk pieces, so it was barely visible.

Sophie moved the chalk markers aside and pulled the paper out. Crumbly white powder stuck to her fingers and hands and fell on her clothes, but she didn't bother to brush it off.

She started to unfold the paper, until all of a sudden, something caught her interest. Now it was fully open, she could see it was covered in words, written in faded black ink in a hand she didn't recognise.

Laying the paper flat on the bedspread, she soon realised she was looking at a letter, dated 3rd May, 1982. She sat up straight, completely focused now and with all her senses alert.

The address at the top was Piping Plover House, and down below, the letter was simply signed, 'Father'.

She read on:

Dear Teresa,

As you can imagine, I have thought long and hard in the past few days and weeks about what to do for the best.

I am shocked, saddened and disappointed by your behaviour. I simply cannot understand how you could bring yourself to be so selfish and reckless yet again.

You have hurt your mother and me more than you can imagine, and betrayed your husband and children in the most despicable way.

As parents, we tried to instil in you the values we hold dear. It seems, however, that you have rejected faith, honesty, hard work and self-sacrifice in favour of lies and self-gratification.

We are deeply concerned not only for you, your husband and daughters, but also for our precious Catholic community here in Rockaway.

As the great poet John Donne famously said, 'No man is an island entire of itself; every man is a piece of the continent, a part of the main'.

We influence each other in ways we cannot imagine and I will not allow you to spread your poison here.

For this reason, it is with great sorrow and a heavy heart that I must ask you not to visit us anymore, unless and until you are willing to go to confession, do your penance and ask our Lord God for forgiveness.

Until then, please do not try to contact me or your mother as turning our backs on you will only cause us more pain.

I hope that one day you will understand our course of action.

In the meantime, I wish you well in the life you have chosen for yourself. I shall continue to pray for you.

Father

When Sophie had finished reading, she folded the paper up again and held it tightly to her chest while she stared into space.

Her eyes were blank but her mind was racing. What on earth had her mother done? Her father called her 'selfish' and said she'd betrayed her husband and children. What could he mean?

Sophie knew her mother had rejected Catholicism and

remained opposed to any sort of organised religion right up until her death.

Returning to the letter, Sophie looked again at the date it was written – the third of May, 1982. Sophie would have been twelve in the March of that year, the same year the Rockaway visits suddenly stopped.

It was also more or less a year to the day before her grandfather's death. Sophie recalled hearing the news and feeling guilty because she wasn't sad enough. She thought she ought to cry, but no tears came.

Her mother told her what had happened in a very matter-of-fact way, as if she wasn't too upset either. But her eyes were red and you could tell she'd been weeping. There was no question of anyone going to the funeral.

Goosebumps ran up and down Sophie's arms and legs, despite the heat, and she hugged her grandmother's bedspread around her.

The letter shed some light on the terrible argument that had torn the family apart, but seemed to raise more questions than it answered.

Why, for example, had her mother refused to tell her what the rift was about, even when she was grown up and quite capable of handling difficult information?

Just as importantly, why was the letter hidden in Pampy's sewing box? Was it a copy? It didn't look like one. Had Sophie's mother ever received it – and how could Sophie find out?

She racked her brains, trying to recall how her mother had explained the argument. 'I'm afraid Pampy and I have had a falling-out. We won't be going to Rockaway any more.'

'Pampy and I...' Sophie had always been led to believe the dispute was between the two women. Yet the letter was written and signed by her grandfather. Why was he never mentioned?

Her left hand crept up to the delicate gold necklace she always wore, with its tiny pendant. It was shaped like a daisy, her favourite flower, and in the centre sat a small, sparkling diamond.

Terry had given her the necklace for her fortieth birthday and she had rarely taken it off since. Little did she know then her mother had already been diagnosed with cancer and hadn't long to live.

A painful lump formed in her throat that wouldn't go down. Terry was only sixty-one when she died. Far too young.

She was just eighteen when Sophie was born, not much more than a schoolgirl. She kept her youthful looks and figure and when Sophie was older, people used to comment they were more like sisters or friends than mother and daughter.

This thought had pleased Sophie, who longed to be really close to her mum. For some reason, however, it seemed that Terry always wanted to keep a slight distance between them. She'd open up a little, only to shut the door again.

The necklace gift had touched Sophie very much, because it reminded her of when she was small, making daisy chains with Terry. Sometimes, they'd press them carefully between the leaves of big fat books so they could keep them forever.

On sunny days, in the middle of a field full of daisies, her mother would turn into a little girl herself, stopping every now and again to admire her work. When her circle was complete, she'd wear it like a tiara. 'How do I look?' she'd ask Sophie, with a laugh. 'Am I a princess now?'

It must have been hard for her, marrying so young and moving with her new husband to England straight away. She'd told Sophie she first met Paul in her early teens, when he was living with his British family in Brooklyn and used to come to Rockaway for weekends and holidays.

He was six years older and treated her more like a kid sister back then. They didn't see each other for several years while he was going through university in England and establishing himself as a lawyer. Then, the summer she turned eighteen, he returned to Rockaway and asked her to be his wife.

Terry made him sound like a knight in shining armour, who swept her off her feet, but Sophie never bought into the romance. Paul was no hero and as far as she could tell, the only thing he and her mother had in common was their Roman Catholic background.

If Terry were lonely or regretted marrying so quickly, she never let on. Sometimes, though, Sophie would find her crying silently in her room. When asked what was wrong, she'd pretend she was fine, or make up some silly excuse that wouldn't fool anyone.

This troubled Sophie. She wanted so much to comfort her mother and make things better, but there was nothing she could do.

Tears sprang to her eyes and she tried to get rid of the

lump in her throat by swallowing hard, but it wouldn't budge. It was as if, all of a sudden, the pain of her childhood, her father's bullying and hostility, her mother's sadness, Celia's contempt, Pampy's rejection and life's many other disappointments had converged into a perfect storm.

If she had been alone in the house she would have howled, but Celia wasn't far away and mustn't know.

Pulling herself together, she sat up tall, straightened her shoulders and took a few deep breaths. When at last the tears started to subside, she carefully tucked the letter back in the container beneath the tailor's chalk and replaced the lid.

It didn't seem wise to put the sewing box back in the tower where it might be discovered, so Sophie carried it downstairs. Just as she reached her bedroom, however, Celia's door swung open at the other end of the landing, making her jump.

'What are you doing?' Celia asked suspiciously. She had wet hair and had changed into trousers and a T-shirt.

'Nothing,' Sophie replied, trying to sound casual and forcing out a smile.

Celia's gaze fell on the sewing box and her eyebrows shot up.

'What's that?'

Sophie thought rapidly.

'Pampy's old sewing caddy. I found it in her room. It's full of wool and cotton reels and stuff. D'you mind if I have it?'

Watching her sister slyly, she started to open the right-hand lid. The two top drawers swung out, revealing a jumble of lace, wool and safety pins, some of which tumbled onto the carpet.

'What do you want that for?' Celia asked with a frown; she hated mess.

'I need somewhere to put my sewing stuff at home. This'd be perfect.'

Celia's frown relaxed. 'Sure,' she said with a shrug, 'if you've got room for it in your suitcase.'

As soon as she'd disappeared, Sophie's heartbeat started to slow and she exhaled deeply. That had been too close for comfort.

Opening the white melamine wardrobe in her bedroom, she popped the sewing box inside, locked the door and hid the small gold key in her purse.

On no account must Celia find out about the letter. Sophie hadn't a clue what she was going to do with it but of one thing she was sure: she didn't want her sister to know.

Seven

It was just as well Sophie had hidden the sewing box, because Celia suggested their next job should be sorting through the clothes in Pampy's wardrobe. Of course she, too, remembered the hidden entrance to the tower, and the first thing she did on walking into their grandmother's bedroom was go up for a look.

When she came down again, Sophie had flung open the wardrobe doors and was sitting hunched on Pampy's bed, overwhelmed by the size of the task.

'She's got so much stuff,' she said with a groan. 'She can't have thrown anything away ever.'

'Just fold it all up and shove it in bin bags. We can do a charity shop run tomorrow.'

Pampy had her own timeless, understated style she'd stuck to religiously. Sophie had never seen such an array of pleated skirts, neat blouses and belted shirtdresses, made of corduroy or cotton and with or without sleeves, depending on the season.

Some of the clothes had been made by Pampy herself, while others came from respectable shops and department stores with a reputation for reliable tailoring and good quality fabrics.

She had been small and slim and even if Sophie had wanted any of the clothes for herself, they wouldn't have fit. Celia could have worn them but she wouldn't have been seen dead in Pampy's cast-offs, so they were packed up and taken downstairs.

The next job after the wardrobe was Pampy's chest of drawers, which was stuffed with knickers, socks, bras, tights and cardigans. Sophie found it difficult to handle such highly personal belongings, knowing she was only going to discard the lot. By the time she'd finished, she was emotionally exhausted.

'I need a swim,' she announced, when she'd bagged up the last items and stripped the bed, too.

Celia didn't reply, but swept Pampy's make-up and scent straight into a black refuse sack. Sophie looked away quickly.

Her neck and back ached with pent-up tension and she stretched her arms above her head, interlacing her fingers and pulling hard.

'I won't be too long,' she said, lowering her arms again with a sigh. 'See you later.'

It was a relief to escape from Pampy's room and go downstairs to get changed. Sophie found her pale blue bikini at the bottom of her suitcase and pulled it out tentatively.

The Lycra had thinned and faded and the bottoms were

a bit saggy. She'd meant to buy a new one, but that was months ago and she hadn't done anything about it.

Still, it was the only one she had. As she tied the halter neck straps together behind her head, she examined herself in the pedestal mirror on the chest of drawers.

Everything above the waist wasn't too bad, she thought. Her shoulders and arms were slim enough and her large round boobs fit snugly into the cups without causing unsightly bulges.

When she pulled on the bikini bottoms and tipped the rectangular mirror down, however, it was a different story. Her tummy, which hadn't seen a single ray of sunshine since the previous summer, looked so white it was almost luminous. The pants seemed to accentuate her wide hips and her thighs resembled lumpy dough. Thankfully, from just below her thighs down, things improved, and she was quite happy with her slim knees, calves and ankles.

Former lovers used to tell her they liked everything about her, including her curves, but she never believed them. In her mind, she still needed to lose at least a stone, probably more.

The image of Celia's slender hips and skinny legs in that denim miniskirt swam before her eyes. Scowling, Sophie took a few steps forwards and spun the mirror round to face the wall.

Bloody bikini. Well, no one would be looking at *her* on the beach anyway. It would probably be heaving with sylph-like girls, prancing around in G-strings.

Grabbing a pink towel from the bathroom, she wrapped it round her chest, tucking in the ends to hold it up. Then, having mislaid her flip-flops, she padded barefoot to the front door and banged it shut behind her.

It was nearly 6 p.m. by the time she reached the beach. The sun had started to fade but the air was still warm and the sand felt delicious beneath her feet.

As it happened, there wasn't a sylph-like girl to be seen. In fact the place was empty, save for a tall man walking a yellow labrador some way off.

Throwing down her towel, Sophie stepped ankle-deep into the chilly spray and gasped; it was much colder than she'd expected. She found herself going up on tiptoe and raising her arms high above her head, as if this would somehow keep her warmer.

Each time a wave reached her knees or thighs, she gasped again and did a silly cold water dance, hopping up and down, backwards and forwards, trying in vain to beat the ocean at its own game.

It was almost impossible to believe that just a few hours ago she'd been boiling hot and desperate for a swim. Getting in was going to be harder than she'd thought.

A giant wave rolled up and slapped her on the stomach, almost knocking her down. Bracing herself, Sophie counted to three and dived straight into the middle of the next roller, holding her breath, closing her eyes and paddling with all her might.

When she emerged on the other side and opened her eyes again, the waves had turned back into ripples. Her body had become accustomed to the temperature, too, and she wasn't so cold any more.

Looking ahead, her feet only just touching the bottom,

all she could see was orangey-blue sky, greenish-grey water, white seagulls and the odd boat bobbing in the distance. She tipped back her head and breathed in and out really slowly, filling her lungs with salty air. Now, she was in heaven.

Laughter gurgled in her throat and for a moment nothing, not even the prospect of selling Piping Plover House, could ruin her joy. Lowering her head, she launched into a strong, rhythmic breaststroke.

She must have done about thirty strokes before deciding it was time to stop and check how far she'd come. Turning round, she spotted her pink towel way off to the right and realised she'd drifted quite far. She'd have to swim hard against the current to get back.

For a while she stuck with crawl, switching to sidestroke, then backstroke only when she started to tire. She was a strong swimmer and wasn't afraid she'd be swept out, but going against the tide was exhausting. When she rolled onto her tummy again, she was relieved to discover she was now much closer to her towel.

As soon as her feet touched the ground once more, she performed a victory roll, pinching her nose with two fingers to stop the spray whooshing up her nostrils.

It was something she'd enjoyed doing as a child – she'd always been a water baby – and it made her feel young and a bit silly.

Next, she attempted an underwater handstand, but it wasn't long before the choppy waves knocked her over. Once upright again, she waded towards land until the water was just below her knees, then jogged the final stretch, vaulting over the bigger waves until the ocean was well and truly behind her.

Her skin tingled pleasurably as she walked up the beach, and her head felt sharper and clearer than before. Grabbing her towel, she gave it a good shake before rubbing herself down and squeezing the sea from her long wet hair.

How Celia could bear not to swim was a total mystery to Sophie. It had been the highlight of her day. There again, the two of them never did have anything in common.

The light was beginning to fade now. Sophie was about to make her way home when a couple of teenagers, clutching bottles of beer, emerged from the alleyway that led from the street.

Drinking any sort of alcohol on the beach was strictly forbidden; there were notices everywhere. This would be why the pair, a boy and girl, had waited till dusk to venture down. What's more, they were probably around sixteen or seventeen years old, maybe less, and certainly not twenty-one, the legal drinking age.

They didn't seem too worried about being spotted, however. They were laughing and talking quite loudly and as they walked, the girl repeatedly bumped into the boy, knocking him sideways, as if it were part of a game.

Soon, Sophie was able to see their features more clearly and could tell the girl was very pretty: slim, athletic and tanned, with long straight dark hair, a wide mouth and big dark eyes. She was wearing a pair of tiny white shorts and a tight pink top with spaghetti straps, showing a lot of cleavage.

He, meanwhile, was the sort most mothers hoped their

daughters wouldn't date, while most daughters wished they could. Bare-chested, his neck, torso and arms were covered with menacing tattoos: an eagle with beady eyes, a sharp beak and talons; a skull and a rather unpleasant snake.

The serpent was slithering from his navel up his chest almost to his jawbone, circling one of his nipples on the way. Its head, resting on the boy's neck, had a wide open mouth, and the creature was flashing its forked tongue.

The boy's bleached blond hair, shaved at the sides and sticking up on top, also screamed danger and anarchy. He might have been mild as a lamb in reality, though, and his face, which was free of garish illustrations, was sensitive and handsome.

The young pair settled down on a dune and proceeded to snog, in between swigs of beer and puffs of something that didn't smell like tobacco. Sophie was intending to pass by quickly, but a short, round, middle-aged woman bustled into view, waving her arms in an agitated sort of way and shouting, 'MARIELLA!' followed by something unfriendly-sounding in Italian.

It was Gigi, who seemed to be red all over – her face, hair, even her chest and neck, above a white, V-neck T-shirt, were puce, and the tips of her ears burned scarlet. Sophie had a strong sense of déja vu.

Gigi didn't even notice Sophie at first, so blinded was she by rage.

'*Sei fuori!*' she shouted, jabbing her finger at the girl. Mariella was clearly her daughter because they looked so similar, with the same high forehead, olive skin and dark, round eyes.

'You, sneaking off, thinking I wouldn't know. Drinking, smoking – and God knows what...' She jutted her chin at this and glared at the boy, who looked shifty and stared hard at his feet.

Then, turning back to her daughter: 'You're lucky the cops haven't caught you. You'll be prosecuted. Did you think about that?'

She didn't wait for a reply but shook her head instead.

'If your Papà gets to hear of this, you'll be mincemeat!' she added, jabbing a finger in the girl's direction.

Conscious she was witnessing yet another family feud and feeling a bit voyeuristic, Sophie started to sidle away. But without warning, Gigi launched forwards like a torpedo, grabbed Mariella's ear, along with a thick clump of dark hair, and yanked hard.

'You little minx!' screamed Gigi. 'You think I brought you up to be some sort of wildcat? *Porco mondo!*'

Mariella wasn't listening, however. She'd managed to get free, ran to Sophie and proceeded to cower behind her, peeping around her shoulder from time to time, using her like a human shield.

'Help!' She was screaming so loudly in Sophie's ear that it hurt. 'Mom's lost it. She's gonna kill me!'

'She won't do that,' Sophie said rather lamely, because Gigi was tensed up and frowning. At any moment she might march over and try to seize her daughter and Sophie wasn't sure whether she should fight for the girl – or run.

Luckily, she didn't have to do either because they were interrupted by a raised voice.

'What's going on? Is everyone OK?'

Spinning round, Sophie saw the tall figure of Joe coming up the beach towards them, with a green bag on his shoulder and a very big fishing rod in his hand.

He was wearing the same clothes he'd had on earlier: dark mirrored sunglasses, canvas khaki hat, baggy tan shorts, white T-shirt and a greenish brown gilet covered in bulging pockets.

All at once the atmosphere seemed to change.

'Joe!' cried Gigi, her face breaking into a wide smile. 'Did you catch anything?'

They were obviously acquainted, then. For a moment, Sophie was surprised, until she realised that Rockaway was quite a small place; everyone knew everyone else, it seemed, or at least knew *of* them.

'I did,' he replied, taking the bag off his shoulder and dropping it on the ground close by. He bent over and set his rod carefully on top. Sophie noticed the golden hairs on his dark brown arms and the fine grains of sand sticking to his skin.

While her mother was distracted, Mariella felt safe enough to step out from behind Sophie's back. She stayed close by, however, hovering at her side.

Joe rose up to his full height again, took off his sunglasses and tucked them in the neck of his T-shirt.

'Is there a problem?' he asked again, looking at each of them in turn. His face was weathered and the lines around his eyes seemed deeper, following an afternoon in the sun.

Gigi was about to reply but Mariella got in first.

'Mom's mad at me 'cause Danny and I were drinking beer on the beach.'

'Ah,' said Joe, tipping back his hat. 'Not a good idea. Lucky the cops didn't get you.'

'Exactly what I said,' Gigi commented, with a self-satisfied nod. She put her hands on her hips. 'She knows the rules perfectly well, she just chooses to ignore them.'

'Here, give me those.' Joe gestured to the empty beer bottles lying on the sand. Obediently, Danny bent down to pick them up. Joe unzipped his bag, put them in and zipped it up again.

'There,' he said with a grin. Then, in a jokey, schoolmasterly tone: 'Now, no one knows anything about any illegal underage drinking. Let's forget all about it, shall we, and go home?'

'Thanks,' said Mariella seriously and Danny mumbled, 'Yeah.'

'You're welcome. Just don't do it again, OK? And don't smoke weed either. It makes you stupid. It also gives you erectile dysfunction and cotton vagina.'

Mariella's dark eyes widened and Danny coughed nervously, while Gigi stared at Joe in stunned silence. Sophie had an inappropriate urge to laugh and was forced to bite the insides of her cheeks – hard.

She made a mental note to Google 'cotton vagina' when she got home. Was it a thing? If so, she needed to know.

All this time, she'd been so engrossed in what was going on that she'd quite forgotten she'd just come out of the sea. A sudden shiver ran all the way from the top of her head down to her toes and it dawned on her that she was terribly cold. What's more, she was standing in front of Joe in her soggy bikini, having dropped her towel back on the sand.

For all she knew, he could see everything through the rather transparent material.

He must have read her thoughts, because he bent down, picked up her sandy towel and passed it to her.

'Here,' he said drily, with a small, sideways smile. 'You must be frozen.' Then he added, deadpan: 'I liked your handstand, by the way.'

So he'd been watching her! Sophie felt her cheeks heat up and quickly wrapped herself in the towel.

'I couldn't stay up long, the-the waves were too strong,' she stuttered.

'Well I was impressed. You love the water, don't you?'

Gigi, Mariella and Danny started strolling towards the alleyway that led to the street, and Sophie and Joe followed. Now he'd helped out her new friend, Sophie decided she wouldn't mind talking to him, just until they reached home.

'What did you catch?' she asked, looking at the fishing rod.

'A couple of sea bass,' he replied. 'Thought I'd drop one off for your sister, if that's all right with you.'

For some reason, Sophie's spirits drooped.

'Of course,' she said. 'She'll be delighted.'

By the time they arrived at Piping Plover House and stopped outside, Gigi was all smiles and had even linked arms with Mariella and Danny as if nothing had happened.

'Come and have a drink on my porch one evening,' she said, looking at Joe then Sophie. 'And your sister, too, of course.'

'Joe was friends with my big brother,' she went on

happily. 'He was round my house the whole time when I was growing up. He was practically family.'

'How lovely that you've known each other so long!' Sophie replied. 'Does your brother live locally?'

'Oh no, he's in Florida.'

Gigi's eyes fell to the ground and the corners of her mouth turned down.

'We had a falling-out – over money, I'm afraid. He got into some trouble and borrowed a lot of cash. Put it this way, I never saw it again.'

'Oh dear, I'm sorry.'

There was an awkward pause and Joe reached out to put a hand on Gigi's shoulder. It was only a small gesture, but she gave him a grateful smile.

'Well,' she said, taking a deep breath and straightening up again. 'Joe, you'd better get your fish on the barbecue. Enjoy!'

'I will. Trust me. Fresh from the sea. Nothing better!'

After saying their goodbyes, he followed Sophie up the steps to the front door of her house.

'Come on in,' she said, when she'd opened up, but he insisted that he'd prefer to stay on the porch.

'I need to get back. Besides, I'm covered in sand.'

She was secretly pleased, but tried not to show it. She didn't want to have to witness Celia fawning all over him again; she didn't think she could stand it.

He unzipped his bag and proceeded to take out one of the sea bass, wrapped in a white plastic carrier.

'Here, can you give this to your sister?'

He proffered the carrier, which Sophie took rather

gingerly, holding it well away from her body and praying that the fish inside was properly dead.

She was about to thank him when they were both distracted by the sound of Celia's footsteps hurrying downstairs.

'It's the other Mary Poppins!' Joe said with a lopsided grin, when Celia stopped short right in front of him. 'I brought you a fish, as promised.'

Sophie couldn't see her sister's face, but her whole body seemed to simper as she wrapped one leg over the other and fiddled girlishly with her hair. It was nauseating.

'Ooh, that's so kind of you!' she squealed, sounding about sixteen years old. 'I didn't think you'd remember!'

'I remembered all right.' Joe removed his canvas hat and placed it on the wooden table nearby, before leaning lazily against it and stretching out his long legs.

'Fancy a beer?' Celia asked, in her silly, squeaky voice. 'I've got some in the fridge.'

Sophie had had enough. She didn't wait to hear his reply.

'I'm going for a shower,' she announced, before plonking the fishy bag in Celia's unsuspecting hands and stalking away.

Eight

Joe was still leaning back against the table, his long, brown legs outstretched. He took a swig of beer from the bottle that Celia had fetched from the kitchen and wiped his upper lip with the back of his hand.

'Who's older – you or Sophie?' he asked at last, replacing the bottle on the table.

'Sophie,' Celia replied with a slight frown, because she thought it was obvious. Thanks to a bit of Botox here and a spot of filler there, her face was virtually unlined, whereas Sophie had heaps of wrinkles. 'There's eighteen months between us. It's just us two, no other siblings.'

She was sitting opposite Joe, on a wooden chair that she'd pulled out from under the table. She crossed and uncrossed her legs before extending them, one ankle over the other, mirroring his stance.

Now that Sophie had gone, there were no distractions and he seemed in no rush to leave. He wanted to know what Celia did and seemed impressed by her job: partner of a busy London GP practice. He asked if she was married and had children and she dropped in the fact that Neil, her husband, worked very long hours.

'We don't see a lot of each other,' she said with a sigh, fiddling with her wedding ring, twisting it round and round. 'He's an investment banker. He's never home before about nine o'clock. He travels a lot, too, mainly to New York, Singapore and Hong Kong.'

'That must be tough for you.'

Celia gave a sad little smile. 'It is.'

There was a slight pause then, 'What about you?' she asked. 'Are you married?'

Joe laughed. 'Me? No. I was once but only for a couple of years.' He scratched his head. 'We were far too young.'

'Anyone since? Girlfriends? Partners?'

'Girlfriends, sure, but nothing long-term. I guess I'm not good at relationships.'

He shrugged and took another swig of beer. There was something extremely attractive about him, Celia decided, and it wasn't just his looks, though they were impressive.

She reckoned his laid-back stance was a bit of an act. Beneath the chilled exterior lurked a sharp, inquisitive brain, and cleverness had always turned her on.

'What do you do for a living?'

'My main job is art, I'm a painter. I don't know if you've seen the murals in Belle Harbor yet?'

Celia shook her head.

'On the walls at both ends of the main row of shops. They're mine. The local business syndicate won a grant from the City to brighten the place up, so I actually got paid for once.' He grinned. 'I also get commissions – for portraits, that sort of thing. Not enough, though. I do painting and decorating on the side. The rest of the time I go fishing. It's not a bad life.' He grinned again. 'Oh, and I write poetry.'

'Do you?' Celia's eyebrows rose. 'What sort of poems?'

'All sorts, you know, whatever's on my mind.'

'I'd love to see some of your work.'

'Really? I'm not sure it'd be your thing.'

Celia, who fancied herself as a bit of a culture vulture, felt rather offended. 'Why not?'

'Well, they're mostly visual poems; that is, they create an image relating to the meaning. It's kind of an acquired taste.'

'How interesting!'

She sat up straight and tucked one leg beneath her, pulling down her skirt to reveal just enough thigh. 'And have any of them been published?'

'Yeah. But unfortunately I don't make a lot of money from that either.'

She was about to ask his surname, so she could look him up online, but he seemed keen to steer the subject away from himself.

'So what brings you to Rockaway?' he asked, and Celia explained about Pampy's will.

'Wow, that's pretty neat. She must have really loved you both. What are you going to do with the house now it's yours?'

'Put it on the market,' Celia said firmly. 'As soon as possible.'

'Really?' Joe looked surprised. 'But it's such a beautiful old place. Why would you want to sell it?'

She pulled a face. 'It's not that beautiful. It's in a terrible state. It needs a complete renovation. We'd have to spend heaps on it, and then we wouldn't use it enough.'

Joe shrugged. 'I guess...'

He was frowning but his expression soon brightened. 'You could rent it out. You'd have no trouble finding tenants. I guarantee they'd be queuing up, even if you only made minor improvements – repainting, putting in a new kitchen, that sort of thing. You wouldn't need to gut the whole house. It's the perfect location, right by the beach. People would love it. At least you'd be able to keep it in the family.'

Celia bit her lip. She didn't want to say Rockaway was a nowhere place and, before meeting him, she couldn't wait to get the hell out of there, never to return. Now, however, she'd begun to think that staying a little bit longer mightn't be quite so bad...

'We did talk about renting it,' she said instead, 'but it'd involve a lot of admin. To be honest, I think my boys would rather have a lump sum and buy themselves something in London.'

Joe ran his fingers through his hair to push it off his face and nodded. 'Still, it's a shame. I'm surprised Sophie doesn't want to keep it. She loves the ocean, right?'

This was delicate. Celia didn't want to portray herself in a bad light or Sophie in a particularly good one.

'She does, but I think she needs the money, too.'

'Ah.'

For a moment, he seemed lost in thought.

'So you're clearing the whole place out? How long will that take?'

She thought fast. She was pretty certain what he really wanted to know was how long they'd be in Rockaway.

'I'm not sure, to be honest. Quite a while, I imagine. It's full of stuff. I'm supposed to be back at work in two weeks, but I'm thinking I might take the summer off. I haven't broken the news to my colleagues yet. They won't exactly be over the moon, but they'll just have to deal with it. I've barely had a day off sick in fifteen years. They'll just have to find a locum to fill my place.'

'And Sophie?' said Joe. 'Will she stay the whole summer, too?'

This annoyed Celia, who detected a trace of hope in his question.

'Oh yeah,' she said dismissively. 'She's always between jobs. She's been a waitress, a barista, a vet's receptionist, a travel agent. I don't think she's found her calling yet.'

Joe's eyes widened a little and Celia feared she sounded catty.

'She's brilliant with her hands,' she added rapidly. 'She was always making clothes for herself when we were younger. And she's a real people person. I think she'd be great in marketing or public relations, maybe. It's never too late…'

Satisfied she'd painted her sister in a negative enough way without being too obvious about it, Celia moved on.

'Have you always lived in Rockaway?' she asked, her head tipped to one side, her eyes fixed on his handsome face.

'No.' Joe crossed his arms over his chest. 'I was born here, but then my dad got a job in LA and we moved there when I was quite little. I went to school in Palm Springs till I was fifteen, then we came back here, then I went to college in Berkeley, California.'

He laughed, noticing her surprise. 'I know, I know. You're thinking, why is this guy, who went to one of the best schools in America, doing painting and decorating for a living. Well, all I can say is, it leaves me free to do the other stuff I like. I was never interested in making big bucks and I'd hate to work for a corporate. I guess I'm not ambitious like that; I'd rather be outdoors and live a peaceful life.'

For a moment, Celia was lost for words. His outlook was so different from her own that she couldn't find a point of connection.

'Well, I suppose if it makes you happy...' she said at last.

'Happy?' He sounded doubtful. 'I'm not sure I know what that is. Content? Yes. I'm definitely comfortable with my choices. But I don't think you can travel all over the world to places like India or Africa and be happy. There's too much that's wrong, too much greed and suffering.'

The conversation had suddenly taken a serious turn. Celia was anxious not to get into a discussion about economics or global politics, suspecting they might not see eye to eye.

'Have you travelled a lot?' she asked, hoping to find something – or somewhere – in common.

He nodded.

'There's not too many places I haven't been, actually. I haven't visited the Democratic Republic of the Congo or

South Sudan, for obvious reasons, but I would if they were safer. And I'd love to see the mountains of North Korea one day – if Kim Jong-un ever gets booted out.'

'Wow, you're very adventurous. I think I prefer nice safe holidays in France or Spain.'

'I like those too,' he agreed. 'And I love visiting the UK. The only place I haven't been is Wales. I want to eat that special cake they make – I think it's called bara brith or something like that. And climb Snowdon.'

A big black car pulled into the drive opposite and a middle-aged man in a dark suit climbed out.

On hearing the door slam shut, Joe rose and did a big stretch, extending his arms way above his head.

'I'd better hit the road,' he said, lowering his arms again. 'I've got a fish to barbecue.'

Celia smiled and rose, too. 'And me. I can't wait.'

'Just put a little olive oil on the grill and some on the fish, too. You can add salt and pepper and other spices if you want, but personally I prefer mine neat. Oh, and make sure the heat's real high. You just need four or five minutes a side.'

He paused. 'You've got a barbecue, right?'

'I think so,' she replied. 'I'm sure I saw one in the backyard. It'll need a good clean.'

'OK,' said Joe. 'Otherwise, you can grill the fish or lightly fry it. It just won't taste quite as good.'

After picking up his bag, he made for the wooden steps and she followed.

Stopping for a moment, he turned round and leaned towards her, slightly inclining his head. It seemed as if he might kiss her on the cheek but he must have thought better of it, because he fist-bumped her instead.

'Let me know if you need a hand with anything,' he said, putting on his canvas hat. 'Moving furniture and stuff. I'll send you my number. Just give me a call.'

'I will. Thank you.'

He bounded light-footedly down the steps on to the pavement.

'And thank you for the fish, too,' she called after him.

She was sorry to see him go and found herself mulling over their chat when she went indoors to prepare a marinade for the sea bass.

He was so very different from Neil, she mused. In fact two people could hardly be more dissimilar. Neil wanted the *best* of everything. His main aim was to earn as much money as possible, so they could afford to live in a luxurious house, drive expensive cars, send their boys to top private schools and eventually retire on big fat pensions.

She'd always thought this was what she wanted, too. There'd been no question of her giving up her job or even working part-time when the boys were little because she hadn't wanted to take the income hit. She was inordinately proud of all the trappings of their success, right down to their Japanese-style garden and the Colefax and Fowler wallpaper in their elegant dining room.

Her parents, especially her father, had revelled in their achievements, too. Before his sudden death from a brain haemorrhage, they'd chosen to spend every Christmas and

Easter with her and Neil, rather than Sophie, whose flat, they said, was cramped and chaotic.

Besides, relations with their eldest were frayed and their father didn't approve of the way Sophie was raising Layla, either. He said Sophie was a lax mother and should take a leaf out of Celia's book. Her boys were an inspiration.

Surrounded by such success and approval, it was hard to understand why, in recent years particularly, Celia had been feeling bitter and dissatisfied.

It was true Neil wasn't the most interesting company. He was even more rigid in his ways than Celia, who rather suspected he might have some form of undiagnosed OCD.

He couldn't bear any mess at all; everything had to be *just so*. For instance, mugs on the kitchen shelf had to be arranged in order of size – from the tallest to the smallest – otherwise he would complain and redo them.

He had a very specific way of loading and unloading the dishwasher and storing cutlery, and his tool shed in the garden was like a ship's cabin, so neatly stowed that he'd notice if one small screwdriver had been moved and put back in the wrong place.

Not only were his shirts and trousers colour-coordinated in his wardrobe, but everyone else's had to be, too.

One Saturday morning, she'd caught him rearranging Rory's clothes and putting his rolled up socks into the special dividers he'd bought for them all, but which they sometimes forgot or couldn't be bothered to use.

'Tidy house, tidy mind,' Neil would say when she commented on his strange ways. She had to agree with him, because life *was* so much easier when you kept on top of jobs and knew where to find everything. Bills were always settled on time, cars taxed and serviced when they were supposed to be and holidays booked and paid for months in advance.

Everything in their world was shipshape and Bristol fashion, yet occasionally she was filled with a burning desire to kick off her shoes in the middle of the hallway or stack kitchen plates and bowls in the wrong cupboards. It would be worth it just to see Neil's face.

Disorder made him pale and jumpy. His forehead would go damp, his eyelid or cheek would twitch and he'd be unable to rest until he'd put things right.

She'd want to laugh, but that would be unkind so she contented herself with puffing on sly cigarettes behind his back instead.

After unlocking the kitchen door, she strolled into the garden and lifted the lid of the metal barbecue. The grill was black and rusty and clearly hadn't been used in years, but she reckoned it would be fine after a thorough scrub.

There was a steel wool soap pad under the kitchen sink and she carried it outside, along with a bucket of water. It was quite satisfying to watch the charred black grate slowly transform into shiny metal again, and her mind turned back to Joe and Neil while she worked away.

It was unlikely her husband would sample the fish if he were here, or even allow her to cook it. He'd worry that it was full of contaminants and unsafe to eat. In general he'd only consume fish and meat from top-end suppliers, sourced solely from approved farms with the highest environmental standards.

Without a shadow of doubt, her boys would want to try it, though. In fact they'd probably want to catch a fish for themselves. It saddened her a little that they had to hide so much from their father. He had no idea they drank spirits and smoked, like her. Sneakiness had entered their DNA at a very early age and they were masters at it by now.

So long as Celia knew what they were up to, she didn't mind that much. It was when they tried to do things behind *her* back she couldn't cope. If they disobeyed Neil, she'd often pretend not to notice, whilst secretly rather admiring their ingenuity and even deploying some of their tactics herself. It was a way of keeping everyone happy, she reasoned. Except that, increasingly, she wasn't happy at all.

How lovely it would be to gorge on white bread sometimes, or turn up the music full blast, without Neil telling her she'd get heart disease or break her eardrums! And he was getting worse, she was sure.

Even sex had become a bit of an ordeal, because he was so worried about picking up infections that he insisted they both hop in the shower almost before they'd done the deed.

Of course she never mentioned any of this to anyone. After all, they were The Perfect Family and so long as the world admired her, she could almost believe the hype.

The barbecue grate was gleaming now and she carried it inside to swoosh off the last of the soap under the tap. There was still no sign of Sophie, so she scouted around on her own for charcoal and eventually found some hardwood lump and a bottle of lighter fluid in a tumbledown shed in the side passage.

Inside the shed, which wasn't locked, she also discovered three old bikes, two women's and one man's. They were battered and rusty and the tyres had gone flat, but she reckoned a little TLC would bring them to life.

She remembered going on the odd bike ride with Sophie when they were young; Sophie was bigger and faster than her and Celia had to pedal hard to keep up.

On one occasion, Sophie had dared her to ride through the river, which had burst its banks and flooded one of the lower streets near their home. Ducks and swans were paddling merrily across the road and folk had to leave their houses in Wellington boots.

Celia was intending to avoid the flood altogether and cycle a different way, but Sophie said it would be fun to whoosh through the water, which wasn't deep.

'Lift up your feet!' she shouted, setting off at a tremendous lick before taking her feet off the pedals and freewheeling to the other side.

Without a second thought, Celia had done as she was told, squealing with joy as the water splashed up her calves. However, when she was halfway across she lost her nerve, wobbled and fell over.

She had a few cuts and bruises but it was her pride that hurt the most. Sophie had waded through the water to help her up and then she had to walk home sopping wet, pushing her bike because she refused to get on it again.

Sophie got a huge bollocking from their father because he said she hadn't looked after her little sister. He'd sent her to her room but she'd climbed out of the window and gone to meet friends. Celia knew because she'd peeped through the keyhole and noticed the room was empty, the window wide open and the curtains were flapping in the wind.

She, meanwhile, had been treated to a warm bath and hot chocolate, yet she remembered feeling jealous of Sophie. It was strange but in her mind, Sophie was the one still having fun while she had become the 'good girl' again, who stayed home and got on with her studies. She couldn't be wild because Sophie had claimed the title and made it all her own.

Celia sighed. This happened many years ago but in some respects, little had changed. Sophie was still a bit crazy and free-spirited. Unhampered by convention, she liked to do things her way and hang the consequences, while Celia was still a goody-goody.

Once she'd stacked the chunks of hardwood lump in the bottom of the barbecue, she coated them in lighter fluid and let them soak for a couple of minutes. The cigarette lighter that she kept hidden from Neil was still in her bag, and she used it to ignite some rolled up paper she'd torn from one of Pampy's dog-eared books.

As soon as she set fire to the charcoal, yellow flames licked around the barbecue base and leaped up through the grill, forcing her to jump back.

It would take ten minutes or so for the heat to reach maximum temperature, then it would sear the fish in no time, browning the surface and scenting it with pure wood smoke. Her stomach rumbled at the mere thought.

★ ★ ★

It was almost dark by the time Sophie came downstairs, all fresh and clean from the shower. Celia had finished eating and was carrying her empty plate from the garden into the kitchen when her sister appeared at the back door.

Sophie was barefoot, dressed in frayed denim shorts that were just a little too tight and a creased navy T-shirt a shade too large. Her hair hung damply over her shoulders. Even so, she looked surprisingly beautiful, Celia thought, though not in a predictable way. She didn't have fake boobs or eyelashes and her skin was pale, freckled and make-up free. You could tell by the slightly clumsy way she moved and held herself that she thought little of her looks, yet somehow oozed sex appeal today.

The key to it, perhaps, was her naturalness, a quality Celia knew she didn't possess. It must be obvious to most people, she guessed, that she spent a great deal of time and money on her appearance. Sophie, on the other hand, didn't even bother with a push-up bra and her clothes could have come from a thrift store.

'How was the fish?' she asked, eyeing the remaining bits of skin and the small bones.

'Delicious,' Celia replied. 'I'm afraid I ate the whole thing. I didn't know if you were coming down again tonight.'

Sophie gave a small shrug. 'That's fine. I don't suppose there was enough for two anyway. I'll find something in the fridge, or I might get a takeaway.'

'I think I'm going to take the summer off and stay here for longer,' Celia blurted.

'Really?' Sophie couldn't hide her astonishment.

'Yes. I can see it's going to take more than two weeks to clear the house. I don't want to rush it.'

'You've changed your tune.'

'I know. I thought I'd be desperate to get out of Rockaway but actually, I'm beginning to rather like it. Not that I want to keep the house,' she added quickly. 'We still have to sell. I just think it might be quite nice to be by the beach for a while. I might as well take advantage of it while I can.'

'Will Neil mind?' Sophie's response wasn't what Celia expected.

'I don't think so, no.'

'Won't he miss you?'

Celia turned and looked squarely at her sister.

'I doubt it. He's usually so busy with work he hardly notices if I'm there or not.'

Sophie's eyes widened. It was news to her, of course, that Celia's ideal marriage wasn't perfect.

'I didn't know—' she began, but Celia raised a hand to stop her.

'There are lots of things you don't know,' she said darkly. 'My relationship with Neil is just one of them.'

Nine

'Are you OK?'

'Yes. Why?'

'You seem a bit distant, that's all. Are you cross with me about something?'

'No.'

Sophie could tell her daughter was lying. Perhaps she was in a rush, running late for something. It was 7 p.m. in the UK, five hours ahead. She might be going out for the evening.

Imagining Layla in her bedroom at their flat, Sophie felt a pang of nostalgia. She'd be lying on the vintage patchwork Indian quilt she'd found in a charity shop. It was bright yellow, pink and blue and very lovely, covered in ornate birds and flowers.

Above the bamboo headboard were three rectangular, embroidered, ethnic wall hangings, and mosaic lanterns hung from the ceiling. The air was always filled with the heady scent of joss sticks. She'd been going through a Zen phase.

'What are you up to this evening?' Sophie asked, and heard Layla sigh.

'Nothing.'

'That's not like you.'

Layla was quite gregarious and had lots of friends.

'I'm not feeling sociable. I can't be bothered to talk to anyone.'

Concern nibbled at Sophie's insides.

'How was work today?' she said, still digging. Layla was waitressing at an Italian restaurant. She'd been there since leaving university a year ago. She claimed she was saving up to go travelling, but money seemed to trickle through her fingers.

'OK,' she replied. 'Bit boring. We weren't particularly busy.'

'Oh.'

There was a pause when no one spoke and Sophie wondered if the conversation had run its course, but then Layla jumped in.

'Mum?'

'Yes.'

'Why didn't you push me more at school and uni? I wish I'd got better grades. You never took my homework seriously. You were always telling me to hurry up so we could watch TV. If I'd done better I might have a decent job. No one wants to know me with my rubbish A-levels and my 2.2.'

So this was the crux of it. The job rejections were getting

her down. Sophie swallowed. She hated it when her daughter was unhappy; she felt it herself, like a bleeding wound.

'I did take your work seriously, I just didn't want to put too much pressure on you,' she replied. 'Your grandfather, Paul, had ridiculously high expectations. It had a terrible impact on me. I didn't want you to go through the same experience.'

Layla laughed humourlessly. 'Surely there's an in-between? I mean, I don't remember you ever commenting on my exam grades. You never said I should try a bit harder. I grew up thinking they didn't matter and you didn't care.'

Sophie was stung. 'Of course I cared. But you were such a happy girl. The last thing I wanted was to cast a shadow over your childhood.'

'All I can see is shadows now,' Layla replied gloomily.

Once they'd hung up, Sophie tried to convince herself Layla was just in a tricky mood. She'd be all right tomorrow; she was probably tired.

Deep down, though, lurked a fear that there was more to it. Sophie and Layla used to be so close, but recently Sophie had sensed a pulling away. She suspected that since leaving university, Layla had spent too much time analysing her upbringing, shining a torch in the dark places and sometimes seeing things that weren't there.

Of course it was tough she hadn't found a proper job yet and didn't really know what she wanted to do. But she was bright, attractive and resourceful. Things would surely come good in the end. She just needed to have faith.

After spending all morning dropping off piles of Pampy's

clothes, books and trinkets at various second-hand stores, Sophie concluded that she deserved a break.

She decided to go for a walk, which would also help to take her mind off Layla. Celia had finally decided to go for a swim and wouldn't be back for a while, so there was no rush.

Belle Harbor was a bit far, but Sophie could vaguely recall visiting a different area of shops and cafés as a child, though she had no idea how to find it. Her mother, Terry, had used Pampy's rattling old station wagon to get about and they had rarely walked anywhere, other than the few metres to the beach.

Sophie could picture them now, heading off in the wagon, waving to Pampy from the back window until they rounded the corner. The car's suspension had gone and it was so low you could feel every bump on the road, but no one minded.

Mum used to describe the car as 'shit brown', which made the girls giggle, but she never swore in Pampy's hearing. Pampy couldn't abide cursing; she said it was lazy and offensive. If you wanted to swear, she said, you'd have to go into the garden.

The air was still hot and heavy at almost 3 p.m., and after crossing to the other side of the street, Sophie walked slowly to conserve energy.

Most of the windows in the houses were closed, the blinds were shut and there wasn't a soul to be seen. Only the sprinklers continued to whirl bravely in front gardens, as if in competition with the silence.

Perhaps the place came alive at weekends, when the second-homers, the rich city crowd, drove into town.

Pampy had been one of them herself once. As a young wife and mother, she'd spent weekdays at the family apartment in Brooklyn and Saturdays and Sundays in Rockaway. It was only after her husband died, and she'd retired from her part-time job, that she'd sold up in Brooklyn and moved here permanently.

On reaching the end of the road, Sophie stopped and looked around, wondering which way to go. Left, right or straight ahead? The area seemed to be entirely residential; there wasn't a shop, church, mosque or any other landmark in sight.

All of a sudden, however, the hair on the back of her neck started to prickle and she felt certain someone was watching her. Sure enough, on glancing to her right she spotted the dark outline of a figure sitting on a raised porch not unlike Pampy's.

With the sun in her eyes and big trees on either side casting a good deal of shade, Sophie couldn't make out the person's features. In normal circumstances, she'd have thought little of it and walked on by. Something made her pause, however, and without thinking, she took a few steps across the front lawn towards the silent figure.

As she drew closer, she realised she was looking at a very elderly woman, in a high-backed wooden chair, peering down at her.

The woman was dressed in a short-sleeved cream blouse, buttoned all the way up, and she had long white hair, secured with a black velvet band and tied in a thick braid that hung over one shoulder.

So bent was she that her neck seemed to shrink into her

shoulders and her chin sagged onto her breastbone. This didn't stop her from looking squarely at Sophie, however, through gaps in the white painted fence, and when their eyes met, a shudder of recognition ran up and down Sophie's spine.

They'd encountered each other before, she was certain. She knew those inquisitive little eyes, half hidden as they were by heavy, drooping lids. They slanted slightly at the corners and the irises were such a dark brown that they appeared coal black.

The woman had a small, squashy nose, narrow mouth and a round, brown face with plump, mottled cheeks flushed pink like an apple. Sophie couldn't place her, but some instinct or long buried memory told her there was no need to be afraid.

Presently, the woman's narrow mouth curved into a funny little closed-lip smile, just as if a small child had drawn it on with a single pencil stroke. It was so unexpected that Sophie found herself smiling back.

When the old woman beckoned with an index finger, her palm facing up, Sophie didn't hesitate to walk right up to the porch steps and stand at the bottom, waiting to see what would happen next.

'Come here,' the stranger said, in a loud, quavering voice. There was a hint of something in her American accent. Russian, perhaps? Or Polish? 'Don't I know you from someplace?'

While Sophie ascended the wooden steps one by one, the old woman dragged and shuffled her chair across the floor towards her visitor. And all the while she was looking intently at Sophie, her head cocked slightly to one side, like a bird.

Once Sophie was close enough, the woman stretched out a plump, knotted hand as if to give a formal shake. When Sophie offered her own hand in return, however, the stranger wrapped her fingers tightly round and gave an affectionate squeeze, just as if she were greeting a relative or long-lost friend.

Her hands were crooked with arthritis, but the skin on the back felt silky smooth, as if it had been buffed and polished like precious metal. She had a slim gold band on the third finger of her right hand, which was so deeply embedded in the folds of flesh that it would surely never come off.

Some yellow honeysuckle twining around a wooden pillar behind her was giving off a sweet, heady scent, and there was a half-filled jug of orange cordial on a small round wooden table alongside.

'Hello, I'm Sophie,' Sophie said, feeling awkward and wanting to pull away, but not wishing to appear rude.

The front door was wide open and she could see that you stepped straight into the living room, as in Pampy's house. It was so gloomy in there, however, that all she could make out were dark shapes – the back of a large sofa and some other heavy furniture.

'Sophie who?' the old woman asked.

From anyone else the question might have seemed impolite, but her smile was so friendly Sophie couldn't take offence.

'Walsh,' she replied, 'Sophie Walsh.'

At last the old woman let go of her grip and put her hand back in her lap to join the other.

'Walsh,' she repeated with a frown, and her eyes appeared to glaze over, as if she were trying to focus on something very far away. After a few moments, Sophie began to feel concerned, fearing the old woman had drifted off into a daze. Then a dog yipped in one of the gardens nearby and all of a sudden she sat up as straight as her twisted body would allow and pressed her palms together.

'Teresa's daughter!' she exclaimed. 'You're Orla's granddaughter! I'm right, aren't I?'

Sophie nodded. 'How do you—'

But the old woman wouldn't let her finish.

'I knew it! You were only young then, but you haven't changed a bit. You've still got that beautiful strawberry-blonde hair. You and your sister used to play in the street outside my house. You were always asking to take my dog, Buster, for a walk. You loved Buster. He was almost as big as you! He passed a long time ago, of course, but he was the best dog, gentle as a lamb.'

Now she thought about it, Sophie did recall a big soppy golden retriever, who would give her his paw and slobber on her face, making her squeal with delight and disgust, rolled into one. Casting her mind back, she could also just about picture its owner, a stout, smiley woman in a flowery frock, with grey-black hair tied in a bun.

Pointing to a wooden chair that was pushed up against the wall of the house, the old woman invited Sophie to pull it out and sit down.

'I don't suppose you remember me,' she went on, shuffling

her own chair round to face Sophie. 'I'd probably have been in my sixties back then – a spring chicken!'

She laughed, and Sophie couldn't help joining in. 'I'm ninety-eight now,' she went on, shaking her white head and giving a pretend sigh. 'I don't get many looks these days but I'll tell you what, some of those greybeards down at the old folks' social club can get a bit frisky. You have to watch where they put their hands!'

'I'm sorry,' Sophie said at last, frowning, 'my memory's vague. I think I do remember you and your dog but nothing much more. Were you friends with my grandmother?'

'Oh yes,' the woman replied, before pausing. 'That is, we were good neighbours, put it like that. I moved here with my husband just after we married – he passed a long time ago, more than twenty years, bless his soul.

'I remember when Orla and Donal moved in. Their only child, your mother, Teresa – some folk called her Terry – she was just a little scrap then, couldn't have been more than five or six. Such a darling, she was. She used to visit me and my husband when they came at weekends and in the holidays. She played with my son, Nicholas.'

Her mouth puckered and she lowered her eyes, as if this were a painful subject.

'Then she grew up,' the old woman went on, gathering herself. 'She moved away and it was a long time before she came back, bringing you and your younger sister. I always wondered why you stopped coming.' She cleared her throat. 'Orla didn't talk about it.'

Her beady dark eyes fixed on Sophie and her bristling white brows rose up, as if they had a mind of their own.

In other circumstances, Sophie might have been tempted to mention the sudden rift that had developed between her mother and grandmother, for reasons never explained.

She might also have said how devastated she'd been when she realised she wouldn't spend summers in Rockaway ever again, how she'd always blamed her mother, being the easiest target, and how, much as Sophie loved her, she'd never quite been able to forgive.

Then there was the letter she'd found in Orla's sewing box. The old woman might know something about that, too.

Keen as Sophie was to find out, however, she held back. Spending time with Celia had reopened old wounds and she felt more vulnerable than she had in a long time. She'd prefer to take things slowly.

'We started spending all our holidays in France,' she said instead. 'Celia and I were learning French at school and our parents wanted us to practise.'

'Ah, yes,' said the old woman, with a nod. 'Languages are very important.'

Lowering her eyes again, she pretended to brush an imaginary speck of dirt off her lap; it was obvious she knew there was more to it than that, but was too polite to press.

'How rude I am!' she said all of a sudden, clapping her hands. 'You must be half parched. I haven't offered you a drink.'

Soon, she was pouring Sophie a glass of orange cordial, and one for herself as well. Now they'd moved away from awkward subjects, Sophie was pleased to have an excuse to stay longer; she was in no hurry to return to Piping Plover House.

'I haven't told you my name. I'm Yana,' said the old woman now, taking a small sip of her drink and replacing it on the table. She pulled a neatly folded, white lace handkerchief from the pocket of her navy skirt, shook it open and dabbed the edges of her small mouth.

'You want some ice?'

A deep, gravelly voice behind made Sophie turn and there was a very tall, middle-aged woman in the doorway, holding a plastic container.

'This is my helper, Donna,' the old woman explained. 'She's am-*azing*. I couldn't do without her.'

Sophie couldn't help staring because Donna was such an unusual sight, with a square-shaped body, very broad shoulders and a large round stomach that rose up to meet her equally big bust. It was hard to tell where one ended and the other began.

Her shoulder-length grey hair had been scraped off her face and secured with a white plastic Alice band, and the T-shirt she wore was tight and pink, with a childish picture of Mickey Mouse on the front.

Her tanned limbs, on the other hand, were very thin and quite unlike the rest of her. In fact her legs, in off-white, calf-length leggings, were so spindly it was a wonder they managed to hold her up.

Lowering her gaze further, Sophie's eyes fell on a pair of broad bare feet as deeply tanned as the arms, suggesting Donna spent a good deal of time outdoors.

Her toes were slightly grubby but the nails were trimmed

into perfect little squares and painted a dazzling shade of turquoise. They must have been done by a professional, as they gleamed like crystal and there wasn't a splodge or chip in sight.

Sophie now noticed Donna's long, pointed fingernails were the same shade and just as immaculate. Everything else about her looked thrown together, as if she'd walked into a child's wardrobe and grabbed the nearest items she could find, never mind whether they fit or not. Only her nails were pristine.

'You shoulda told me you were expecting company, Mrs L. I would've made crab canapés.'

Sophie later learned the L stood for Yana's surname, Lebedev.

'I was planning on serving the rest of the cold cuts for dinner, with potato salad. If I'd known we had company I'd have gone to the grocery store.'

Donna's tone was reproving, but her face told a different story. Although her sparse, grey eyebrows were raised in mock exasperation, she was smiling at Yana at the same time. It was clear they were very fond of one another.

'Oh, I'm not staying for dinner,' Sophie said quickly, not wishing to disrupt their routine. 'I was just passing…'

She started to rise, but Yana reached out and touched her arm.

'Don't go yet,' she pleaded. 'We've only just started. It's not often I get visitors…'

She glanced at Donna. 'Scrabble can wait, can't it? We can play later.' She turned to Sophie. 'We have a game most days. It keeps our minds sharp.'

Donna bent over to sweep a few crumbs off the little round table into her other hand.

'Sure! You just give me a shout when you're ready.'

Before leaving, her gaze settled for a moment on Sophie.

'You're English, aren't you?'

Sophie nodded.

'I love your accent. You sound so...' she paused for a moment, 'so ladylike.'

Sophie laughed. 'I'm afraid I'm not – much of a lady I mean.'

But Donna wasn't listening. 'I'd love to visit London one day,' she said with a sigh. 'I want to see Buckingham Palace, Big Ben, Prince William and Catherine...' Then, lowering her voice, she whispered, 'Have you ever met them?'

For a moment, Sophie thought she was joking, but her expression was deadly serious.

'I'm afraid not.'

Donna's face fell.

'But I did once watch William and Harry playing polo,' Sophie went on. It had been many years ago, but who was to know? 'They were this far away from me,' she added, stretching her arms to about a foot wide.

'Oh my!' Donna's brown eyes bulged, lemur-like. It was all Sophie could do not to laugh.

'She's crazy about your royals,' Yana whispered, inclining her head, as if Donna wouldn't be able to hear. 'She's got enough books and magazines to fill a library!'

When Donna padded back into the house, Sophie and Yana were alone once more. It was clear that the old woman wanted to talk, and Sophie listened patiently while she harked back to her early childhood in a village outside Moscow. When she was about four years old, she had emigrated to New York with her family.

'We went by sea, and Mama threw up almost the whole way. My brother, Andrei, was only about two years old and I had to look after him. Apparently I wasn't very good at it and Mama said it's a miracle he lived to tell the tale!'

Her parents both found jobs in retail and eventually opened their own clothes store on the Lower East Side. Before long, they had a chain of successful shops and Yana helped with the family business until she met her husband, a car mechanic.

'His father owned garages on the Rockaway Peninsula,' she explained. 'Well! I'd never even heard of the place. But I was madly in love and when he said he'd found us a house in the neighbourhood and we were going to get married and his parents would buy the house for us, of course I agreed. That was this place. I've been here over seventy years. Imagine that! By the time my husband showed it to me and I realised how far it was from the city, it was too late.'

Her hands fluttered sideways and she shrugged her shoulders, as if to say that she'd made a terrible mistake.

'But you've been happy here, haven't you?' Sophie asked, with a slight frown. She wouldn't want to think otherwise.

Yana's shoulders relaxed. 'Oh yes, I couldn't imagine being anywhere else now, but I must confess, I never have got used to being so near the ocean. I can't stand cold water!'

They both laughed again because it was absurd, of course. For most folks, the beach here was the major draw.

'That said, Nicholas loved it here,' Yana went on, and Sophie noticed her eyes cloud over once more. 'I'm glad he grew up with so much fresh air and space around him. It did him the world of good.'

There was a pause and when Sophie spoke again, she'd plucked up enough courage to ask something that had been troubling her for a very long time.

'You know my mother died, don't you?' she began.

Yana nodded. 'Orla told me. About five years ago, right? I'm sorry for your loss...'

'Thank you. Of course it was sad but also a blessing in a way; she'd been so ill...'

Sophie leaned forwards, eager to get to the nub of her question.

'Did my mother seem happy when you knew her?' She swallowed; her mouth had gone dry. 'Was she – you know – content with life?'

Yana seemed to flinch slightly, or had Sophie imagined it?

'I think so, yes. Why do you ask?'

Sophie took a deep breath. 'Oh, I don't know. I just sometimes wonder. When I was a child, I'd quite often catch her looking sad or crying, when she thought no one was watching. I didn't understand and it made me sad, too. On the face of it, Mum had everything she wanted. When I asked if she was OK, she always insisted she was fine. I wanted to believe her but couldn't. She had unhappy eyes. I wish I could ask Pampy, but it's too late.'

A slight breeze made the garden leaves rustle and Sophie caught a whiff of the honeysuckle twining around the porch pillar.

Yana rubbed her arms as if she were chilly, though the air was still warm. Her palms made a soft, scratching noise against her skin, like fine sandpaper.

'I, too, have many things I wish I'd asked my loved ones before they died,' she said quietly.

She looked tired all of a sudden and glanced at the open doorway, perhaps hoping to see Donna.

'But, you know, sometimes I think there's a reason…'

Sophie's ears pricked. 'Yes?'

A pair of dark eyes fixed on her and she felt a strange scampering, as if a small creature was trapped inside her gut, struggling to get out.

'…there's a reason we don't ask,' Yana continued. 'It's because we don't really want to know the answer. The truth can hurt, you see. Sometimes it's better not to go there at all.'

Ten

Yana definitely knew more than she was letting on, but Sophie was afraid to push any further right now. If she probed too far, the old woman might clam up and refuse to see her again, taking any secrets with her to the grave.

However, Sophie did ask one more question.

'Did you know Donal, my grandfather, too? He was nothing like Pampy.'

Yana nodded. 'He was a devout Roman Catholic. I don't think your mother liked that side of him very much. She used to tell me she hated going to Mass; she found it boring. In those days, the Catholic folk tended to stick together, same as the Jews and Muslims. There wasn't much mixing.

'I remember she got friendly with a Protestant girl for a while and your grandfather put a stop to it. The girl's family were Northern Irish, I think; they were staying here for the summer. I used to see Teresa out and about on her bike with that girl and her brother; they were all much of an age.

'It seemed like they were having a lot of fun together,

but then the next time I saw your mother, she was alone. When I asked where her friends were, she told me she wasn't allowed to see them any more. It was a shame, really. The family must have left the area, gone back to Ireland, I expect. I never saw them round here again, anyway.'

Yana looked tired and Sophie decided she should let her rest.

'May I come and see you again?' she asked, bending down to kiss Yana's cheek, which was baby soft and smelled of violets and talcum powder.

'Of course. Any time,' the old woman replied. 'I'm always here, either on the porch or indoors. I don't go out much these days. I've enjoyed your company. Don't leave it too long.'

Sophie resolved to head back to Piping Plover House. As she passed Gigi's home, Nino came out of the front door, along with an older boy and girl, wrapped around each other.

Nino, in a black, back-to-front baseball cap, grinned when he saw Sophie.

'Hi!' he said, walking towards her. 'Meet my brother, Eddie. Eddie, this is Sophie. She's English.'

Eddie was quite short and solid, dark haired and olive skinned. He looked like a weightlifter but his face was lean and handsome, and he had dark brown eyes, a straight nose, full lips and a square jaw. Small gold studs flashed in his earlobes and there were tattoos on his muscly upper arms.

Sophie was about to ask after Gigi when she heard footsteps and a clanking noise. It was Celia walking towards them, pushing a rusty bike.

Her hair was wet and she was still in her black bikini,

with a loose white shirt on top, also damp. She couldn't have been out of the water long.

'Do you happen to have a pump I could borrow?' she asked, looking first at Nino, then Eddie. 'I found some old bikes in the shed but they've all got flat tyres.'

Eddie was in a rush. 'Sorry, I gotta go.' He took a set of keys out of his pocket and with a flourish clicked open the silver Nissan parked in the driveway. 'Sure we've got a pump. Nino will dig it out for you.'

Nino walked around the bike, eyeing it suspiciously.

'Can I try something?' he asked Celia. 'Brakes need fixing,' he said with a frown. 'And I'm pretty sure the tyres have punctures. They'll need more than just air.'

'Oh dear.' Celia looked disappointed.

'We can try and find a bike repair shop,' Sophie suggested, but Nino shook his head.

'You don't need to do that. I'll fix them up for you.'

'Would you really? We'll be happy to pay you.'

'I don't want any money,' Nino replied. 'I like messing around with bikes, taking them apart and putting them back together. It'd be my pleasure.'

Soon, he had two bikes on the grass in front of his house, along with a puncture repair kit, some spare inner tubes and brake pads, a tyre lever and pump, a can of lubricant, assorted tools and a bucket of water. Celia went home to have a shower and get changed, while Sophie stayed to watch.

Nino clearly knew what he was doing and became utterly absorbed in the task, the tip of his tongue sticking out of his mouth while he concentrated. He was quite slow and methodical, but after about an hour and a half, both bikes were fully operational and ready to ride again.

'Do you want to give it a go?' he asked, standing up and wheeling the biggest bike over to Sophie.

He sniffed and wiped his nose with the back of a hand, leaving a dark, oily smear on his face.

'Ooh, yes!'

She jumped up, climbed on and circled round the grassy island in the middle of the road while he watched, grinning with delight. It was a while since she'd cycled and she wobbled a bit.

'It's fab! Thank you so much,' she said. 'I can't wait to take it on the boardwalk!'

She was about to wheel both bikes back to her house when Eddie's silver car pulled up again in the drive and Eddie got out. Sophie was expecting to see the girl that he'd been cosying up with earlier get out, but either she was going mad, or it wasn't the same one. This one was tallish and blonde, while the other had been small and dark.

Without acknowledging either Sophie or Nino, Eddie cupped the new girl's face in his palms and proceeded to give her a big snog, right there in front of them.

'Guess what, bro?' Nino called, seemingly unperturbed. 'I just fixed two bikes.'

'Uh? Mm,' Eddie muttered, managing a thumbs up while his lips were still glued to the girl's. Then he rubbed her bottom, grabbed her hand and pulled her, giggling, inside, leaving Sophie staring after them.

'Who's she?' she whispered to Nino. 'She wasn't the same one as before.'

Nino shrugged. 'No idea. Never seen either of them till today.'

'Really?' Sophie couldn't hide her surprise. 'Eddie seems very familiar with them both.'

Nino pulled off his baseball cap and scratched his head.

'You don't know my brother. Girls go crazy for him. He has a hard time keeping them all happy.'

'Do they know about each other?' she asked. It was none of her business, but she couldn't help being intrigued.

'I guess not,' Nino replied, replacing his cap on his head. 'They'd probably get jealous. Eddie doesn't like hurting people's feelings, especially not girls'. He never breaks up with them, they just overlap.'

'Well that's one way of putting it!' Sophie said with a laugh.

She was still smiling when she opened the side gate to her house and wheeled in the bikes one by one. Now that she'd met all three of Gigi's children, she could see why Gigi found them a handful.

The afternoon had almost slipped away and it would be getting dark in an hour or so. Sophie thought Celia would have started sorting through another room, but she found her lying on her bed reading a book.

'Do you fancy cycling along the boardwalk and watching the sunset?' she asked and rather to her relief, Celia said no.

Bicycle access to the boardwalk was up a steep ramp several blocks along from Pampy's street. Once there, the concrete surface was smooth and easy to ride along and you could see for quite some way in all directions.

Sophie set off at a pace, enjoying the feeling of the wind in her hair. She was intending to go to the very end of the boardwalk, until she spotted a sign saying 'Ice Cold Fresh Green Coconut Water' and realised she was very thirsty.

Leaning her bike against the railings, she walked over to the kiosk and ordered one. She took a sip as she walked back to her bike. The coconut water was ice cold, sweet and delicious. Greedy for more, she settled on a bench overlooking the beach and closed her eyes, savouring every drop until the drink was finished.

She was contemplating going back to the kiosk for another one when she was startled by a very deep voice.

'My! Looks like you needed that!'

It was only when her eyelids fluttered open she realised a man had sat down beside her.

It took a moment or two to recognise him, then the penny dropped: it was Terrell, the guy from the liquor store the other night.

He had the same small beard and tattoos, but now his squashy topknot had been replaced by neat black cornrows, flecked with a little grey. He was dressed in a bright orange vest and shorts and had an orange waterproof jacket on the bench beside him.

Recalling that he was a lifeguard and thinking he'd probably just finished a shift, Sophie smiled and he grinned widely back. There was a gap between his two front teeth, which made her smile even more.

'How are you doing? I hope your young friend managed to avoid a beating from his dad?'

When she said he had, Terrell laughed. 'Well that's good, I'm glad.'

He seemed in no hurry to leave and when he offered to buy her another green coconut, she accepted gladly. He chose a virgin piña colada for himself, and she had a sip.

It was made with pineapple juice, coconut cream and lots of ice and it was so dreamy she resolved to have one another time.

'Look!' she said suddenly, pointing to the tangerine sun, which was now halfway below the horizon.

'It's going so fast,' he commented, as the shining semicircle shrank to an arc then a sliver, then just a pinprick of light before it was gone. Meanwhile the sky was splashed with candyfloss pink, gold and scarlet, just as if someone had got carried away with a paintbrush.

'No, *we're* going so fast,' Sophie replied.

As darkness fell, lights went on around them and a band started playing under one of the nearby gazebos that was attached to a bar.

'How long are you here?' Terrell asked, and he seemed pleased when Sophie said she wasn't sure, but possibly most of the summer.

He was sympathetic when she explained how her sister was adamant about putting the house on the market, while she would have liked to keep it.

'I guess it's not a situation where there's an obvious compromise. I get why you don't want to sell.'

They'd both finished their drinks by now and he rose and

put her empty coconut and his plastic cup in a nearby bin. Imagining that they'd go their separate ways, she wasn't at all prepared for what he said when he came back.

'Do you like to dance?'

He was smiling and his eyes were very bright.

'Yes,' she said, surprised. 'I'm not very good at it, though.'

'That doesn't matter.'

He held out a hand and she took it, thinking she really wasn't in the mood.

'I love this song,' he murmured, pulling her towards the gazebo where the band was blasting out an old Motown number.

His hand was warm and reassuring and as soon as they reached the edge of the dance floor, he turned towards her and started to move his hips and feet.

There was nothing for it but for her to do the same, and as she got into the beat, she was aware he was keeping to her rhythm, all the while smiling and watching her face.

He was a very good dancer but it was a long time since she'd danced herself and at first she felt silly and self-conscious. Little by little, however, she loosened up and began to enjoy it.

As she relaxed, he did, too, and before long, he started doing his own, free-flow thing, snaking his hips, gliding forwards and backwards, stomping his feet and sometimes leaping athletically into the air.

Neither of them was dressed for the evening. She was still in her slightly-too-tight, frayed denim shorts and he in his lifeguarding gear, but it didn't matter.

At last, Sophie said she needed to go.

'Sure you don't want another drink?' Terrell asked, nodding to the bar, but she said no. She was tired and hungry and although she really liked him, they barely knew each other and she didn't want to stay out late. Besides, she had no lights on her bike and was anxious about bumping into the cops.

He walked with her to her bike and they said goodbye. He seemed slightly agitated, as if he wanted to say something more, and just before she pedalled off, he asked if she'd like to go to a yoga class with him.

'There's one on the beach tomorrow at eight a.m. I usually go before my shift. It's a beautiful time of day.'

Although it was too dark to see his face properly, she could tell he was embarrassed by the way he shifted awkwardly from one foot to another. She was both amused and rather touched.

'I'd love that,' she replied, and he explained exactly which part of the beach to go to.

'See you tomorrow!' she called over her shoulder as she cycled away.

The journey back seemed to take forever, especially once she left the boardwalk. She stuck closely to the pavement for most of the way, keeping her eyes peeled for cars and police.

Hoping Celia would be upstairs by now, she was dismayed to see the light on in the porch. As she drew closer, she was even more appalled to spot the outline of two figures sitting side by side on the swing bench and she heard the low murmur of voices.

Whoever was there didn't see her open the side gate and wheel her bike into the passage. When she came out again, however, Celia was waiting for her at the top of the porch steps.

'You've been ages,' she said in her squeaky voice. Her eyes shone like glass and she giggled, unsteady on her feet. She was wearing a sexy pink sundress, high, rope-heeled sandals and lots of black mascara. 'Joe's here. We're having a drink.'

Sophie ground her teeth. She could tell booze had been consumed. Drinks, plural, more like.

'Oh good,' she said, because she couldn't think of anything else, other than swear words. 'I need to eat, then I'm going to bed. You missed a wonderful sunset, by the way.'

Celia stood back as Sophie passed, but before she could escape inside, Joe rose and walked towards her.

He wasn't as drunk as Celia but he'd clearly had a few, too. His movements were slower than usual and his fair hair was all over the place. His white T-shirt was crumpled as well.

'Your sister called me,' he said in a thick, apologetic voice. 'We were about to come and find you. She was worried about you. '

That Celia had used Sophie as an excuse to get him over made her skin prickle with annoyance.

'Not so worried that she didn't decide to get pissed first,' she muttered under her breath.

Joe looked at her strangely. 'I guess I'll make a move,' he said after a short pause. 'Now you're back safely.'

'Don't go yet. Have another drink.' Celia swayed forwards and backwards then suddenly lurched to one side, losing her footing. Joe reacted quickly, catching her just before she fell.

She giggled, quite unfazed by her near accident. 'Whoops.'

He had an arm round her, propping her up. She didn't seem in any hurry to be free so he walked her over to the nearest chair against the wall.

'Here, you'd better sit down.'

'I don't think I can walk upstairs. I think I need you to carry me,' she said in a silly, babyish tone.

'Oh my God.' Sophie couldn't help herself. 'She's pathetic.'

Celia raised her chin and sniffed in an effort to appear haughty, but spoiled it by concluding with a loud hiccup.

'Don't worry,' Sophie went on. 'I'll sort her out.'

'Are you sure?' Joe scratched his head, staring at Celia in bewilderment. 'I can give you a hand? We can carry her together?'

But Sophie wouldn't hear of it.

'No, honestly. I can manage. She's going to feel terrible in the morning.'

'We shouldn't have had that last drink. I'm sorry. I didn't realise she was that bad.'

Celia made a snuffling noise and her eyes closed. She was asleep already.

'It's not your fault,' Sophie replied. 'It's strange, though. I've never seen her drunk. In fact I've never known her have more than one glass of wine before. She used to be so disciplined. I was the one who was always pissed and out of control. I don't know what's come over her.'

Eleven

Celia was still fast asleep at seven thirty the next morning when Sophie put her head round the door.

It had been a struggle getting her to bed the night before. After Joe left, Sophie had half carried and half dragged her sister upstairs. She'd removed her shoes but not her clothes or make-up and now she was lying flat on her back, open-mouthed, with mascara smeared over her face and pillow. It wasn't a pretty sight.

After softly closing the door, Sophie tiptoed downstairs and filled a plastic bottle with water from the tap. Then she went outside to fetch her bike.

Guessing her sister wouldn't be doing a lot of work in the house today, Sophie had already resolved to enjoy every moment of the yoga class and take her time coming home. She might even drop in on Gigi at the café afterwards and treat herself to an ice cream or some frozen yoghurt.

She hadn't brought any gym gear with her to Rockaway

and was wearing a pair of grey, cotton jersey shorts with a tie waist and a loose, beige T-shirt.

It was about half a mile to the remote Fort Tilden Beach, where the class was being held, and a concrete path flanking the Atlantic Ocean ran most of the way.

At this time of day, she wasn't expecting to see many people, but at first there were quite a few folk on bikes and scooters, as well as dog walkers.

Numbers dwindled, however, the further west she travelled as the landscape became wilder and scrubbier, a mix of coastal dunes, forest and beaches surrounded by dense vegetation.

When the concrete path ended, she pushed her bike through the sand until it connected with another concrete path, called Shore Road, which ran about halfway along Fort Tilden Beach.

The actual fort behind it was once an army base, dating back to 1917, and evidence of its history was still eerily visible.

She passed by two abandoned silos, largely buried under dunes, and wondered how many missiles had been launched from there. Behind them lay the crumbling remains of old buildings and graffiti-strewn batteries.

Initially, the place appeared to be deserted, save for a lone fisherman at the water's edge with a long, sturdy beachcaster rod. Feeling rather isolated all of a sudden, she pedalled on, and was relieved when, before too long, she spotted a small group of men and women in the distance, whom she took to be yogis.

As she drew closer, she could see Terrell talking to a thin, tanned older woman with long grey plaits, wearing a bright green vest top. When he spotted Sophie, he grinned and waved.

'You made it!' he said when she was close enough to hear. 'I'm glad.'

'Wouldn't have missed it for the world,' she replied. She wheeled her bike a little way away from the group and rested it against a dune. 'I don't have a yoga mat so I've brought along a towel. I hope that's OK?'

'Absolutely fine. It's super relaxed and informal.'

There were eight of them in all, including the yoga teacher, the woman Terrell had been chatting to. Known as Bunny, she told Sophie she was seventy years old and had been practising yoga for more than four decades.

'I trained in India in Iyengar – that's structurally accurate yoga. I still think it's the best, but I tend to incorporate a bit of everything in my classes now. It keeps things interesting, I guess, and my students seem to prefer it.'

Bunny started the class with everyone in seated positions on the ground. Sophie was soon in complete awe of her. She had amazing strength and flexibility and also a beautiful aura. She seemed to sparkle with joy and vitality and she had such a calm, soothing voice that you were lulled into a state of blissful relaxation, even when holding a difficult position. She was self-assured without being cocky, and enviably comfortable in her own skin.

Terrell was right in front of Sophie, who had deliberately put her towel at the back. She liked yoga but wasn't a regular class attender and was aware she had a lot to learn.

He, on the other hand, had clearly being doing it for

years. He knew the routine off pat, segueing smoothly from one movement to another. He'd also mastered some very difficult arm balances and could stay for ages in a backbend and headstand.

Sophie reckoned he must have limbs of steel and iron abs. He also had a very cute backside, encased today in navy Lycra shorts, which she was able to admire secretly, especially when he was in downward dog.

The middle-aged man next to him wasn't nearly as athletic. Sweating profusely, he seemed to struggle with most of the poses, even balasana, or child's pose, which was supposed to be restful.

He was overweight, had a strange, spiky haircut and his joints cracked when he stood up. He did a lot of puffing and grunting, but at least he was trying, Sophie thought. Everyone had to begin somewhere and she wasn't exactly super fit herself.

When it came to garudasana, or eagle pose, however, he staged a mutiny. Sophie watched him try to move his right thigh over the left but it wouldn't wrap around, and there was no way he could get his right foot to rest on the calf of the left leg.

He lost his balance and toppled over on the first and second attempt and she had to stifle a laugh. When it happened a third time, he shook his head, muttered, 'Jeez!', threw up his hands and plonked down huffily on his mat, crossing his arms and legs.

There he stayed, until the class drew to a close and it was time for shavasana, or corpse pose.

This wasn't difficult and even he could manage it. All you

had to do was to lie on your back, let your feet fall to the sides, bring your arms alongside your torso, palms facing up, and close your eyes.

They stayed like this for about five minutes, breathing in and out deeply, their bodies still, their minds empty. With the warm sun on her face and the gentle sounds of the sea in the background, Sophie felt herself nodding off. The overweight man must have done so, too, because she was soon woken again by the rattle and clunk of his loud snores.

Unfortunately, it was at this moment Terrell leaned up on his elbows and turned to look at Sophie.

She was still lying flat, peering at him through half-closed lids. He had a huge grin on his face and as soon as she caught his eye, a giggle exploded from her mouth and her hand shot up to try to smother it.

Pushing herself up, she tried to recover her equanimity, but Terrell was shaking with silent laughter and her next giggle came out as a hoggish snort.

'Oops,' she said, covering her mouth again. Terrell could barely contain himself. Tears dribbled down his cheeks and the only way Sophie could make herself shut up was by rolling onto her tummy, shoving the towel in her mouth and burying her face in the sand.

Bunny must have noticed what was going on but didn't lose her cool. As the rest of the class slowly came out of their meditation, she tiptoed on bare feet to where the overweight man lay, crouched down and gently shook his shoulder.

'Wyatt?' she whispered, then, more loudly and with another shake, 'WYATT?'

He gave one final volley of snores, which sounded like a tractor engine starting up, opened his eyes and gazed around him in a daze.

'What? Wh-where am I?'

By now, everyone else was sitting up cross-legged. Bunny padded back to the front, settled into the lotus position and pressed her hands together at her heart. Finally she bowed deeply to the class and everyone said in unison, 'Namaste'. It was over.

Sophie imagined they'd say goodbye now and go their separate ways. She bent down to pick up her towel but when she rose again, she saw Terrell and several others taking off their clothes.

'Coming in the water?' he asked.

'Sure,' she replied, thinking it was a good job she'd brought her blue bikini. She must remember to buy a new one next time she passed a clothes shop.

Wyatt, as she now knew the overweight man to be called, was wearing red swimming shorts, patterned with toucans with yellow bibs and bright orange bills.

While Sophie struggled with her bikini, she heard him telling one of the other women, in her thirties, that he was a hair stylist with his own salon, Lookin' Good, in Belle Harbor.

He seemed pleasant and friendly and listened politely while the other woman complained to him about her hair, which was frizzy, brown and shapeless.

'Come and have a consultation!' he said. 'We can talk through some ideas.'

Once she'd fastened her bikini top, Sophie set off down

the beach with Wyatt, Terrell, the woman with frizzy hair and Bunny. The others had gone on ahead and were already in the water.

Bunny looked very elegant in a sleek, black, all-in-one bathing suit, with her long, silver grey plaits hanging down her back.

At one point, when they were close to the shoreline, Bunny took Terrell's hand. He didn't seem surprised, but quickly dropped it and was the first to run into the water. His skin glinted in the sunlight and the coloured beads on the ends of his cornrows bobbed merrily as the cold waves splashed around his legs and up to his waist.

After a few moments, a bigger wave approached and he dived straight in. When he reappeared on the other side he was facing them, smiling widely and beckoning them in.

Sophie seized the opportunity to ask Bunny how well she and Terrell knew each other.

'Oh, we go back a long way,' she said slightly wistfully. 'He's one of my best students.'

She seemed to imply they were just good friends but still, Sophie wasn't sure. There again, they'd make an odd couple, with some twenty years between them.

'Is he married?' she asked next, realising she didn't know. She hoped she didn't sound too interested; she wouldn't want Bunny saying anything to him.

Bunny laughed. 'Terrell? No. He's a free spirit. He doesn't like to be pinned down.'

'Ah.' Sophie thought she had it sussed: Bunny carried a torch for Terrell and he liked her, but not in a romantic way. She was glad she'd worked it out.

'Right,' she said. 'The time's come!' And with that, she left Bunny's side and ran into the sea herself, gasping as the cold water slapped against her skin before closing all around her.

Once she was fully immersed, Terrell swam over to join her. He showed off like a kid, doing backflips and forward rolls, so she made him take part in an underwater handstand competition, which she won.

When they'd finished their silly game, they stood for a moment facing each other. She was on tiptoe but the water reached to just above his chest, leaving his broad shoulders exposed. The skin on them was drying fast, but a few droplets sparkled in the sunlight and she had a sudden urge to lick them off.

'I really like you,' he said with a grin, as if reading her mind.

'I really like you, too.'

'So, tell me about yourself. I want to know everything.' He was smiling still, but his tone was serious.

'Well…' she began, and she relayed some of the bare facts – she had a daughter, Layla, the relationship with Layla's father hadn't lasted, in fact none of her relationships had lasted, come to that. Her last boyfriend, Richard, was more interested in computers than her so she'd kicked him out.

She also said she'd always worked, but never had a career, unlike her sister, who was a bit of a star. And she lived in a smallish London apartment, which she didn't own.

'Where are you staying? Remind me.'

She mentioned Piping Plover House again, and he nodded.

'I know that place. It's really cool. It must be worth a lot.'

'I guess,' she agreed, 'but it's very run-down.'

'Do you want to go someplace to eat Saturday night?' he said, as they walked side by side towards the sand.

Her stomach fluttered and a warm feeling spread through her. She didn't hesitate to say yes.

'Great, I'll pick you up at six thirty.'

If she could still cartwheel, she'd have done one right there and then. She had a date! With the gorgeous Terrell! She'd been beginning to think her dating days were over.

They didn't talk much after that because he was in a rush to get to his lifeguarding shift. His car was parked some way away, so he dressed quickly and said goodbye.

Sophie, Bunny and Wyatt were the only ones left – the rest had already gone – and Sophie wheeled her bike as they strolled together to the end of Shore Road.

'Thanks for the class. I'll definitely come again next week,' she promised.

It was almost 11 a.m. by the time she reached her neighbourhood. She hadn't the energy to continue on to Gigi's café, but stopped instead at an ice cream stall on the boardwalk and bought a vanilla cone and a can of Diet Coke.

She ate the cone standing up, leaning over the railings and looking out to sea. The beach was pretty full now, even on a weekday, and some of the lifeguards in their orange bathing suits had climbed down from their towers and were patrolling up and down, keeping a close eye on the children, especially.

Behind her, folk were milling around the old, 1930's art deco bathhouse, an elaborate, long, low red-brick structure. Once abandoned and allowed to fall into disrepair, it had recently had a new lease of life and was now home to local food vendors and live music events. You could also rent beach umbrellas and chairs.

Having finished her cone, Sophie started on the Coke, leaning back against the railings and watching the passing crowd on the boardwalk.

Gigi's daughter, Mariella, was buying something from one of the food stalls. Sophie recognised her boyfriend, Danny, first, in a red T-shirt and droopy black board shorts. He was standing to one side, waiting for her.

Mariella looked stunning in a pink top and teeny white shorts that barely covered her bottom. When she turned round, holding a carton of something in her hand, she noticed Sophie on the other side of the boardwalk and gave a big, friendly wave. The boyfriend nodded and smiled.

Instead of waiting to find a bench to sit on, they opened up the carton straight away. Both peered in, their foreheads touching. Then they pulled out something to eat and popped it in their mouths before strolling on.

They looked very relaxed, content and comfortable with each other. Sophie thought of Layla and felt sad. Layla didn't have a boyfriend, hated her job, felt miserable and was stuck in a rut.

Next time they spoke on the phone, Sophie would invite her here for a holiday. She deserved a break; she hadn't had one for ages.

A few weeks in Rockaway would do her a power of good. Also, getting away from London might just clear her head and help her focus on making the right changes when she returned home.

Sophie was hard up, but would find money for the air fare somehow. It would be wonderful to see Layla. The only problem was, she could be incredibly stubborn. There was always a chance she'd refuse to come.

Once she'd finished her drink, Sophie threw the empty can in the bin and set off again on her bike.

After such a great morning, it seemed as if nothing could spoil her good humour. Almost as soon as she got home, however, her mood took a downturn.

In her absence, a large yellow skip had arrived, which had been left in the driveway beside the house. While Sophie manoeuvred her bike around it to reach the side gate, Celia appeared carrying a tatty old suitcase in both hands.

It was bulging and obviously weighed a lot, because she had trouble lugging it down the porch steps. Her hair was wet and she must have had a shower, but she looked pretty rough all the same. Her complexion was sickly grey and she was make-up-free, which was unusual. She also had dark puffy cushions beneath her eyes.

'Here, let me give you a hand,' Sophie said, propping her bike against the gate.

Celia didn't answer, but tried to haul the bag up high so that she could sling it in the skip.

When she realised she couldn't do it alone, she grudgingly allowed Sophie to help.

'Wow! That was heavy. What's in it?'

It seemed an innocent enough question, but Celia didn't
seem to think so.

'Broken radios, hideous lamps, chipped china. That
sort of thing. Not that *you'd* care. Where have you been
anyway?'

Sophie felt a whoosh of blood to her head.

'What's that supposed to mean? I went to a yoga class, if
you must know. I knew you wouldn't be able to get up this
morning 'cause you got pissed last night with your friend
Joe.'

'Ha! You're a right one to blame *me* for drinking!'

It was true Sophie got drunk many times as a teenager
while Celia was swotting away in her bedroom.

'Do you think your drunken escapades had no effect on
me?' Celia went on. She didn't wait for an answer. 'Well, it's
not true. You caused so much tension when I was growing
up. All I can remember is your endless rows with Dad, you
running away, you getting suspended from school, you
failing your exams. You gave Mum and Dad hell. It was a
nightmare for me, stuck in the middle of all that shit. You
should look at your own behaviour before you start having
a go at me.'

Black thoughts flitted through Sophie's mind like evil
spirits. It was as if all the injustices she'd experienced as a
child were assembling like an army in her brain, preparing
for battle.

'Poor little Celia!' she said in a nasty voice, before she
could stop herself. 'Don't expect me to feel sorry for you.
You were such a fucking goody-goody, Daddy's favourite
little girl. He did terrible things to me, he was verbally and

emotionally abusive. You never stuck up for me, ever. He was constantly putting me down, saying I was stupid and worthless. But you could do no wrong, could you? You were perfect. How do you think that made me feel? No wonder I rebelled. I couldn't wait to leave home and get away from the toxic atmosphere. My life was a misery until I got the hell out of there. You revelled in being the favourite. You absolutely lapped it up…'

Her volume had risen and she was suddenly aware that she could probably be heard up and down the street. She started to walk towards the front door, hoping to cool off inside, but Celia hadn't finished.

'Wait!'

Sophie felt a jab in her back when she reached the porch.

Turning, she saw Celia right behind her on the highest step, her eyes flashing with anger.

'How dare you say that,' she hissed. 'Do you really think I wanted to be the good girl all the time?'

Sophie's eyes narrowed in suspicion.

'I was under huge pressure. Dad expected me to come first in everything and if I didn't, I knew I'd let him down. I was jealous of you, actually.'

'Of me?' Sophie laughed humourlessly. 'Don't be ridiculous.'

'It's true,' Celia insisted. 'And you know why? Because even though you got all the flak, at least you were able to go out with your friends and have fun and do silly things and let your hair down. I had to slave away to live up to Dad's ideal. I couldn't rebel. I didn't have a life.'

'You're kidding yourself,' Sophie said quietly. 'You

loved getting top marks, you got off on it. And you adored showing me up in front of Dad. I remember that superior look on your face when he was telling me off, like butter wouldn't melt in your mouth. Whatever I did, you had to do one better. You wanted Dad to worship you. Well, congratulations! You certainly got your wish.'

It seemed as if time stood still for a few moments. The air, which was thick and stifling, sat on them like a quilt. Even the flies settled listlessly on ceiling and walls and looked half asleep.

Sophie was thirsty, but couldn't move. It was Celia who broke the silence.

'It was years before I understood why I was the favourite.'

Sophie's ears pricked, because this was the first time anyone in the family had acknowledged their father's favouritism.

'I always prayed you'd stop doing bad things so he'd have no excuse to shout at you,' Celia went on. 'Then he told me something huge. I wish he hadn't.'

Sophie had no idea what her sister was talking about, but her change of tone was chilling.

'He made me promise not to tell you, so I didn't,' she went on. 'In hindsight, I think that was unfair.'

Sophie coughed nervously, half convinced Celia was exaggerating, half frightened of what she was about to reveal.

'You'd better sit down,' Celia said suddenly, walking over to the table and pulling out a chair.

Sophie followed obediently, although she felt like bolting. She noticed the greyness had gone from Celia's face and her cheeks were flushed and slightly feverish. The whites of her eyes were bloodshot, too.

'Have you ever wondered why we look nothing like each other?' Celia stared at Sophie, who shook her head and shivered, crossing her arms tightly over her chest.

It wasn't true; she *had* thought about it.

'I'm surprised,' Celia continued. 'I used to wonder a lot. I mean, we weren't just physically different, we were completely different characters, too.'

'Where's this leading?' Sophie sounded shrill. Her mouth was dry and she needed water badly, but she was rooted to the spot.

'We've got different fathers,' Celia blurted. 'Mum fell pregnant with you when she was seventeen. She married Dad soon after and he adopted you. Then they had me.'

Sophie's head swam and she felt sick. 'Are you lying?' she said hoarsely. 'Because if you are, it's really cruel.'

Celia's thin fingers picked at a hangnail on her right hand.

'No, I promise. Dad told me when I was in the Upper Sixth at school. You'd left home and you were partying a lot and doing drugs. I stayed overnight with you once in Notting Hill – do you remember?'

Sophie vaguely recalled Celia at one of her boozy gatherings, being surprisingly fun for once and crashing on the sofa later.

'Afterwards, I told Dad I'd had a great time,' Celia continued. 'He was annoyed and said I shouldn't have gone. I was applying for medical school and I think he thought you were a bad influence and you'd make me go off the idea.

'Later that day, he sat me down and said he had something important to tell me. He said your father was an Irish boy from Belfast. He and Mum had a summer fling in Rockaway. Mum found out she was pregnant after he'd gone back to Ireland. She wrote to him but never got a reply.

'Grandpa Donal was appalled, not least because the boy was Protestant. There was a lot of shame back then and he didn't want anyone to know. Luckily, Dad... my dad,' she added, correcting herself, 'had been in love with Mum for years. He offered to marry her, save her from the shame and pretend you were his.'

Tears came to Sophie's eyes. It was too much to take in.

'Is this true?' she asked again, holding on to the hope that it might still be a bad joke, but Celia nodded.

The image of the man Sophie thought was her father swam before her and she wanted to shout and scream.

'He shouldn't have been allowed to adopt me.' She sounded calm, but shock and anger were bubbling just below the surface. 'He didn't have the capacity to love someone else's child. It was wicked of Mum, too. She knew how he treated me. She should have kicked him out.'

She rose, knocking the chair over by accident and it crashed to the floor and broke. She wanted to be alone with her grief and dismay. Right now, she needed to bury her face in a pillow and howl.

'Wait! Hear me out – please.' Celia's arm shot out to try to stop her leaving.

Sophie swallowed and winced, because the lump in her throat hurt like hell. She didn't move, though.

'I told Dad I didn't understand why it was still a secret,'

Celia said. She was speaking quickly, anxious to get the words out while she could. 'I mean, none of our friends in England would judge and I thought you had the right to know. But Dad said it might kill Mum if you found out. Grandpa was dead by then but it wasn't fair on Pampy, either, even though we'd stopped seeing her for whatever reason.'

'So my needs didn't even come into it,' Sophie said bitterly.

Celia frowned. 'Neither did mine.'

'What do you mean?'

Celia took a deep breath.

'As I said, it wasn't easy keeping this secret from you and not telling Mum I knew, either. Actually, I think I sort of guessed something wasn't right when I was quite little, even before Dad revealed the truth. Children pick up on things and I just had this feeling that he, Mum, Grandpa and Pampy were hiding a secret. I was troubled and angry with them and didn't much like coming to Rockaway. I always felt uncomfortable here.

'It was much worse, though, when my suspicions were confirmed. I was furious. I still am. I was petrified of blowing up the family if I mentioned anything. Even Neil doesn't know.'

'Really?' This surprised Sophie, who thought he and Celia were thick as thieves, but Celia nodded.

'I couldn't risk it. I thought he might blurt it out to one of the boys. Then they might talk to Terry – and, God forbid, Layla.'

'Didn't you think you should at least tell me?' Sophie

could stem the tears no longer; they were dribbling down her cheeks, which felt hot and stingy. Her nose and ears were blocked, and her head had started pounding so loudly she thought it might explode.

Celia's thin shoulders drooped. She seemed to fold in on herself.

'I'm sorry,' she said, with a catch in her voice. 'I wanted to talk to you for years, but I was too scared. Now it's come out because I was so angry with you. I wish I'd done it sooner and in a better way.'

'Well it's too late now.'

Sophie stepped over the broken chair and walked on wobbly legs towards the open front door. As soon as she was out of sight, she half pulled, half dragged herself upstairs and crashed in a heap on her bed.

Twelve

Who am I? Where do I come from? Do I really exist? Gripped with panic, Sophie curled up, foetus-like, on the duvet, too shocked even to cry.

So this is what it felt like to discover the man you'd called Dad your entire life wasn't in fact your biological father. She felt betrayed by everyone she'd once cared about, including her mother and even Pampy.

So much made sense now and she understood at last why her dad had been so cold towards her. But whilst the shattering news certainly answered some big questions, it also raised a myriad others.

Sophie wanted to know, for instance, whether Terry, her mother, actually chose to marry Paul. It was painful to imagine her hand had been forced and that perhaps they'd never been in love.

Also, who was the Irish boy she slept with, what did he look like and why did he let her down? Was he alive and if so, where did he live and with whom? Perhaps he was rich and successful, or maybe he lived a sad and lonely existence. He might have an incurable disease, which Sophie was destined to inherit, or other children, who'd be her half-brothers and -sisters.

Only a short time ago, she'd thought of herself as predominantly English, because she'd been born in London, with a bit of her mother's Irish-American in her, too. Knowing now that it was mostly Irish blood coursing through her veins made her feel lost, alone and empty, as if her very identity had been stolen away by thieves, leaving just a hollow shell.

She must have fallen asleep for a long time, worn out by the thoughts and feelings tormenting her. When she opened her eyes, the bright sun outside her window was starting to fade and a gnawing pain in her stomach reminded her she hadn't eaten or drunk anything for hours.

Sitting up made her feel sick and light-headed, so she remained on the bed for a little while, breathing in and out slowly to try to stop the panic from rising again.

Her gaze fell on her wardrobe, the door of which was firmly locked, and she remembered her grandfather's letter. After a while she got up, fetched the key from her purse, opened the door, removed the letter from the sewing box and read it once more.

As parents, we tried to instil in you the values we hold dear. It seems, however, that you have rejected faith, honesty, hard work and self-sacrifice in favour of lies and self-gratification.

We are deeply concerned not only for you, your husband and daughters, but also for our precious Catholic community here in Rockaway.

Sophie bit her lip and frowned. What did he mean by saying Terry had rejected the values he held dear in favour of lies and self-gratification? Hadn't she obeyed his wishes, married Paul and lived a lie in a desperate bid to make amends and save the family's reputation?

She must have done a really dreadful thing later in life to enrage her father so. Sophie was convinced that whatever it was had something to do with her conception and the subsequent cover-up. Now, more than ever, she needed to discover the truth and find out what part Pampy might or might not have played in the affair.

After placing the letter and sewing box back in their hiding place and locking the wardrobe door again, Sophie left her room and went downstairs in bare feet.

Still feeling unsteady, she walked slowly, holding on tightly to the banister rail and listening out for her sister.

The house and everything in it seemed strange and unreal. Was the pastel paint on the kitchen walls always this grubby? Had the tiles behind the sink always been peppermint green?

Even her own hand looked unfamiliar, the fingers whiter, the nails longer, the cuticles more ragged. She wondered if she'd recognise her face in the mirror now that she was no longer the daughter of Paul, but of some man from Belfast whom she'd never met and might never know.

Nothing and everything had changed. She wasn't the

same person who'd arrived in Rockaway only a few short days before; she was a stranger even to herself.

She drank two glasses of water standing up and ate a slice of brown bread with cream cheese, from the fridge. No longer hungry and thirsty, the aching emptiness was still there, however, threatening to overwhelm her.

Celia wasn't around, which was a relief, as Sophie didn't wish to speak to her. All of a sudden, she realised she wanted nothing more than to see Layla and hold her in her arms. Layla would bring comfort; she was the only one who could.

Leaving her glass on the kitchen table, Sophie hurried upstairs to find her mobile phone. Perching on the end of the bed, she quickly dialled the number, desperate to hear her daughter's voice.

The phone rang three or four times then stopped. Was it the signal? She tried again and when the same thing happened, disappointment washed over her.

After a third attempt, it dawned on her that Layla was clicking the Decline Call option. Sophie couldn't even leave a voicemail.

According to her phone, it was 5.15 p.m., soon after ten o'clock at night in England. Her dismay turned to relief as the penny dropped. Of course! Layla would be at the restaurant. But then Sophie remembered she wasn't allowed to have her mobile on her while she was waitressing; she had to leave it in a locker.

Puzzled and concerned, Sophie sent a text message – *Where are u? Please call asap. Thx. Mum xx*

It wasn't often she asked for an urgent response, and she told herself Layla would be in touch soon, for sure. The problem was, she didn't know what to do with herself in the meantime.

Her mind kept flitting from one dark thought to another and she was too weak and jittery to start on any jobs in the house. She couldn't possibly focus on a book or magazine, either.

She tried Layla once more and got a message saying, '*The person you have called is unavailable right now. Please try again later.*' This only made her feel worse.

All by herself in her silent room, Sophie thought that she'd never felt so alone. She was about to go for a walk, just to see some other people and try to quieten the noise in her head, when a knock on the bedroom door made her jump.

Celia hovered awkwardly at the entrance with one hand on the knob.

'How are you?' she asked with seeming concern, but Sophie wasn't buying it.

'Shocked, raw, devastated,' she replied sharply. 'How would *you* feel?'

There was a pause and it was only then Sophie noticed what her sister was wearing: smart jeans, white trainers and a clean white shirt with a navy jumper tied round her shoulders. She was overdressed for Rockaway and looked rather hot.

'Can I get you anything?' she said, but Sophie shook her head.

'I can look after myself, thanks.'

Picking up her phone, she stared at her screenshot, hoping Celia would get the message and leave, but she didn't.

'I'm going home,' she said suddenly. 'I've booked an overnight flight.'

Sophie looked up. 'Cheers.' Her voice dripped with sarcasm. 'Don't worry, I can manage on my own.'

Celia cleared her throat. 'I-I think it's for the best,' she said with a stammer. 'We can't carry on in this atmosphere.'

She glanced at Sophie, who stared back blankly, giving nothing away.

'I'll ask Neil or one of the boys to come and help you. I'll book their flights as soon as I'm back.'

'Don't bother.'

'I shouldn't have come in the first place. It was never going to work.'

'No.'

'I really am sorry for telling you the way I did. I wish—'

'Just go,' Sophie said wearily. 'Don't make things worse.'

Later, Sophie heard Celia dragging her suitcase downstairs. The doorbell rang and she watched her sister climb into the yellow taxi without a backwards glance and slam the door shut.

As darkness fell, she padded round the house like a lost soul before deciding the lookout tower was where she needed to be. Layla hadn't called back and was still unobtainable. There was nothing to do but wait.

Sitting on Pampy's chair, watching the stars twinkling in the coal-black sky, Sophie tried to imagine what was going through her grandmother's head when she wrote her will, leaving the house to her granddaughters.

Did she do it to assuage her guilt? If so, she might have died happy – or happier, anyway. For Sophie, however, happiness seemed as elusive as the pot of gold at the end of the rainbow, as unattainable as true love.

'Ladies and gentlemen, we're about to experience some turbulence. Please return to your seats and keep your seatbelts securely fastened.'

On hearing the pilot's words, Celia frowned, put down her book and stared out of the cabin window at the black night sky.

There was nothing glamorous about flying, she thought, even when you could afford first class. She'd sipped Champagne, watched a film and picked at her smoked salmon starter. Despite these distractions, however, she still couldn't get away from feeling cooped up and uncomfortable, breathing in other people's germs along with the rank, recycled air.

Neil had been surprised to hear she was coming home so soon and had offered to pick her up from the airport.

Was she looking forward to seeing him? She wasn't sure. On the one hand, it would be a tremendous relief to return to some normality. She'd missed her husband's steady presence and the comfort of their routine. On the other hand, she dreaded his questions and wondered what and how much to tell him.

Where would she begin? With her father's shattering revelation all those years ago, or her final row with Sophie? Celia could imagine Neil being shocked if she told him the whole truth. He might even take Sophie's side.

Admittedly this was unlikely, because he was very loyal,

but the mere possibility made Celia go hot and cold at the same time. In his eyes, as well as her own, she rarely put a foot wrong. She couldn't bear the thought of falling from her pedestal.

Guilt and shame were relatively new emotions to her. In fact she'd rarely felt bad about anything she'd done. For the past few hours, however, she seemed to see Sophie's distraught image everywhere. Her blue-grey eyes, so different from Celia's own, stared at Celia reproachfully, while tears trickled down her pale cheeks.

The fact Celia had kept the secret of Sophie's parentage for so long didn't especially trouble her. After all, she'd made a promise to her father, and he'd frightened her into believing that to tell would have dire consequences.

However, she couldn't seem to forgive herself for the way she'd delivered the news. She'd always thought Sophie was tough, but not on this occasion. The information had devastated her.

It was quite a surprise to Celia that she not only felt guilty, she was actually worried about her sister. When she walked out, she truly believed she was doing the right thing, saving them both from further arguments and heartache. Just a short time later, though, she'd started seeing her actions in a different light. She'd left Sophie in great distress and what's more, knew she'd be too proud to call to apologise and check she was all right.

If only she could talk to somebody she trusted and ask for advice. The problem was, she didn't have friends, not real ones, anyway. She was on cordial relations with some of the mothers from the boys' old schools. And she sometimes had coffee at the gym with a group of local women. She and Neil gave dinner parties, too, but their guests were mostly work colleagues they wanted to impress.

None of these acquaintances really *knew* Celia. In fact she wouldn't be surprised if they were somewhat intimidated by her. After all, she was careful only ever to reveal her very best side. She never showed stressed and anxious Celia, with an almost-out-of-control eating disorder. Even Neil didn't know much about that.

An air steward came by with a trolley and took away Celia's half-eaten meal.

'Can I get you anything else?' she asked, with a smile. Celia said no.

Pushing back her seat as far as it would go and raising the leg rest, she wrapped herself in a blanket. She was sure she wouldn't be able to sleep properly, but a doze would be better than nothing.

On reflection, she thought, closing her eyes, it would be better to keep her own counsel and not mention exactly what had happened to anyone. A great believer in self-promotion, she reckoned it would be too difficult to spin things the right way and put her actions in a suitably glowing light.

Her stomach growled and she wondered if she should have allowed herself to eat more of her meal. '*Don't be silly, Celia,*' said the sharp little voice in her head. '*Do you want to stay seven and a half stone or not?*'

She certainly did, she thought, and smiled. If there was one thing she was really good at, it was being thin. No one in the world could deny her that.

* * *

When dawn broke the following morning, Sophie was awake, too. Having tossed and turned most of the night, it was a relief to see light creeping through the window and hear the distant chime of church bells. At least she wouldn't have to lie here any longer, praying for slumber.

She checked her phone for the umpteenth time: still nothing from Layla. Sophie decided she'd call Layla's best friend, Zoe, later this morning to see if she knew of her whereabouts.

As well as being concerned, Sophie also felt angry and wronged. At twenty-one, she thought Layla should know better. It was true she had no notion of what her mother was going through right now, but Layla was certainly wise to the fact that Sophie worried if she didn't know where her daughter was. It really was too bad.

Tears sprang in Sophie's eyes again. She was surprised she had any left to shed. It was no good being a victim, though. Determined to pull herself together, she rose and went to the bathroom to have a shower. As the tepid water splashed over her face and body, she gave herself a stiff talking-to.

Today was a new day, like a blank page in the diary of her life. She could choose to fritter it away, feeling sorry for herself and drowning in resentment and blame, or she could move her life forwards.

Remembering that she'd faced numerous challenges in the past and survived somehow, she told herself she'd deal with this latest crisis, too. The first step was to get dressed, have breakfast and begin the next job.

There were still piles of items in the front room either to go to landfill or be taken to charity. For a while, Sophie went back and forth to the skip, chucking out anything broken or useless.

She began conservatively but became more ruthless as the morning wore on. Out went any books and sheet music not in tip-top condition. The wooden piano stool was tatty and the lid had come off its hinges, so that went, too, along with two rugs, which had seen better days, and all the curtains and cushions.

It was backbreaking work, but it helped to take her mind off her troubles and she stopped only twice for a glass of water. She started carting boxes of the saleable books to the car.

Once it was piled high and there wasn't an inch more space, she drove to the first suitable donation centre. A volunteer helped her unload and she made two more such journeys until all the books were gone. It was surprisingly satisfying.

By the time she'd finished, it was after 2 p.m. There was still no word from Layla, so Sophie sat on the swing bench in the porch and called Zoe.

It took several rings before she answered and Sophie almost wept with relief.

'Do you know where Layla is? I can't get hold of her,' she blurted. Zoe tried to reassure her.

'I'm sure she's fine... I'll ask her to call you...'

Soon after they'd hung up, Zoe sent a text saying Layla was at work and would be in touch at the end of her shift. It was comforting news, though Sophie felt even more hurt that her daughter had responded immediately to a friend, but not to her mother.

There wasn't much food in the house but despite not being hungry, she made herself eat a piece of buttered toast.

Her next task was to arrange a free pick-up in a few days' time, for the unwanted furniture she'd decided to donate to a homeless charity. She'd only keep back a few things necessary for her stay here, including her bed, her wardrobe and Pampy's rocking chair. The kitchen table and chairs and even the piano would be taken away and sold by the charity, with luck for quite good money.

There were several mediocre paintings, which someone might want. The only items she intended to take home with her were the sampler, a small watercolour of the beach, signed and painted by Pampy, and the sewing box, of course.

Being busy meant that she'd scarcely thought about Celia, but as soon as she sat down, her sister's revelations started preying on her mind once more.

Swinging to and fro again on her favourite chair in the porch, she thought how Celia would be back in London now, relieved, no doubt, to have left Sophie and Rockaway far behind.

The idea of her sending Neil or one of her boys to help out was anathema, and Sophie quickly texted, telling her not to.

No need to reply, she added. *Just don't do it. There aren't any beds – everything's gone to charity.*

This wasn't quite true, of course, but she hoped her small lie would kill off the idea.

The chair swung gently to and fro as she pushed with

the tip of one foot, while listening to the happy sounds of children's voices in a nearby garden.

They reminded her of her own garden in London when she was a child. It was long and narrow, with a swing and a metal climbing frame at the far end. She must have played in it, but her abiding memory was of climbing over the fence into the neighbours' garden to hide from her father, or the man who pretended to be him.

Sometimes, the neighbours spotted her in the bushes and would invite her indoors. They were a kind family, with a smiley, stay-at-home mum and a dad who never shouted at the children, but took them swimming every Sunday morning without fail.

'Yoo-hoo!'

Snapping out of her reverie, Sophie opened her eyes to find Gigi gazing up at her from the pavement.

'Can I come up?' Gigi asked. 'I've got something for you.'

'Of course.' Sophie rose, and it was only now she noticed that Gigi was holding quite a large, white cardboard box.

Sophie opened the lid and took a peek. Inside were four delicious-looking cakes: a chocolate muffin, an éclair stuffed with fresh cream, a round bun with white icing and a cherry on top, and a slice of something made with flaky pastry, jam and nuts.

'Oh my!' Sophie said, stealing a bit of toasted almond from the pastry and popping it in her mouth.

'I just came from the café,' Gigi explained. 'I know you're working real hard. I guessed you and your sister would appreciate something sweet!'

Sophie thanked her warmly and invited her to stay for a drink.

'I've got something to tell you,' she said, once she'd made the tea. 'Celia's gone home. I'm afraid we had a row.'

Intending to leave it at that, she started to ask Gigi about her day, but Gigi interrupted.

'You look terrible!' She leaned forwards with a frown and scrutinised Sophie's features. 'You've been crying, I can see.'

Taken aback, Sophie could only nod. Her eyes were already filling with tears again, no matter how hard she tried to stop them.

'Oh, you poor darling!' Gigi moved her chair up close and put an arm round Sophie's shoulders. 'Tell me what happened. I want to know everything.'

Her voice was full of compassion and the hug felt warm and comforting. It was a long time since anyone had held Sophie tight and she realised how much she'd missed it.

Before long, she was narrating almost word for word exactly what Celia had said the day before and how she felt about it. Gigi was a good listener and butted in only occasionally, when she couldn't help herself.

'What a wicked man,' she said with feeling. 'He used Celia, yes, but that's no excuse for her to be mean to you. I couldn't have lived with myself.'

When Sophie mentioned the letter, Gigi's ears pricked up and Sophie had to go and fetch it from the sewing box. When she'd finished reading, Gigi let out a big sigh.

'The depths to which some human beings will sink amazes me. It's beyond belief he'd turn his back on his own daughter and grandchildren. I don't care what your mother did or didn't do – and I bet it wasn't anything dreadful – he was nothing short of a monster. And all supposedly in the name of God, too. Pah!'

She swatted away an invisible fly with her free hand.

They'd been talking for quite some time now and the cakes were still untouched in the box. Sophie offered to make more tea, but Gigi said: 'I think we both need something stronger!'

As there wasn't any alcohol in the house, she went to get a bottle of chilled white wine. She made Sophie eat the chocolate muffin, insisting that she needed the boost, and had half the éclair herself.

'First things first,' she said at last, licking cream off her fingers and brushing the crumbs from her lap. 'I'm going to help you with the house. I'll get my kids involved, too.'

Sophie started to protest but Gigi was having none of it. 'You can't do it on your own. Apart from anything else, you'll hurt your back with all that lifting. I won't be able to come when the café's open, obviously, but I can do stuff in the evenings. Nino's got nothing whatever on at the moment; he's loafing round all day. It'll do him good to get stuck in.'

'That's so kind,' said Sophie warmly, thinking it *would* be a relief to have another pair of hands.

'Thank goodness that's settled.' Gigi sat back comfortably in her chair. 'I'm glad you've finally seen sense.'

Now, she asked Sophie if she were sure she wanted to discover why her mother and Pampy ceased speaking, and Sophie said yes.

'It might upset you,' Gigi warned. 'You won't know until you find out the truth, and by then it'll be too late.'

'I couldn't be more upset than I already am.'

This answer seemed to satisfy Gigi. 'All right then, I'll try and help you with this, too.'

Living in the same house for more than twenty years and owning a busy café meant she knew a lot of local people. She said she'd ask around and try to find anyone who remembered Pampy and Donal in their younger days.

'There are bound to be some folk who knew Terry, too. Maybe someone lived in Brooklyn during the week as well and went to the same school, or met her here on the beach. If I keep hassling, I'm sure something will come up.'

Sophie was grateful. However, having spoken to Yana, one of Rockaway's oldest residents, and gleaned little information, she was doubtful anyone else would be of much assistance.

But Gigi was an optimist. 'Nonsense!' she said, wagging an index finger at Sophie. 'Don't be so defeatist! Your mother and grandmother weren't invisible. Someone somewhere will have crossed their path.'

The sun had already sunk below the horizon and the sky was changing from light grey to charcoal black.

Gigi sighed. 'I need to go and start on supper. My husband's off work today. He put in an order this morning for home-made stracciatella soup and veal Milanese.'

She pulled an exasperated face. 'No rest for me. A woman's work is never done.'

'Poor you,' said Sophie. 'Can't he make dinner for once?'

Gigi shook her head and rose, kissing Sophie lightly on the cheek.

'No, *cara*, you don't understand. He's very fussy. He only likes my food, he says it's the best in the world.'

She shrugged, and a big smile spread across her face.

'You see, I'm a victim of my own success!'

Sophie laughed. 'You are.'

When she was alone again, Sophie sat for a while, reflecting on their long chat. It had lifted her spirits more than she could say and she was deeply grateful.

Gigi's family were lucky to have her and whether or not she could help shed light on the mysterious letter, Sophie felt lucky, too. She might have lost a sister, but she'd gained a friend.

Thirteen

'Why didn't you call when you got my message? I've been worried sick.'

Sophie didn't mean to start the conversation this way; the words slipped out and she immediately wished she could take them back.

She could sense Layla's annoyance before she'd even spoken. Her mobile seemed to prickle like heat rash in her hand and ear.

'For God's sake, Mum! I'm twenty-one. I've got a job, remember? I'm busy.'

'I know, but how often do I ask you to ring urgently? You must have realised it was important. You managed to answer Zoe straight away...'

Glancing out of the front window, Sophie could see lights blazing in the house opposite. By contrast, she found the darkness in Pampy's front room quite soothing.

Sitting in her grandmother's rocking chair, with her feet

pulled up beneath her, she wanted Layla to be gentle and soothing, too.

'What did you want anyway?' Layla asked crossly. 'You know it's one o'clock in the morning here?'

'How come you're back so late? It must have been a very long shift.'

Layla clicked her tongue. 'The last customers didn't leave till midnight. In case you've forgotten, it's Friday, and someone had a birthday. Then I waited for my boss to finish so she could give me a lift home. Any more questions?'

Sophie tucked her knees under her chin, so she was curled up tight, like a ball.

'No,' she said meekly. 'You must be tired.'

'I'm completely knackered. I hate my job, I hate my whole fucking life, actually. It's shit. I'm never going to have children. I wouldn't want to put them through it.'

'I'm sorry you feel like this. I wish I could help.' Sophie's eyes stung and her lips felt dry and cracked. She was exhausted, too. 'Can't you look for another job? Just a temporary one, I mean,' she said quickly. 'Something with better hours? Just until you find what you really want…'

There was an exasperated sigh at the other end. 'I'm not going to get a job I want, Mum. I just have to accept it. I'm not good enough to get into TV. I haven't got the grades and I haven't got parents in the business.'

Her anger had lessened and she sounded bitter and hopeless. Sophie wanted to kiss her and make it all better, as she used to when Layla was small. Those days were long gone.

'Of course you—' she began but Layla jumped in.

'Don't tell me to keep trying and everything's going to be all right. It's not OK. I'm not OK.' Her voice cracked. 'Why didn't you make me keep in touch with my dad? Maybe he could've helped.'

'Oh, Layla. We've been through this. I did try.'

But Layla wasn't listening.

'I was only young when I stopped seeing him. I didn't know what I was doing. You were the adult. It was up to you to lead the way.'

Guilt stabbed at Sophie's insides. It was a familiar pain, which she'd suffered from off and on for virtually all of Layla's life. Sophie was twenty-four when she moved in with Layla's father, Luke, and twenty-five when Layla was born.

They decided to have a baby in the early stages of their relationship when they were madly in love. By the time Layla came along, however, the love was already waning.

Luke wasn't cut out for family life; he was too restless. He was a chef when they met but it didn't suit him so he switched to sales. Soon after, he decided he wanted to be a photographer and Sophie, who was then eight months pregnant, offered to go back to work and support them both. He could look after the baby during the day and complete an online photography course.

A few months into that, however, he concluded he didn't want to be a photographer after all, he hated England and wanted to move to southern Spain. He didn't much like looking after Layla, either.

By then, she was ten months old. Sophie said she and the baby would follow when he'd found work and suitable accommodation, but he couldn't seem to settle to anything and kept moving.

Weeks turned into months and in the end, Sophie and Luke both realised that she and the baby wouldn't be going to Spain after all. Whatever they'd once had as a couple was no longer there, and Sophie had grown used to being a single mother. She was also resigned to the fact she'd receive little or no support from him.

He did settle in Malaga for a while and had some success as a property developer. When Layla was old enough to fly on her own, she stayed with him for a week in the summer holidays. She didn't like his girlfriend, his apartment or his lifestyle, however, and at the age of thirteen, declared she'd never go again.

Sophie tried to reason with her but Layla knew her own mind and dug in her heels. Luke was angry and hurt and blamed Sophie for turning their daughter against him. When he changed jobs and girlfriend and moved yet again, he didn't pass on his new contact details and they didn't try to find him.

Sophie did her best to give her daughter a happy childhood. The sense of guilt, however, was never far away. She wondered if, for Layla's sake, she should have done more to keep the relationship with Luke alive.

'Celia's gone home,' she said suddenly, hoping to move the conversation on.

'Why?' asked Layla.

'Oh, something came up and she had to rush back.' Sophie was being deliberately vague. She'd resolved some minutes ago not to mention the real reason after all; it wasn't the right time. 'I was thinking,' she went on. 'How about packing in the job and coming here to meet me? I'll pay your air fare.'

But the idea only seemed to upset Layla more.

'See! You're doing it again! You're not taking what I do seriously. I can't just walk out on work. It's a shitty job but I still need to give them notice. Anyhow, I can't afford not to be earning. I know you're skint, too, you can't pay for me as well.'

It seemed nothing Sophie said could lift Layla's mood, not even the prospect of a break. She felt useless.

Layla yawned loudly, making it obvious she wanted to bring the call to an end.

'I need to get some sleep.'

'Will you be all right?' asked Sophie, wanting to hold on to her for a moment longer. 'On your own, I mean?'

'I don't have a choice, do I?'

'You could ask a friend to come and keep you company? Zoe, or someone else?'

'Nah. It's too late. I'll be fine.'

Only slightly comforted, Sophie made Layla promise not to ignore her calls again and they said goodnight. It was only once she'd put the phone down she realised her daughter hadn't pursued the matter of why she'd sent the urgent text in the first place, or asked one single question about how she really was.

The following morning, Sophie woke with a headache. She felt a bit better after washing down a painkiller with a mug of tea, then remembered with a jolt that it was Saturday. Terrell was supposed to be picking her up at 6.30 p.m. and taking her out to supper.

Her first thought was to cancel. The previous few days had taken their toll and she wasn't in the right frame of mind for socialising.

On the other hand, the prospect of spending all day and night alone with her thoughts was unappealing, too. Terrell was kind of hot and he made her laugh. Perhaps an evening with him was just the medicine she needed.

She hadn't forgotten Gigi's offer of help the previous day, but wasn't expecting Nino to turn up on her doorstep at 9 a.m. when she was wearing nothing but pink knickers with her baggy yellow T-shirt.

'Mum said you've got some jobs for me,' he said with a grin, quickly followed by a mock bow. 'At your service, ma'am.'

He'd come in work clothes: a frayed black T-shirt and torn joggers, too short for his tall, gangly frame. He must have grown a lot recently.

Sophie was touched by his cheery enthusiasm, a pretty rare quality in a teenage boy. She'd been dreading clearing out the spare room, which was full of junk, so she suggested they do it together. There was nothing worth passing on; literally everything was to go in the skip.

After changing into her denim shorts and a navy T-shirt, she collected an axe, a saw and some other tools from the outside shed and carried them to the top floor, where Nino was waiting.

The big items needed to be broken up before they

could heave them downstairs. The damaged chair wasn't a problem as it came apart quite easily, but the same couldn't be said of the iron bedstead.

All the nuts and bolts were rusted and it took a long time and a great deal of effort to unscrew them. Nino's skinny arms belied the fact that he was quite strong, but once or twice even he almost admitted defeat.

To and fro they went from room to skip, carting an old mattress, sections of iron bedstead, a rolled up carpet, heavy velvet curtains and the wonky ironing board with the torn cover.

Everything was covered in dust and Sophie shrieked when she lifted the lid of a large leather trunk to discover mouse droppings inside. There were several battered suitcases, as well, and she decided to dump them after a quick check to make sure they weren't concealing anything important.

Mariella called in at midday, with a tray of cold drinks and sandwiches Gigi had prepared before leaving for work. She said she was meeting up with her boyfriend and didn't stay long, but promised to lend a hand another day.

Sophie and Nino devoured the food at the kitchen table before resuming their task. It took more than five hours to clear the room completely and when they'd finished, Sophie vacuumed the carpet, wiped the window sills and skirting boards and closed the door firmly behind them.

'I'm incredibly grateful,' she told Nino when they were downstairs again. 'I couldn't have done it on my own.'

She tried to make him accept some cash, but he wouldn't.

'Then I'll just have to give it to your mum for you,' she said fake-crossly, but he shook his head and smiled.

By the time he left it was almost 3 p.m. Remembering her date tonight, Sophie looked at herself in the bathroom mirror and frowned.

Her reddish-yellow hair was lank and greasy and her face tired and sweaty. Glancing down at her hands and feet, she noticed the ends of her finger- and toenails were almost black and there were ugly scratches on her knees and calves.

What to do? A thought flashed through her mind and she quickly Googled the nail salon she'd checked out when she was buying groceries with Celia. It was called Pink Blossom Nail and Spa and if she came immediately, they could see her straight away.

Without a second thought, Sophie hopped in the hired Toyota and drove to Belle Harbor. The street was quite busy, but she managed to find a parking slot and half walked, half ran to the shop, hoping that they could effect some sort of miraculous transformation.

She felt quite embarrassed. The place was immaculate: all glass and steel, with white walls, a gleaming pale grey floor, squashy white armchairs and white washbasins and foot bowls. Even the staff wore crisp white, short-sleeved overalls, and she was sure they were secretly eyeing her up and down.

Rows of shelves on the walls to left and right were stacked with little pots of nail polish in every colour imaginable: whites, blacks, blues, purples, pinks, reds, corals, nudes, greens, sparkling silvers and browns.

Unable to resist, she walked over to one display, took down several pots in turn and checked out the names, as sumptuous and evocative as the colours themselves: Palm Springs, Fiesta, Strawberries and Cream, Blackberry, Bush Baby and Pillow Talk.

While she was still browsing, one of the technicians came over. She was a very small, slim, graceful-looking woman with wide, black, deep-set eyes and a jet black bun.

'Hello, miss, do you know what colour you want?'

She crossed her arms and Sophie noticed her delicate, almost childlike wrists and hands. 'My name is Cilla. I'll be doing your mani-pedi today.'

Unsure which polish to choose, Sophie hesitated for a few moments.

'Um, oh dear,' she said, replacing a bright orange and taking out a plum-coloured varnish. Even as she did so, her eye was caught by an unusual, vivid, sky blue shade. It was rather ethereal and reminded her of Van Gogh's *The Starry Night*.

'This is the one,' she said firmly. 'I've never had blue nails before.'

'Good choice,' said Cilla. 'Please follow me.'

She led Sophie towards the back of the salon, where there were six squashy armchairs, in a white, faux leather fabric, with footbaths attached.

Once settled, Cilla showed her how to adjust the backrest and use the electronic seat controls. Sophie felt like a kid in a sweetshop, pressing different buttons to test the neck, upper and lower back massage options while the footbath was filling.

To her right, a tanned, gum-chewing girl in pink shorts with a yellow ponytail looked blissed out. She was leafing through a magazine while a male technician massaged one foot and lower leg as the other languished in foamy water.

On her left, an older woman with a short grey bob was having her toenails painted coral pink.

'D'you like the colour?' she asked, noticing Sophie looking her way. 'I'm not sure. I usually go for a darker red.'

'It's lovely, very fresh,' Sophie replied with a smile. 'I've picked blue. I hope I won't regret it.'

Cilla tapped Sophie on the shin.

'You can put your feet in the bath now,' she said. Sophie settled back with her eyes closed, enjoying the soothing sensation of warm, swirling, scented water.

Her eyes sprang open when the massage she'd chosen suddenly became quite painful, pummelling her neck and shoulders and making her squirm. She soon discovered how to adjust the strength, however, and was able to relax again.

Cilla was silent and focused during the first part of the treatment, when she wrapped Sophie's feet in warm wax, massaged them, scraped off the dead skin and trimmed and buffed her toenails.

Once she started to apply the polish, however, she became more chatty, asking Sophie where she was from and how she liked Rockaway.

Sophie, in turn, discovered Cilla grew up in Hanoi, Vietnam, and moved to the US about ten years ago, when she was sixteen.

'Do you have a husband?' Cilla asked, looking up.

Sophie was momentarily taken aback. Cilla's pretty, heart-shaped face and delicate bone structure made her appear fragile, but like most Americans, she wasn't afraid of being direct.

'No, I'm single,' Sophie replied, wondering if that sounded sad.

On the contrary, Cilla seemed rather impressed.

'Sensible lady!' she cried, bobbing up and down on her footstool. Sophie hoped she wouldn't smudge the nail polish.

'We don't need a man to make us happy,' Cilla went on. 'Men are no good. They're all selfish, not like women.'

She shook her head and jiggled the bottle of varnish vigorously.

'Women make the world go round.'

Sophie couldn't help laughing.

'What makes you such a feminist? Personal experience?'

Cilla nodded sagely. 'My last boyfriend didn't tell me he was married with two children. Imagine! When I found out, that was the end of that. The one before him was so boring. And the one before that was only interested in one thing.' She gave Sophie a knowing look. 'I'm done with men. I have a nice job, nice apartment, nice life. I'm happy. I don't want to cook and clean for a man or wash his clothes. I'd rather cook for myself, thank you.'

It was Sophie's turn to be impressed. 'Well done you,' she said, adding, 'We mustn't settle for second or third best.'

She wondered whether to let on she had a date tonight, but decided against it. Cilla might try to put her off.

Sophie couldn't help gazing in delight at her toenails once they were done. They were neat and square-shaped and the glossy blue polish shimmered like oil on water.

Now her feet looked beautiful, there was only the rest of her to worry about, she mused, as she followed Cilla to one of the manicure stations at the front of the shop.

Cilla had mentioned a walk-in hairdresser a few blocks away, and this was Sophie's next stop. She was told she'd have to wait half an hour for a wash and blow dry. She'd be pushing it for time, but decided to go ahead anyway.

On the rare occasions that she went to salons, she always quite liked her hair. It somehow looked less gingery, more reddish-blonde and as sleek and shiny as polished wood. However, it certainly didn't go with her rather tight, tatty denim shorts and baggy T-shirt, or her grubby face, come to that.

The car was parked outside a shoe shop. Sophie was about to open the driver's door when she saw Joe, emerging from the drugstore opposite with a small white paper bag.

Hoping he wouldn't notice her, she bobbed down and began to climb into her seat, but she was too late.

'Mary Poppins!' he called, strolling across the road to join her. 'How're you doing?'

He didn't have a hat on today and Sophie could tell that he'd been to the hairdresser, too. His fair hair no longer straggled around his neck but had been cut into a neat short back and sides.

It was quite a transformation and Sophie couldn't hide her surprise. He looked almost preppy.

'You-you look completely different!' she stammered, inwardly kicking herself for being gauche.

'What, this?' He grinned and ran a hand across his head,

ruffling the crown. 'Yeah, I reckoned I needed a haircut. It had gotten far too long.'

He was wearing the baggy board shorts she'd seen him in before, and a plain black faded T-shirt that might have been washed a thousand times.

'I could say the same – about you,' he went on and when she raised her eyebrows questioningly. 'The hair. You've had it done. You look completely different too.'

Sophie's cheeks flushed pink.

'I'm out tonight,' she explained, standing up straight and trying to muster some dignity.

'Where? A ball? I hope you're not wearing those.' He pointed to her shorts and flip-flops. At least she had clean feet and gleaming blue toenails. 'Do you have a fairy godmother? You'll be like Cinderella!'

A small smile was playing on his lips. He was teasing her again.

'I'm going home now to get changed,' she said tartly, fiddling with her car keys to show she needed to leave. 'My sister's gone back to London,' she added for no apparent reason.

'Has she?' His expression didn't change and she was half disappointed, half pleased, though she wasn't sure why.

'She had to get back to work,' Sophie lied.

'So Mary Poppins is all alone.' Joe made a mock-sad face.

'I'm fine,' she replied firmly. 'In some ways it's easier when it's just me. I can really get on with things.'

He stroked his cheek, as if brushing off a small insect or a speck of dirt. She imagined how the skin might feel beneath his fingers – all soft and smooth, perhaps smelling of soap.

'Excuse me, I must get going,' she said quickly. She'd started walking back to the car when she heard him call her name.

'Sophie?'

'Yes?' she said, stopping and turning.

'It's fabulous, by the way. Your hair!'

He was standing very tall, looking straight at her and smiling widely.

'What? Oh! Thank you.'

She smiled back in spite of herself, and her hand rose up instinctively to tuck some strands behind an ear. Just for a moment, their eyes met. He was so focused she might have been the only person in the world.

He seemed to be searching for something in her gaze, but she was probably imagining it. She glanced away and the next time she checked, he was striding up the street in the opposite direction.

Fourteen

Terrell was bang on time. Sophie had just finished her make-up when she heard the bell and scuttled downstairs to greet him.

'Wow!' he said, when she opened the door, and he followed up with a wolf-whistle. 'You look beautiful!'

Sophie had never been good at taking compliments and her cheeks went red for the second time that day. 'Thank you. I just need to find my shoes. Come on in.'

She ran upstairs and when she came down again, Terrell had his back to her in the kitchen. He was in front of the window, gazing out at the overgrown garden.

'It's a great place you've got here,' he said, hearing her footsteps and turning around. 'How many bedrooms?'

Sophie did a mental tally. 'Six,' she said eventually. 'Seven if you include the tower, but you have to walk through another bedroom to get there, so I guess it doesn't really count.'

He whistled again. 'It's a big old house, that's for sure, and you've got sea views?'

'Oh yes,' Sophie replied.

'You could do a lot with it,' Terrell went on. 'I mean, you could knock all the way through if you wanted, to make one giant space. No one needs a walk-in food cupboard these days.' He nodded at the pantry, which he'd clearly peeked inside. 'And you could probably extend out the back as well.'

'I know, but like I said, we have to sell. There's no other option.'

Terrell frowned. 'That's a pity, it really is.' He paused for a moment. 'Maybe we can do something about that. We'll have to see…'

Sophie didn't know what he meant and besides, she was eager to go out and enjoy their evening together. He'd made quite an effort and looked very handsome, in a slim-fitting, white designer polo top, which showed off his muscly, tattooed arms and flat stomach. His black jeans were freshly cleaned and ironed and quite tight too, and he had sparkling white trainers on his feet, which looked brand new.

Around his neck he wore a thin gold necklace, to match his gold earrings, and there was a glossy sheen to his skin, as if he'd bathed in essential oil or smothered himself in body butter.

The beard had gone but the cornrows were still there, with multicoloured beads on the ends that seemed to dance when he moved his head.

'Where are we going?' Sophie asked, as they left the kitchen and strolled into the front room.

'Wherever you want. What do you like to eat?'

She was a little surprised, as she'd imagined he'd have booked somewhere in advance, but maybe you didn't need to reserve a table in Rockaway.

'Anything,' Sophie replied. 'Indian, Chinese, Japanese, Mexican. I'm easy.'

'We don't have much Indian food here. It's not a common thing.'

'Japanese, then?' Sophie said hopefully, but Terrell shook his head.

'I wouldn't recommend the Japanese restaurants round here. They do good burgers in Beefy's. It's over in Sheepshead Bay, southern Brooklyn. It's about a twenty minute drive. We can go there if you like?'

'Burgers it is.' Sophie tried not to look disappointed. She'd been hoping for something spicy and a bit different but there again, she hadn't eaten out in a while and ought to be grateful for anything.

'Will I need a sweater?' she asked.

'I doubt it, but take one just in case.'

She was wearing a strappy, olive green jumpsuit and platform espadrilles. It was a while since she'd walked in heels and she felt a bit unsteady as she followed him to his car.

He had a smart black SUV and she sank gratefully into the comfy, tan leather front seat. It was very clean inside, and smelled of a delicious, lemony aftershave she couldn't identify.

Butterflies fluttered when he clambered in beside her, closed his door and started the engine.

'What kind of music do you like?'

'Anything – you choose. Maybe Johnny Cash?'

'You're a country and blues girl, huh?' He turned to her and grinned. 'OK, I got it.'

Terrell was a confident but impatient driver, weaving in and out of traffic and wedging into faster lanes. He bibbed his horn a lot and the other cars hooted back. As they weren't in a hurry, Sophie wasn't sure why he bothered.

'You OK?' he asked. 'You're very quiet.'

'All good,' she replied, not wanting to dampen the atmosphere. 'I'm enjoying the music.'

They parked at the top of Emmons Avenue and started walking. Sophie couldn't remember ever having visited Sheepshead Bay before and was intrigued.

In fact it was predominantly a restaurant and party-boat area overlooking the water. According to Terrell, the bay had once been a ritzy getaway for New Yorkers, known as Brooklyn's French Riviera. It wasn't as upmarket now, but still had a slightly European holiday feel.

All along the waterway, people were dining at tables outside, under colourful awnings. There were lights everywhere and jaunty displays of flowers around porches, windows and doors.

'Follow me,' Terrell said, taking Sophie's arm. Together they walked to the other side of the road, pausing to look out across the bay.

It was quite a sight. The water was ablaze with colour, with a myriad twinkling, fluorescent lights from the nearby Manhattan and Brighton Beaches.

'Coney Island's only a few blocks away,' Terrell explained. 'You know what that is?'

Sophie nodded. 'It's like a big funfair. I remember going as a child.'

'Mm. And Nathan's hotdogs. You tried those, too?'

'I think so. They're famous, right?'

'Uh-huh. You can't beat 'em.'

When they reached the docks area, Terrell suggested a detour and Sophie followed him down a long wooden pier, one of ten dotted along this stretch of the water.

From here they had a good view of the boats, which came in all shapes and sizes. There were fishing tugs for hire, smart dinner boats, beautiful sailboats and large cruisers.

'Why is it called Sheepshead Bay?'

Terrell explained it was named after a fish, native to the Atlantic Coast, all the way from Nova Scotia to the Gulf of Mexico. The silvery, black-banded sheepshead fish allegedly had teeth like a sheep.

'The original inhabitants were Canarsie Indians. They lived here until the eighteenth century, then the European settlers arrived and kicked them out.'

'Same old story,' Sophie said, with a sigh.

''Fraid so.'

As they strolled back along the pier, passing a crowd of noisy young partygoers heading towards one of the vessels, she shivered slightly and crossed her arms.

'You cold? Here, wait a minute.'

Terrell bent down and gently undid the pale grey sweater from around her waist. Then he draped it around her shoulders, rearranging the folds so it looked right. Finally, he looped together the arms, which were hanging down in front like a scarf.

It felt strangely intimate and when he'd finished, he stood back to admire his work, casting his gaze over her face, neck and shoulders.

'Perfect,' he said with a slightly cheeky smile. 'Better?'

'Much, thank you.' Sophie smiled back.

After crossing the road again, they fell into step and she felt happy and comfortable by his side. She knew they both looked good, though he was the one who attracted the most attention. He had the air of a proud matador, perhaps, or a lion.

'Here we are,' he said at last, coming to a halt outside the brightly lit entrance of a restaurant. There was a large, red and white striped canopy overhead and above the door was a sign saying 'BEEFY'S ON THE BAY'.

Sophie was hungry but to her dismay, the place seemed very busy. The tables on the pavement were all full and inside, she could see a queue of folk waiting.

Sensing her concern, Terrell touched her lightly on the arm.

'Don't worry, I've got it. Stay here.'

Before she knew it, he was weaving his way through the throng to get to the back of the restaurant. His hand seemed to have left a warm, tingly imprint on her skin. Her fingers fluttered up instinctively to feel for the exact place.

Terrell seemed to be gone a long time and she began to wonder what he could possibly be doing. When he finally reappeared, he had a waitress with him: a young, attractive woman in a red and white striped uniform.

'This is my friend Dahlia. Dahlia, meet Sophie,' he

said, with a grin. The waitress nodded and gave a cool, businesslike smile.

'Dahlia's fixed us up with a table, right here.'

He pointed to an area under the awning where a group of four were rising from their seats.

'C'mon, quick. Mind the chairs.'

It was only once they were both seated that Sophie remembered to glance over her shoulder. She was curious about the folk queuing in front of them.

There seemed to be a bit of a commotion going on inside. One of the waiters was surrounded by a group of angry-looking customers. She could see them shouting and pointing in her direction. She looked away quickly.

'Oh dear! Did we jump the queue?' she whispered, leaning across the table.

Terrell had settled back comfortably in his chair. He waved a hand in the air. 'Nah, we're fine. It's all cool.'

'I hope Dahlia won't get in trouble,' she went on. 'For giving us the table, I mean.'

'Relax!' He caught the eye of another waiter, who handed him the wine list. 'Dahlia's not stupid. She told her boss I'd made a reservation with her directly; she'd just forgotten to write it down.'

Sophie was surprised, but decided not to let it spoil her evening. Besides, she was far too hungry to get up and leave. Fortunately, she was facing out towards the bay, and couldn't see the customers they'd upset.

However, she did notice a middle-aged couple march past with faces like thunder. She looked down quickly and pretended to admire her shiny blue fingernails.

Terrell was examining the drinks list when Dahlia appeared with the food menu.

'I'll have a beer,' he said, glancing up.

He must have forgotten Sophie hadn't seen the drinks list yet, because it was only now that he asked what she wanted.

'I, um, a glass of white wine?'

Dahlia gave her a sniffy look.

'We have lots of different white wines. Do you want Chardonnay, Sauvignon, Pinot grigio…?'

'Pinot grigio would be perfect. Thanks,' Sophie said quickly.

Terrell must come here often because he knew exactly what he wanted to eat. However, Sophie took a while to choose. Burgers weren't the only items on the menu, but she didn't fancy pizza or a salad. In the end, she plumped for a plain steak burger and fries, while Terrell went for a double-decker cheeseburger with bacon. They agreed not to have a starter but to go for dessert instead.

Once they'd ordered, Sophie took a sip of wine and sat back.

'How do you know Dahlia?' she asked, and Terrell shrugged.

'Just from being round here, I guess, hanging out with some of the same people, you know? She's a Rockaway kid, same as me.'

'She's very pretty.' Sophie took another sip of her wine, which was cool and delicious.

'Yeah, bit skinny.' Terrell pulled a face and laughed. 'I prefer a bit of chunk.'

While they waited for the food to arrive, he asked Sophie about her family. He was interested to find out what Pampy was like and how long she'd lived in Piping Plover House. When Sophie said it had once been her weekend and holiday home, he wanted to know where the Brooklyn apartment was and when it had been sold. He also asked where Neil and Celia lived and about their jobs.

'So how come you two don't get along?' he said.

'We're very different characters. I think we just rub each other up the wrong way.'

Terrell raised his eyebrows. 'I can't imagine you falling out with anyone. There must be more to it than that?'

Sophie paused. His voice was deep and coaxing. In one way, she wanted to share the story about her real father with him, but also told herself she didn't know him well enough yet.

'Go on,' he said, gently. 'I can see there's something you want to tell me.' He reached out and placed his hand on her hers. 'You know what they say? A problem shared is a problem halved. I'm a good listener.'

She took a deep breath. 'OK. Thank you.'

When she'd finished speaking, he stretched his arms above his head and whistled.

'Jeez! That's some tale.'

Leaning forwards again, this time he took both her hands in his and gently stroked the tops with his thumbs.

'You've been through a lot, Sophie. Remember, you're not alone. I'm here for you.'

Dahlia brought their food just as Terrell was gazing into Sophie's eyes.

'Excuse me,' she said sharply.

Sophie sat back just in time, before the hot plate landed with a smack on the placemat in front of her. It was lucky the fries didn't go flying.

Terrell got the same treatment, but didn't seem to mind.

'Can you get me the ketchup and mustard?' he said.

'She seems rather cross,' Sophie commented, picking up a chip.

Terrell reached for the salt and sprinkled it liberally all over his fries.

'Nah, she's all right. She hates waitressing, that's all. She gets antsy with the customers. I told her to smile more, or she'll get fired. She knows she doesn't need to smile for me!'

Terrell's burger was twice the size of Sophie's, but he still managed to pick it up in both hands and bite into it without making a mess. She was so hungry she devoured hers rather too quickly, which meant nibbling on her fries while she waited for him to catch up.

Afterwards, she ordered two scoops of salted caramel ice cream and he had Key lime pie. They had more drinks, too. She was about to ask him about his family when a strange woman leaned over the low wooden barrier separating the restaurant from the street and tapped Terrell on the shoulder.

'Hey, you!'

She was tall and striking, rather than pretty, with big features and lots of long blonde hair. Sophie reckoned she was in her mid to late fifties.

'Hannah!' Terrell's face had broken into one of his wide grins. 'How're you doing? It's been an age!'

He didn't introduce Sophie, who felt like a wallflower.

Hannah, it seemed, had been away for a while, visiting friends in Canada.

'I bought this in Montreal. Like it?'

She pointed to her wraparound top and did a flirty twirl. It had an unusual, blue-green geometric pattern and was tied in a big knot just above her navel. There was quite a lot of flesh on display.

'I do,' Terrell replied. 'You look great.'

Sophie stared into her bowl and said nothing.

'I'll call you,' Hannah said, glancing at his untouched pie. 'Sorry I've interrupted your meal.'

It was a bit late now, Sophie thought. She'd finished her ice cream and virtually scraped the bowl clean.

'Cool,' Terrell replied. 'You do that. Great to see you again.'

Oblivious to Sophie's annoyance, he started tucking into his pie.

'Mm, this is good.' He glanced up. 'Want to try some?'

Sophie shook her head.

'You know a lot of people,' she said, trying not to sound tart.

'I do, I'm Mister Sociable.' He placed both hands, outspread, on his chest and took a deep breath. 'I've also got eyes bigger than my belly. I might take the rest of this pie home in a doggy bag.'

They had one more drink before Terrell asked for the bill. At first, he insisted on paying, but in the end Sophie managed to persuade him to go fifty-fifty. When Dahlia saw her twenty per cent tip, she couldn't quite bring herself to smile, but did manage a muted 'thanks'.

'See you soon,' she said to Terrell, with a knowing smirk.

He frowned and shot her a fierce look. 'Yeah. You know how much I like these burgers. I'll be back.'

It was quite a relief to leave the restaurant and head out once more into the warm night air. The street wasn't as busy now and there were fewer lights shining on the water.

'Wanna go some place else?' he asked as they strolled back towards the car. 'We could grab a coffee somewhere?'

Sophie thought about it for a moment. He was good company and very attractive, but something about him didn't seem quite right. His driving, the restaurant lie, the fact he was familiar with so many women. There again, there was nothing wrong with having friends of the opposite sex. She was probably just being prudish.

Invitations from handsome men were few and far between. You have to live a little, Soph, she told herself.

'Why don't you come back to mine? I'll make coffee,' she said.

There was a momentary pause.

'Great, yeah, thanks. That'll be great.'

Fifteen

It was still warm enough to sit outside. At first, Sophie sipped her coffee on the swing bench, while Terrell perched on the low wall opposite.

Before long, however, he joined her on the swing. It felt quite natural when he put an arm around her shoulders and stroked her skin lightly with his fingertips.

'I just love these long summer nights,' he said softly. 'It's so quiet here. Listen.'

She pricked her ears and they both listened. A sprinkler was whirring in one of the gardens, but there were no cars and no voices. They couldn't even hear a dog bark, only the occasional creak of rope when the swing started to slow down.

'I wish I could stay here forever,' she said with a sigh. 'I love Rockaway.'

Terrell took her mug and placed it with his own on the ground. When he sat up, she hoped that he'd put his arm around her again because it had felt so comforting.

Instead, he lunged forwards and before she knew it, his wet mouth was on hers and his tongue was disappearing down her throat.

Startled, she tried to pull back, but his right hand was clamped around the back of her head, pushing her in closer. Shutting her eyes, she willed herself to get into the kiss. It was what she'd wanted, wasn't it? She just hadn't expected it to happen now, not on their first date. Maybe just a teeny smooch when they said goodbye.

His other hand reached up to her jumpsuit strap and tugged it down. Then it was inside her bra, squeezing her breast and pinching her nipple hard. So fast! The strength and speed of his movements made her dizzy.

His breathing was heavy and urgent. He shifted his weight forwards even more, so that her back squashed painfully against the end of the seat. Then he took his left hand out of her bra and thrust it down to the top of her knickers.

'No, wait!' Her head was stuck and her arms were clamped, but she managed to free them enough to give him a shove.

He let her head go immediately but his hand was still stuck down the front of her clothes.

'I'm not ready for this.' She was out of breath and tearful.

He pulled out his hand and sat back, wide-eyed with surprise. 'But I thought—'

She shook her head, pulling up her bra and jumpsuit strap at the same time.

'I'm having a really hard time. Sorry. I didn't realise how upset I was about my real dad.'

The penny seemed to drop and his mood shifted instantly.

'Don't you be sorry,' he said, reaching out to stroke her hair. She flinched at first, but his touch was soft and reassuring again. 'I should've known. It was stupid of me.'

Then he took her hand, interlacing her fingers in his.

'You're a beautiful woman, a beautiful person, you know? I can wait. What's the rush? We can get to know each other properly, like in the old movies. We'll go courting. It's romantic! I'm fine with that.'

He laughed, and she did, too.

'Thanks for being understanding.'

But her heart was still pumping faster than usual and she was relieved when he let her hand go.

'Madam, I must leave you to your slumber,' he said. He rose, and she followed him to the stairs.

'I enjoyed the meal,' she said in a small voice.

'Me too. I'll give you a call.'

Afraid he might be about to lunge again, she took a step back. She needn't have worried, though, because he bounded down the steps, turning only once to wave a cheery goodbye. He seemed so normal, it was as if nothing had happened and he hadn't a care in the world.

As soon as he'd driven away, Sophie went inside and locked the door. She checked the downstairs windows and the back door, too, just to be sure.

It took her a long time to get to sleep. Confused about what had taken place, she went back over her actions that evening, trying to work out where she'd gone wrong. The only mistake she'd made, she concluded, was to invite him in for coffee.

For some reason, Hannah sprang to mind, the woman

who'd chatted to him for ages while they were eating. She'd seemed pretty keen on him. It was a good job she was home from Canada now to keep him company.

While Sophie was trying to nod off, Celia had just risen from her bed. It was 5 a.m. in London and still fairly dark outside, but she couldn't bear to lie awake for a moment longer.

She padded over to where her white waffle dressing gown lay on the back of a chair and put it on. The thick beige carpet felt soft and luxurious beneath her bare feet. She bent down to pick up her grey felt slippers.

Neil was still fast asleep, snoring lightly as he always did when he'd rolled onto his back. He'd pushed off the duvet so that only his lower half was covered with a white, Egyptian cotton sheet. His naked chest, with its smattering of soft grey hair, looked pale and vulnerable. There was a dent in the breastbone like a small well, and you could see the outline of his ribs as they rose and fell with his breathing.

Today was Sunday, when they'd usually both have a lie-in. Not wanting to disturb him, she tiptoed out of the room, still carrying her slippers, and closed the door gently behind her.

Both boys were out last night and had slept over with friends, so she had the house to herself. She always enjoyed walking down the wide staircase, with its gleaming wooden banisters smelling of polish. She often paused to admire the multicoloured stained glass on the front door. It was original but had been in a mess when they'd moved in. She'd had it restored by an expert and it was beautiful again. Everyone commented on it.

She wasn't in the mood to gaze at it now, though, and scarcely even noticed the vase of wilting lilies on the little mahogany table in the hall either. The carpet stopped at the bottom of the staircase and became wooden floorboards. After sliding her feet into the felt slippers, she made for the kitchen. There, she filled the silver kettle and sat on a bar stool by the island with her eyes closed, while she waited for the water to boil, her elbows resting on cool white marble.

She'd never felt like this before. No one knew what had happened with Sophie, and guilt, worry and shame were making Celia ill. For a change, she didn't have to control her eating because she didn't want any food anyway.

The pounds were dropping off effortlessly and all her clothes were loose. Once, she'd have been delighted, but now she couldn't care less. Intrusive thoughts filled her mind and she'd started to think she was a really bad person.

She could sense the safe, protective edifice, that she'd been at pains to build around her, crumbling. She didn't know which way to turn and thought she might be going mad.

When the kettle boiled, she rose to fetch a mug from the cupboard, the blue and white spotted one, which was the biggest they had. Opening the cupboard next door, she found a box of her favourite tea – Twinings English Breakfast – and popped a tea bag in the mug before filling it with water, stirring a little to release the flavour before adding some milk.

This time, she took her mug over to the pale leather

armchair at the other end of the kitchen and sat down. Through two giant glass doors, which opened onto the terrace and then the garden, she watched a robin pecking for worms in the dewy grass. The leaves on the pink and red geraniums in terracotta pots were turning brown; they needed watering. When you had a big house, there was always so much to *do*.

Her tea was still very hot, so she blew on it before taking a tentative sip. In a way, both she and Sophie were in crisis, she thought, putting the mug down on the floor beside her.

She scratched her elbows, which had become red and itchy with stress. Blood sprang from the scaly, cracked skin and she rolled up her sleeves to stop it getting on her clothes.

Now she'd told another person about the secret her father made her keep, now she'd heard herself say the words and watched Sophie crumple, his actions seemed more heinous than she'd ever realised.

All her life, she'd pretended to herself and others that she'd felt lucky to be Daddy's favourite, though he expected a lot in return. Now, she almost wished she'd had a different father, too, because her own was unforgiveable. She'd believed she loved him. Instead, she hated him now. The hurt and damage he'd caused was inestimable.

'What's up? Can't you sleep?'

Celia turned to see Neil walking in. He'd put on slippers and some blue stripy pyjama bottoms, but his chest was still bare.

'I had a bad night,' she replied. 'I couldn't get to sleep for ages, then I woke again at four. I didn't want to disturb you, so I came downstairs.'

Neil scratched his hair, which was mostly grey and sticking up on top. He spotted Celia's mug on the floor. She could tell that he was itching to tidy it away, so she picked it up quickly and took a sip.

As she did so, the sleeve of her gown slipped back and she pushed it up, away from the drying blood.

'What's that?' Neil said, noticing. 'What's wrong with your arm?'

'I think it's eczema, or something. It's on my other elbow, too.'

She started scratching again and he told her to stop or she'd make it worse.

'You've never had eczema before, have you?' he asked, examining the wound. 'It looks nasty. You'd better see that dermatologist friend of yours, Dr Stacey.'

He made himself a mug of tea before pulling up another chair and sitting beside her. She must have looked rough, because he took her hand and patted it.

'Why couldn't you sleep? That's not like you. Something bothering you?'

She shook her head. All he knew was that she and Sophie had argued, so she'd come home early. He wasn't surprised. He said he knew what Sophie was like.

'I could murder that sister of yours,' he said suddenly. 'She's nothing but trouble. I wish you'd never gone to Rockaway. You haven't been yourself since coming home.'

Celia was taken aback; she thought she'd hidden her feelings rather well. His concern was touching, but for once, she didn't think she deserved it. Sophie didn't deserve to take all the blame, either.

Remembering how surprised Sophie had been when she heard that Neil didn't know about their mother and the Irish boy, it dawned on her quite suddenly she mustn't keep the secret from her husband any longer.

'Sophie's been very wronged,' she said in a sombre voice.

Neil listened quietly, occasionally nodding or shaking his head, until Celia said for the third or fourth time that she was riddled with guilt.

'Enough,' he said firmly. 'I agree it's unfortunate you told Sophie in that way, but you're not to blame for keeping the secret from her. The fault lies firmly at your father's door.'

He rose, and started pacing around the kitchen. He seemed agitated all of sudden.

'What are you thinking?' Celia asked when she couldn't stand the silence any longer.

Neil halted, cradled his head in his arms and let out a heartrending, otherworldly groan, which frightened Celia. He sounded like a dying animal, or a father lamenting at his child's grave.

'What I can't understand, Celia, is why you didn't tell *me*. I could have helped you. We'd have decided together what to do. I thought you trusted me. I thought we told each other everything.'

There was a break in his voice and his eyes were damp. Celia had never seen him cry before.

'Oh, Neil,' she said, running to him. She flung her arms round his waist and buried her face in his chest. 'I'm so sorry. I should have told you ages ago. It was like a heavy object, which I'd buried so deep. I was frightened of bringing it out of the ground; I was scared of the consequences.'

To her relief, his arms snaked round her back and he held her tightly, brushing the top of her head with his lips.

'My darling,' he whispered several times. 'Thank God it's in the open at last. Secrets are terrible; they can kill you.'

It was a long time since Celia had felt this close to her husband and his chest was damp with her tears. She wanted it to be like this always. Taking him by the hand, she led him away from the kitchen into the sitting room, where they sat arm in arm on the pale blue sofa.

An early morning jogger went past the window; Celia could see him through the black railings bordering their front garden.

After taking a deep breath, she said there was something more Neil needed to know.

'I'm not as nice as you think,' she began, before explaining how jealous she'd always been of Sophie, because she seemed to have more fun.

'I know you think she's stupid and feckless, but at least she's *lived* a little. It feels as if all I've ever done is work. I never went to parties or got totally legless or took drugs. I didn't go backpacking on my own or kip on the beach. And I never slept around. In fact I've only had three boyfriends in my life, and one of them is you. I even flirted with this guy, Joe, just to prove he liked me more than her,' she went on. 'How horrible is that!'

Fearing Neil's response, she shut her eyes tightly, as if it would somehow defend her from his anger. But to her surprise, he laughed.

'That's pretty mean,' he agreed. 'Poor Sophie.'

There was a pause before he went on. 'What did this guy look like? Not as handsome as me, I hope?'

Now it was Celia's turn to laugh. 'Well, he was pretty fit, to be honest, but I don't think my strategy worked. He was definitely more into her than me.'

'Good,' said Neil, giving her a squeeze. 'You're not for sharing. Seriously, though, if you want to work less and have more fun, for God's sake, go ahead. We're not getting any younger and let's be honest, I earn enough for us both. Have some adventures if you want. Go travelling. I'll come with you when I can, or you can ask a friend. My only stipulation is – no flirting.'

He gave her a look, which made her smile.

'And finally…' He cleared his throat and she wondered what was coming next. 'We need to decide what to do about Sophie.'

'What do you mean?'

'I'm not sure yet. It's going to require some thought.'

They were both tired and spent the rest of the morning doing very little. At around eleven o'clock, they went for a walk in the park, strolling hand in hand past wild deer and ponds crowded with noisy ducks, coots, swans and Canada geese.

The sun was quite hot and Celia wished she'd brought something to drink. After a while, they came to a kiosk and bought bottles of sparkling water and two lattes, which they drank on a bench underneath an old oak tree.

They sat in companionable silence for a while, until Neil coughed.

'Celia?' he said, sounding nervous.

'Yes?' She was dismayed; she thought they'd done enough serious talking for one day.

'I'm worried about you. You've lost weight. You were too thin before, in my view. Now there's hardly anything of you. I don't think you eat enough. I know it's a sensitive subject but—'

'It's OK,' Celia said quietly, feeling her pulse quicken.

She *was* very sensitive about it. She knew he rarely raised the matter because in the past she'd bitten off his head. She'd told him she was a doctor, for heaven's sake, and far more knowledgeable about health and nutrition than most people. What she ate was none of his business and she was perfectly fine, thank you very much.

But the last few days had made her realise she wasn't really fine. She needed help, and Neil was doing his best to give it to her.

'I'll go and see someone,' she said, touching his arm. 'I haven't been able to eat much since I got back from Rockaway. I've been too stressed. But I know I had a problem before, too. In fact it's been with me most of my life. I'll find someone who specialises in eating disorders.'

He squeezed her knee. 'Please do. Clever girl. Well done. Thank God.' He let out a long sigh. 'I've been wanting to mention this for a long time. We'll tackle it together.'

Rory was at home when they got back, but he was clearly hung-over and spent most of the day in his room. Celia roasted a chicken and they ate it in the kitchen at around 3 p.m.

Rory did come down for that, but vanished again almost immediately. Rupert rang to say that he was with his girlfriend and would go straight from her house to work the next morning.

In the evening, once the sun had set, Celia went into the back garden to do some watering. The air was still beautifully warm and she fancied the plants and flowers were bowing their heads at her, thanking her for their much-needed drink.

It hadn't rained for days and the soil was bone dry, so everywhere needed a dousing. Watering seemed to release the scent of the roses and honeysuckle, the lavender and tobacco plants, and she breathed in deeply, enjoying the sweet, heady perfume.

Neil was watching something on TV when she went back in the house. It had taken her all day to pluck up the courage to do what she felt was the right thing and now that she'd run out of chores, she could find no more excuses.

Fetching her mobile from her bag in the hallway, she sat at the kitchen island and scrolled through her list of contacts until she reached the one she wanted.

'Just do it, Celia,' she muttered to herself. 'You're a big girl now.'

The phone rang several times and she rather hoped she'd have a reprieve; she could try again tomorrow.

Then, all of a sudden, there was a voice at the other end. 'Hello?'

'Layla?' Celia said, feeling her heart pitter-patter.

'Yes?'

'It's your aunt here, Aunt Celia. Please can I have a word?'

Sixteen

The following week, Sophie focused on finishing the house clearing. Back and forth she went to various charity shops, having sorted carefully through Pampy's remaining items, trying to ensure they ended up in the right place where someone would be able to use them. The house felt empty and sad now. At least this might make leaving less difficult.

Terrell rang on Monday, Tuesday and Thursday, asking if she fancied doing something after work. She managed to put him off, saying she had too much on, but feared that he hadn't got the message. She hoped she wouldn't have to spell it out for him.

Gigi stopped by a couple of times to say she'd been asking around about Sophie's mother and real father, but had so far drawn a blank.

Eddie, Mariella and Nino also popped in at different times and offered to lend a hand. Mostly, though, they ended up sitting on Sophie's porch, having a drink and a chat with her. She was on top of the house-clearing now, enjoyed their company and welcomed the opportunity for a break.

She hadn't seen Joe for a while, but on Friday morning she met him by chance on the beach, having decided to take an early swim.

As she swam out, further than usual because the water was so calm, she spotted a lone figure in a sunhat on the other side of the breakwater, holding a fishing rod and casting a long line out to sea.

It looked like Joe, but she couldn't be sure. She would have swum back in the opposite direction, but he must have seen her, too, because he waved his hat and beckoned to her.

He watched her as she came out of the water, feeling self-conscious in her worn bikini. She'd been through such a lot recently, buying a new one had gone way down her list of priorities.

'Mary Poppins!' he said as usual, adding with a smile, 'More like a mermaid, today. Here, use this.'

He handed her a black towel, which she took gratefully, rubbing herself down before settling on the sand beside him.

'What brings you here so early?' he asked, fixing his eyes on the water again.

'I fancied a swim before the crowds descend. Have you caught anything?'

He shook his head. 'How's the house? Are you winning?'

Sophie said that she was.

'Well done. It's a big job.'

He'd brought a flask of iced coffee and he gave some to

her in a plastic cup. While she took a sip, he reeled in his line and cast far out again.

'I get the feeling I'm not going to have much luck today. The beach is too crowded this time of year; it scares the fish away.'

There was something very peaceful about sitting quietly, watching him hold the line as he scrutinised the water. Although he was concentrating hard, his handsome face looked completely relaxed and his strong, brown arms made her feel safe.

Gone was the swagger and he didn't seem in the mood for teasing, either. He seemed in his element here, at one with the earth, sea and sky.

'Is this usually the best place to fish?' asked Sophie, who knew nothing about the sport.

'Actually, I think Jamaica Bay's better, but it's easier to get here from my place. I hardly ever fish on the beach right across from where I live. The neighbours always seem to join me. I don't mind their company, they're nice people, but I don't want to get dragged into long conversations with them. I find that really bugging. '

She frowned. 'I must have been to Jamaica Bay as a child but I can't remember. What's it like?'

There was a pause. Joe's expression didn't change but he appeared to be pondering on something.

'I could take you now, if you like?' he said at last.

Sophie was about to say no, but then she thought of returning to the near-empty house with all its memories. The clearing up job was almost finished and she had no leads to follow about her real father. What difference would a few hours make?

'I'd like that, thank you. If you're sure?'

'I'm sure.'

It took no time to pack up his gear and he left her at Piping Plover House while he went to fetch his car. She ran upstairs to change out of her wet bikini and popped it in a bag, in case she wanted to swim later.

Her denim shorts were dirty so she decided to put on a cotton tie-dye sundress she hadn't yet worn. It was blue and white and had a round neck and thin straps. It reached to just above the knee and as she rather liked the lower part of her legs from the knee down , she hoped it was reasonably flattering.

Her hair was still wet so she left it loose and rubbed sun cream on her face, neck and shoulders.

She was waiting for him on the porch when he pulled up in his white Audi. It looked quite new, but there was a fair amount of rubbish inside: a couple of crumpled sweatshirts, some empty cardboard coffee cups, the wet black towel that she'd used earlier, an old sandwich packet and assorted sunglasses cases. She was relieved to discover he was a safe, considerate driver.

It didn't take long to reach Jamaica Bay. At first Sophie was a little disappointed. Surrounded by commercial, industrial and residential developments, it was hard to believe Joe hadn't been teasing her again when he told her this was a wildlife refuge.

Apparently, there were more than thirteen thousand acres of water, salt marsh, meadowland beaches, dunes and woodlands, and the area was also home to hundreds of migratory birds and fish. To Sophie, though, it looked more like a wasteland.

As they walked along a gravel trail towards the bay, however, she began to see what he meant. The path was lined with holly, grasses of different heights, wildflowers and even prickly pear cacti.

At the mouth of the estuary, they stopped to gaze across the water at the shimmery Manhattan skyline, rising majestically in the distance. Sophie had never experienced quite so powerfully that sense of nature not just surviving but thriving in the middle of an urban industrial landscape. She was blown away.

'It's stunning,' she said, looking left and right, taking it all in.

Joe put down his bag. 'Glad you like it. This is as good a spot as any. Let's see what's out there.'

She watched, fascinated, while he assembled his rod, his nimble fingers tightening the reel and threading the line through the guides.

While he worked, he explained that July and August weren't the best times for fish, as oxygen levels in the water dropped and baitfish and predators tended to flood out of the bay.

He was hopeful, though, of catching something on the outgoing tide, maybe some bunker, spearfish or even bonito. If they had no luck, they could go further inside the bay, where they might catch cocktail blues and snapper blues feeding. Sophie had never heard of any of the fish, but liked the names.

When the rod was ready, Joe asked her to open up one of his Tupperware boxes. She peeked inside and let out a scream when confronted by dozens of fat, wriggling sandworms. She almost dropped the container.

'Get one out for me, will you?' Joe said, deadpan.

She wasn't sure if he were joking or not.

'Absolutely no way,' she replied, and he laughed. 'They're disgusting.'

'Let's hope the fish like them.'

He'd brought a tripod with him this time, which he set up by the water's edge. They stood and watched the line in silence for a while, until he wanted to know if she were hungry.

'I stopped by Monique's, down the peninsula, to pick up some cauli bowls. They've got charred cauliflower, grilled lemon pepper chicken, arugula, and feta with a lemon vinaigrette – no sandworm,' he added, with a grin.

'That's very kind of you,' said Sophie. 'They sound delicious.'

They sat on a sand dune while they ate and at first he hardly took his eyes off the line. Sophie decided there was no harm in telling him about her real father, and he said he wasn't surprised the news had so shocked and devastated her.

'I can see why you're angry with your sister. I'm angry with her, too. She shouldn't have left you here alone after that.'

His concern was touching and the more they talked, the more she realised how much she liked him. Far from being annoying and a bit sarcastic, as she'd first thought, he was actually quite gentle and sensitive. Live and let live was his philosophy, but he also had a strong sense of right and wrong and was quick to condemn cruelty and injustice.

His late father, it seemed, had been a successful banker, killed by crazy working hours.

'He was forty-eight when he died of a heart attack, and I was sixteen,' Joe explained, taking a bite of chicken. 'I really missed him, so did my mom. They never got to do all the stuff they'd talked about doing when he retired. They wanted to go travelling together, but my mom ended up having to go on her own.

'I decided I was going live a very different life. What's the point in slogging away at some job you don't even like if you never get to enjoy the fruits of your labour? I always wanted to paint and write poetry, but I knew unless I got really famous it wouldn't pay the bills. Luckily Dad left me a bit of money. I'm not rich but I'm all right and I'm doing things my way. I think my dad would be happy with that.'

His thinking appealed to Sophie, who told him her passion had always been to live by the sea and run a small retreat for artists, writers and anyone else wanting somewhere peaceful to work.

'I had a dream of turning Piping Plover House into that type of place. It'd be perfect for it,' she said with a sigh. 'Unfortunately, it's not to be.'

Joe agreed it was a great idea, and just what Rockaway needed. 'If it can't be Piping Plover House, you'll find somewhere else just as good. I have every faith in you.'

'I wish I had,' she said with feeling.

She watched as he opened a can of soda and took several

long swigs. She liked his neck, which was strong and muscular like the rest of him, and the way his Adam's apple moved up and down with each swallow. She had to control the urge to reach out and touch it.

After putting down the can, he did a large, involuntary burp.

'Excuse me,' he said, covering his mouth, too late, with a hand.

'No worries,' she said with a grin, realising she didn't mind and he didn't seem embarrassed, and wondering what that meant.

Talking to him felt so easy and natural that when he asked about her love life, she was happy to recount her many disasters. In fact, they ended up laughing because he, too, had had a chequered romantic career.

He'd been let down badly by a previous girlfriend, who'd made fun of his paintings, poems and lifestyle choices and had eventually left him for one of his friends. After hearing this, Sophie concluded his habit of teasing was perhaps a defence mechanism, though he didn't seem to be doing it quite so much any more.

She'd quite forgotten about the fishing. It was a shock, therefore, when Joe suddenly jumped up and grabbed the rod off the tripod.

'We've got a bite,' he said. 'It's putting up quite a fight; I think it's a big one.'

She watched, mesmerised, as he swept the rod backwards. Then he got in several turns of the reel before doing it again.

'You have to tire the fish out first,' he explained, keeping his eye on the line all the time. Whatever was on the end must have been strong, because it required quite a lot of effort to keep hold of the rod. Joe didn't panic, though.

'You play it and let it run. You don't want it to spit out the hook or break the line. Eventually it'll slow down and stop dragging.'

The fight seemed to go on for a long time as the fish twisted and thrashed, making the water bubble and boil. Every now and again, Sophie would notice the tip of a fin, part of a striped back or what looked like a silvery forked tail, before the creature plunged beneath the surface once more.

When the line finally stopped dragging quite so much, Joe asked for the landing net, which he'd folded and tucked into a special pocket on the back of his jacket.

'You catch him once I've reeled him in,' he commanded, while she worked out how to unfold the net. 'It's shallow so you'll have to go right in the water. Careful you don't fall.'

It was a big, angry fish and trapping it wasn't as easy as she'd imagined. Once she had it securely in the net, Joe helped her to pull it out of the water and place it on the sand. Then he carefully removed the hook and weighed it.

'Twelve pounds,' he announced with a grin. 'Impressive!'

Sophie admired its blue-black oblique stripes and shiny scales, mostly silver, with a hint of green and light blue. One glassy black eye seemed to stare at her accusingly.

'It's beautiful! I feel a bit guilty, though.'

'It'll be fine,' Joe assured her. 'It'll swim off when we put it back in. You'll see.'

He passed her his phone for a picture before lifting the

fish carefully out of the net. After she'd taken the snap, he said he'd do the same for her.

'What does it feel like?' she asked tentatively, realising she'd never held a live fish before.

'You'll soon find out. Here.'

Before she knew it, the slippery fish was in her hands and she did her best to look natural and smile for the camera, all the while praying she wouldn't drop her prize. She was relieved when Joe said soon after that they should put it back in the water.

'Do you want to do it?' he asked, before following her to the shore.

There, she crouched down, placed the fish underwater and gently took her hands away. For a couple of minutes, they both watched in silence while it floated, motionless, and then all of a sudden it came to life and darted off.

'That was amazing!' Sophie said, turning to Joe with a big smile on her face. 'I never realised there was so much to it!'

'I'm glad you enjoyed it. That was pretty neat for your first catch!'

Realising she was thirsty, Sophie went to fetch some water from his bag and had several big swigs before offering the bottle to him.

Remembering she hadn't applied any more sunscreen, she checked her arms and shoulders.

'Am I burning?' she asked anxiously. 'I hope I don't look like a lobster.'

Joe shook his head, before checking her back. She felt him gently lift the loose hair and his fingers ever so lightly touch her neck. This made her shiver, though she wasn't cold, and she hoped he wouldn't notice.

'You're fine,' he said at last, 'but you'd better get some shade now. We've been out quite a few hours.'

There were no trees nearby and she was sorry when he insisted they pack up and go home.

'I don't want to be responsible for burning that beautiful Irish skin of yours.'

Without any warning, her eyes started to well up. She turned her head away but it was too late; he'd already seen.

'What is it? What did I say?' His handsome, tanned face was full of concern, which only made her want to cry more.

'No one except my grandmother has ever called my skin beautiful. I used to hate being so pale. My sister called me albino and I got teased all the time about my freckles. Now I've found out my father was Irish, at least I know where they come from.'

She managed a slight laugh, but it was hollow and the tears wouldn't stop. Joe leaned forwards and tried to wipe them away with his big, warm thumbs, only for more to appear.

'Come here,' he said at last, not knowing what else to do. He opened his arms, she walked right in and he wrapped them around her, resting his chin on the top of her head.

'You cry all you want,' he crooned, rocking gently to and fro. Her body shook with sobs, but he didn't let go, just held her tighter. 'That's it, let it all out. Things will get better, you'll see.'

Strangely, she didn't feel ashamed or even embarrassed about having a meltdown in front of him. When she finally calmed down and took a step back, however, she did try to laugh it off.

'I'm so sorry—' she began, wiping her eyes with the back of an arm, but he raised a hand to stop her.

'What you're going through would make anyone upset,' he insisted. 'It's a huge deal. If I can help in any way, I will.'

'You've helped already just by being here and putting up with my histrionics.' Her nose was running and she didn't have a hanky, so she took the unladylike option and sniffed. This time, she didn't even apologise. 'I'm a mess, honestly. I've never felt so confused in all my life.'

Feeling tired and feeble, she didn't protest when he took her hand as they walked back to the car. His strong grip was reassuring and without it, she might have sat down and wept again.

As he drove home, he told her funny stories about escapades from his youth. She knew he was being kind, trying to distract her, and it seemed to work, partially, at least.

When they rounded the corner into her street, he asked if she'd like to come fishing with him another day, or they could hire kayaks or paddleboards, or just find somewhere quiet to swim and sunbathe.

She said she could think of nothing nicer.

She was sorry when he finally drew up outside Piping Plover House because she didn't want to say goodbye. They both got out and he fetched her bag from the back seat.

'Here you go,' he said, passing it to her slowly.

Something different in his tone made her glance up. Catching his eye, all of a sudden she was overcome by a giddy feeling, which made her stomach flutter and her mouth turn dry. His dark brown eyes glittered and a soft smile played on his lips…

'Hey, Sophie! I've found you at last!'

Startled, she turned to see Terrell advancing towards her. He looked extremely attractive in a white vest top, white trainers and black board shorts. Today, however, his wide smile and confident, rolling gait made her feel slightly sick.

'Hi!' she said coolly, when he was close enough.

'You've been playing hard to get,' Terrell said, still grinning. He looked curiously at Joe and stuck out his hand. 'I'm Terrell. Do I know you?'

Joe hesitated before taking the hand and shaking it. 'I think I've seen you on the beach. You're a lifeguard, right?'

Terrell nodded. 'Uh huh. You too?'

'No,' said Joe, 'but I go fishing a lot.'

'I guess I confused you with someone else,' Terrell replied, with a dismissive shrug. 'You OK, babe?' He didn't wait for a response. 'I had such a great time last weekend.' He winked, as if they shared a special secret. 'We'll go someplace else tomorrow night. There's a little Greek place in Astoria. I know you like Greek. I won't take no for an answer.' He grinned again.

Caught on the hop, Sophie racked her brains to think of a good excuse. While she was doing so, he reached out and gave the fleshy part of her upper arm a squeeze, which made her shrink.

'Wear that dress, it suits you.' He sounded as if he owned her.

Horrified, she stepped back, away from his grip, and

glanced at Joe, hoping to be rescued. He was frowning but wouldn't meet her gaze.

'I need to get going,' he said firmly.

She wanted to explain and beg him not to leave, but the air between them had turned frosty and, besides, Terrell was watching.

'Bye,' Joe said, reaching for the keys in his pocket and clicking open the car door.

'Wait!' Sophie cried, but he was already climbing in the driver's seat and starting the engine. He seemed to be in a big rush.

'Weird guy,' Terrell commented, watching as Joe drove away. 'So, whaddya say about tomorrow night?'

'I can't,' Sophie replied, quick as a flash. 'I'm sorry but I don't want to go out with you again.'

She thought that Terrell might be upset and ask why, or act angry and defensive. Her words, however, seemed barely to register.

'I said I won't take no for an answer,' he repeated. The grin remained but his eyes looked mean. 'I'll come by at six thirty.'

Seventeen

If only Celia were still here. The thought sprang to Sophie's mind and took her completely by surprise.

Angry as she was with her sister, she knew that if there was one person who could frighten Terrell off, it was Celia. But Sophie was alone now and would have to handle this herself.

She made straight for the kitchen and poured herself a big glass of water, which she drank in one go. After that, she sat on Pampy's rocking chair in the sitting room, with her legs pulled up, eyes closed and head resting on her knees.

Terrell's behaviour was bad enough, but Sophie was even more upset about Joe. He'd clearly jumped to the conclusion that she and Terrell were involved with each other, and must be wondering why she hadn't told him.

She hated to think he might believe she'd intended to deceive him, or that she was the kind of woman who toyed with men and perhaps had several boyfriends on the go at once.

Joe struck her as sincere and kind. She was certain he'd look for the same qualities in the people he hung out with, especially potential girlfriends. They'd so nearly kissed; she could almost feel his lips on hers and smell his warm, sweet breath. Just thinking about it made her giddy again. But now he'd been put off by Terrell and she might never see or speak to him again.

Of course it crossed her mind to ring Joe and try to explain, but she didn't think he'd believe her. Terrell had given the impression they'd slept together last weekend. It would be her word against his.

When Joe held her in his arms at Jamaica Bay and wiped away her tears, he told her that things were going to get better. Well, they'd just got a whole lot worse.

Feeling low and anxious, she would have liked to call on Gigi right away, but her friend wouldn't be home from work until about 5 p.m.

Stretching out her legs, she noticed that her feet were grubby. Her hands felt sticky, too. She'd have a shower and wait for Gigi's return.

Standing naked under the lukewarm water, Sophie observed two thin white marks on her shoulders where the straps of her dress had been. She must have picked up a little bit of colour after all. Her legs were less pale, too, and even her stomach had lost its luminosity. Once, she would have been thrilled to have a slight tan but now, nothing could have mattered less.

After drying off, she put on a pair of khaki cotton shorts and a white T-shirt. Then she combed her hair before lying down on her bed and closing her eyes. Gigi would know what to do about Terrell, she decided. Thank God she still had one friend in Rockaway.

She must have dropped off to sleep because when she looked at her mobile phone again, it was five thirty. Her hair had dried in a funny way, so she quickly tied it back in a ponytail and hurried downstairs to find her flip-flops.

It was a relief to see Gigi's car in the drive; she hadn't gone anywhere after work, then. As soon as Gigi opened her front door and saw Sophie's worried expression, she invited her in and made cold drinks for them both, which they took into her back garden.

It was a biggish, square garden, wider than Pampy's and longer. All around the edges, the borders were filled with blue, white and pink hydrangeas, while leafy shrubs had been planted up close to the fence and had grown so tall they provided complete privacy.

The grass had been mown into perfect stripes and was beautifully green, thanks to what Gigi described as her husband's ferocious, automatic sprinkler system.

'It comes on religiously at five in the morning and seven at night. You wouldn't believe the number of times I've forgotten about it and been caught out. I get absolutely drenched. Everyone else seems to think it's very funny.'

An oval wooden table and chairs stood on the paved area nearest to the house, where Gigi also kept her pots. These, too, were brimming with colour and herbs, including rosemary, basil and thyme. Sophie could smell the rosemary from where she stood.

'Sit down,' said Gigi, pulling out a chair for Sophie and settling on one herself. 'I've got some news for you.'

It seemed that an elderly gentleman had come into the café earlier in the day with his daughter and granddaughter.

'He's named Sean O'Keefe, but I always call him Mr O'Keefe. I hadn't seen him in a while. He must be well into his eighties and his walking isn't good. I don't think he gets out much.

'Anyway,' Gigi went on, 'I'd forgotten about him, to be honest, but I know he's lived in Rockaway all his life. I asked him about your mom and grandmother, and he said he remembered your mom quite well.'

Sophie's ears pricked up.

'He used to own a candy store and she'd go in quite often to buy candy. When she was older, he'd see her out and about on her bike. She didn't seem to have many friends, but one particular summer, she hung out a lot with an Irish girl and her brother. Mr O'Keefe said he thought your mom was sweet on the boy.'

'How did he know that?'

Gigi nodded. 'I did ask him about it. He said it was just a feeling he had. The two of them would park their bikes and go into one of the stores to get ice cream. He said they looked very happy and sort of absorbed in each other, as if they were more than just friends.

'But now here's the interesting bit,' said Gigi, leaning forwards. 'He said he knew they visited Mrs Lebedev, Yana Lebedev.'

Sophie's eyebrows shot up. 'Yana? The old lady round the corner?'

Gigi nodded. 'The very same.'

'She didn't tell me they called on her, she just said she'd seen them.'

Gigi shrugged. 'Maybe she forgot? Anyway, Mr O'Keefe told me he saw your mom and the Irish boy a few times leaving their bikes in the front yard and going in. He seemed very confident of his facts. He even remembered that the boy had red hair. Said he was a nice person, from what he could tell. He didn't much like your grandfather, I'm afraid.'

Sophie pulled a face. 'No one did.'

'And he said your grandmother wasn't very sociable. She was when she was young, but she became a bit of a recluse in later years. She hardly spoke to anyone and even stopped going to church. Mr O'Keefe said the family used to be devout Roman Catholics, but rumour had it she'd lost her faith.'

Sophie picked up her drink of orange cordial and took a sip. She was thinking hard.

'Why would they go to Yana's?' She was speaking as much to herself as to Gigi.

'I can't imagine. Yana did have a son – Nicholas, he was called. He would have been older than those two, but maybe they went to visit him? He died in a car crash some thirty years ago. He was only in his forties, apparently.'

'How sad!' Sophie remembered the old lady's expression when she spoke of him. 'Yana must have been devastated. I remember now, she did say my mother used to play with him when she was little.'

'MOM!'

A loud voice startled them both. They looked up to see Mariella's head sticking out of a bedroom window. Her hair was wrapped in a pink towel and she was clutching a white towel around her chest.

'Can I borrow your Chanel purse?' she asked Gigi, waving a dainty black quilted evening bag in the air. The white towel slipped and she bobbed down to pick it up.

When Mariella reappeared, Gigi had risen from her chair.

'Put it back this instant!' she said angrily. 'You shouldn't have got it out in the first place.'

Mariella tipped her head to one side and fluttered her eyelashes. 'Pleeease, Mom. It will really go with my outfit. I'll look after it, I promise.'

But Gigi was having none of it.

'I know what you're like. You lose everything. That purse was a present from your father. He'll be furious if it goes missing.'

All semblance of cuteness vanished and Mariella's eyes narrowed into black slits.

'Have it your way,' she said nastily, before doing a very obvious V-sign.

Gigi's face turned bright red. 'You little—' she began, but her daughter hopped away from the window and vanished from sight.

'That girl will be the death of me,' Gigi muttered, shaking her head. 'She took my gold necklace once and lost it, and she lost a watch of my mother's. She's borrowing that purse over my dead body.'

Sophie didn't say anything, but had a sneaking suspicion

Mariella would get her way somehow. Gigi was a soft touch, really. The fierceness was all show.

Once Gigi had calmed down, they returned to the subject of Yana. Gigi said Sophie would have to go and see the old lady again, but this time, she would come too.

'She knows me quite well. Maybe I can put her at ease. I'll be backup for you, too. If you forget to ask something, I will.'

They agreed to go the following morning, Gigi would only work for a few hours. 'There's enough staff to cover for me. And someone else can lock up for once. I do it most days.'

It was only then Sophie remembered about Terrell. It had been a relief not to think about him for a while, but now the sick feeling returned with a vengeance. She recounted her tale to Gigi, who was appalled.

'He sounds horrible. I don't know him, but I wouldn't have anything more to do with him. Text him now and tell him you're definitely not going tomorrow and you don't want to hear from him again. You don't have to be rude, just firm, and don't respond to any more texts or calls. You'd better be out of the house at six thirty, just in case he turns up anyway. We'll go to a movie or something.'

The plan sounded good and Gigi made Sophie message Terrell straight away. She also insisted on Sophie blocking his number.

Gigi didn't have an immediate solution to the Joe problem, but she promised to think about it.

'He's such a great guy and obviously really likes you. I'm

sure he'll come about. He's proud, though. It might take a little while for him to get over it. I can try talking to him,' she offered, as an afterthought, but Sophie said no.

'He might take it the wrong way and think I've been gossiping about him. I need to try and sort it out myself.'

When Sophie looked at her watch, it was almost 7 p.m. and time for the dreaded sprinkler system to get going.

'Oh my God!' she said, jumping up. 'I'd better be off. I don't fancy getting soaked.'

'Me neither.' Gigi rose, too. 'I'd rather have my shower in the bathroom, thank you very much.'

She followed Sophie to the front door and was just about to open up, when Mariella hurried downstairs in a tight white minidress and sky-high black sandals.

She had blown dry her glossy dark hair into loose waves and she was wearing dark red lipstick and extremely long, fake, spidery black eyelashes.

On seeing her mother with Sophie in the hall, she stopped, eyes wide with surprise.

'Oh,' she said. 'It's you.'

'Are you getting a lift?' Gigi asked crisply, looking her daughter up and down.

Mariella raised her eyebrows. 'Yes, Mom,' she said, with a sigh. 'Any more questions?'

Sophie couldn't help noticing she was standing in a slightly odd way, with one arm behind her back.

'Can I go now please?' she asked tartly.

Gigi was about to lean forward and give her daughter a goodbye kiss, when her eyes fell on an object in Mariella's hand.

'What's that?' she asked shrilly. Sophie's stomach lurched, imagining herself in the girl's shoes.

'Nothing,' said Mariella, trying to sound nonchalant, but it was too late. Gigi darted around her daughter's back and spotted the treasured Chanel purse nestling against her thigh.

Incandescent with rage, she seemed to grow at least a foot in height.

'Give me that!' She made a grab for the purse, but Mariella was too quick. Slipping off her sandals, she bent down, picked them up and bolted through the front door.

There was a car waiting for her on the other side of the street with the passenger door open. Sophie watched as Mariella hopped in and the driver roared away, before Gigi had even reached the pavement.

'I'm going to kill her,' she said through gritted teeth. 'That girl acts like a princess. She thinks she's entitled to anything she wants.'

'It was pretty brazen,' Sophie agreed, sympathising. 'What will you do?'

Gigi threw up her arms in despair.

'The same as usual, I expect. I'll get mad at her and ground her. She'll say sorry and be really, really nice to me, then in a couple of days, there'll be some party she wants to go to. She'll beg like mad and in the end, I'll cave in because I hate seeing her unhappy. Then she'll probably steal my purse again and the whole cycle will restart. I'm a hopeless mother,' she added mournfully.

Sophie held out her arms and gave her friend a hug.

'You're a wonderful mother, silly. You've got three great

kids. They're all really good people and they certainly know right from wrong. Like all teenagers, they just push the boundaries. It's normal.'

'But I have no control.' There was a catch in Gigi's voice. 'I say one thing and they do another. The problem is, I've never set proper rules. What I need is a disciplinary system, like schools, or the police. I should have written one down years ago and stuck it on the wall.'

Sophie thought about this for a moment.

'You do have a system.'

'I do?' Gigi raised her eyebrows hopefully.

Sophie nodded. 'Absolutely. You're consistently inconsistent. If you say no one day, there's always a chance you'll say yes the next. There's a certain logic to it, don't you see? If I were your child, I'd find it lovely and comforting,' she added with a wry smile.

She called on Gigi at eleven o'clock the following day and they walked together to Yana's house. Although Sophie didn't really expect to learn anything new, she had butterflies in her stomach and was grateful for her friend's company.

Sophie was determined to dig more deeply this time. For now, at least, Yana was her only hope.

It was another hot, airless day and the old woman was sitting hunched in her high-backed wooden chair on the porch, as before. She looked incredibly old.

'Come on up!' she called in a quavering voice when they reached the bottom of the steps. Then, over her shoulder, she cried, 'Donna, bring some juice. We have visitors!'

She was smartly dressed again, in a cream blouse and pale pink, pleated skirt. This time, her long white hair was plaited into two braids, then coiled and pinned on either side. To Sophie, they looked like fluffy ear defenders.

She introduced herself again, and Yana seemed quite offended.

'Of course I remember you,' she said impatiently. 'You're Orla's granddaughter. I wouldn't forget a thing like that.'

When Gigi put out her hand, Yana batted it away.

'Come here,' she said, opening her arms wide.

Gigi bent down and Yana gave her a hug, patting her affectionately with knobbly, arthritic hands.

'I knew you'd be back,' she said, looking at Sophie over Gigi's shoulder. Sophie wondered what she meant, and her stomach fluttered again.

'I brought you some cakes,' said Gigi, straightening up and opening the lid of a white cardboard box. Yana peeked in.

'Oh my! Éclairs! My favourite. Are you trying to fatten me up?'

Soon Donna appeared, carrying a tray with a jug of orange juice and three glasses.

For a while, they made small talk. Yana complained about the weather and asked after Gigi's husband and children.

'They drive me to distraction,' Gigi said with a smile. 'But, you know, I wouldn't be without them.'

'Of course you wouldn't,' Yana said seriously. 'You're fortunate to have them in your life. Treasure them. I know you do.'

After about fifteen minutes, Gigi glanced at Sophie

and nodded. It was her cue to start asking questions. She'd already decided the best way to begin would be to tell Yana exactly what Celia had revealed about her parentage.

'I do believe it's true,' she said at the end, 'and I desperately want to find out about my real father. Please, can you tell me anything more at all?'

Yana had listened attentively and in silence while Sophie was talking and her expression had barely changed. Now, though, she let out a big sigh and cleared her throat.

'When you came the first time,' she said, looking intently at Sophie, 'I didn't want to do anything to upset you. I knew about your mother, or at least I had my suspicions. She used to visit me quite a lot, you see. I think she saw me as a sort of mother figure.'

The blood rushed to Sophie's head and her heart started to race.

'After the Irish boy left,' Yana continued, 'your mother hinted at a few things. I began to notice some physical changes, too. She seemed sad and anxious and I wanted to help, but she wouldn't tell me what was troubling her. Then she disappeared for quite a few months and the next time I saw her, she had a husband and baby – you. I thought about the timings and let's just say, I put two and two together, but I never mentioned it to anyone. I thought I'd take the secret to my grave, but now you know the truth, I can talk freely at last.'

Gigi leaned over and gave Sophie's hand a squeeze. There was a lump in her throat, but Sophie was determined not to cry because it would waste valuable time. She could cry all she wanted later. Now was the moment to find the answers to her most burning questions.

'What was he like – my father?'

Yana smiled. 'I remember him quite well, actually. He was quite tall and he had this mop of wonderful, curly red hair. It was very striking. He had a nice face, sort of friendly and open. He had a wicked laugh, too. I do remember that. He was always goofing around and telling jokes. He made your mother cry with laughter sometimes. I think he was good for her in that way; they were good for each other, actually. They seemed very happy and relaxed together, as if they'd known each other a long time rather than just a couple of months. He seemed to adore her and I think she felt the same way about him. It's a shame they had to part.'

The 'had to' hung in the air between them like a black cloud, but Sophie decided not to go there. Instead, she asked what they did at Yana's house.

'Oh, we'd have a little chat and they'd drink soda and eat cookies on the porch or in my backyard. Mostly they came to see my son, Nicholas, though.'

'Why?' Sophie asked. 'I mean, what for?'

Yana frowned. 'I can't recall…'

It seemed she had nothing to add, but then all of a sudden, her eyes lit up.

'Billy! That was his name!'

Goosebumps ran up and down Sophie's arms.

'Whose name? My father's?'

Yana nodded.

Billy. Sophie silently mouthed the word, turning it over

in her mind and testing how it felt. It was cute and kind of funny, she decided. A bit childish, perhaps, but it conjured up the image of someone friendly and fun. In other words, someone who was as unlike the man she'd once thought was her father as you could possibly imagine. Billy. She liked it; it was cool.

'Nicholas, Nicky, I used to call him, he did a lot of sketching. He could draw anything he wanted. He'd just do a few strokes and bam! There was a cat, or a mouse or whatever. It was a talent he had.

'Well now, Billy loved sketching too. He said he wanted to be a cartoonist. Your mother, Teresa, must have told Billy about my son and she introduced them to each other. Nicky would have been about ten years older. He was probably twenty-six or twenty-seven then. He was still living at home. He had a job with an engineering firm, but he liked drawing in his spare time. He and Billy used to sketch together. I think Billy learned a few new techniques. My son probably picked things up from him, too.'

This was fascinating news to Sophie, who felt a sense of awe and wonder. Little by little, she was starting to paint a portrait of her father. It was like piecing together a jigsaw puzzle, but there were still plenty of bits missing.

'I wish you knew his surname,' she said with a sigh. 'I'd so love to find out what happened to him.'

Gigi leaned forwards. She'd been quiet the whole time, leaving Sophie and Yana to do all the talking.

'Do you know anything at all about Billy's family? His father's and mother's names, the street where they lived? The school he went to? Who his friends or relatives were in

Rockaway? I'm thinking if we had just a bit more to go on, we might be able to track him down.'

'I'm sorry,' said Yana, shaking her head. 'I never did know who he was staying with and it was so long ago now. As far as I'm aware, he never came back here. He did once do a sketch of me. I've still got it somewhere. Would you like to see it?'

Sophie couldn't believe her ears.

'You've got a drawing done by my father? Of course I want to see it,' she cried.

'Oh well, it was only a quick pencil and paper thing, you know.' Yana craned her head and tried to spot Donna through the open front door.

'It's lucky I kept it, really. It tickled me, because I thought he'd captured me so well, warts and all.'

Donna was nowhere to be seen, so Gigi went inside to find her. Sophie found herself asking about her father's features: his nose, eyes and mouth, the colour of his skin and the breadth of his shoulders.

Yana's memory of these was vague and she was beginning to look weary.

'Can I cut you a piece of this éclair?' Sophie asked, pointing in desperation at the last, melted cake on the nearby plate. Perhaps a sugar rush would do the trick.

But Yana declined the offer: 'I couldn't eat another thing.' Her chin drooped further onto her breastbone and her eyelids started to close.

'Ta-da!'

At just the right moment, Gigi and Donna reappeared.

Yana half opened her eyes. 'You know that picture...' she

began in a sleepy voice, struggling to keep her lids up. At any moment, they'd shut again.

'We've got it!' Gigi said triumphantly.

It was only then Sophie noticed that Donna had a scroll of white paper in her hand.

'Here it is! It was in one of the drawers of that desk, under the stairs. I knew I'd seen it somewhere.'

Feeling sick with excitement, Sophie carefully unrolled it, then walked over to the table and spread it out almost reverentially on the surface.

Now she could study it properly, she was entranced. It was, as Yana said, only a quick pencil on paper thing, but she could recognise immediately who it was and it made her smile.

Her father had portrayed Yana as a sort of Lara, the romantic Russian heroine in *Dr Zhivago*. She was racing down a snowy mountain in a horse-drawn sleigh, dressed in a sumptuous fur hat and coat, her long, thick hair streaming out behind her.

She had Yana's round face, squashy nose and narrow mouth but she was beautiful, nevertheless, and Billy had captured her gentleness perfectly, as well as her slanted, inquisitive dark eyes.

'Isn't it great?' Gigi was standing beside Sophie. 'He was very artistic.'

Sophie's gaze drifted to the left, where a bare tree rose up out of the snow. Some thin pencil lines at the base resembled grass or fallen twigs, but when she looked again, they seemed to be letters. She rubbed her eyes. It was a bit like one of those baffling optical illusions.

'What does that look like?' she said, pointing.

'Grass?' Gigi replied. 'Or dead leaves, maybe?'

'No, look again. Isn't that a B?'

Gigi seemed doubtful. 'Mm. Possibly.'

'And there's an I, two L's and a Y.' Sophie started trembling and her voice had risen to a squeak.

There was a small space, then all of a sudden she could clearly make out another whole word.

'LIGHTBODY,' she squealed. 'That's his name, Billy Lightbody.'

'Fuck me!' Gigi couldn't help herself. Donna was beside her now, too.

'Jesus wept!' she said, altering the tone. 'You're bloody right!'

A loud snore made them all turn round. Yana was asleep. She looked so peaceful, with her head on one side and a small smile playing on her lips, that it seemed a shame to wake her.

'We'll leave her for a while,' Donna said. 'She's had a lot of excitement for one morning.'

Sophie could hardly wait to get onto Google. She practically ran home, clutching the precious sketch, which she'd promised she'd return.

'Slow down!' Gigi cried, puffing behind her. 'I can't keep up!'

Together, they burst through Sophie's front door. Sophie plonked down on the sitting room floor, Gigi took the rocking chair and they both got out their phones.

'Let's see who comes up with something first,' Gigi said, starting to type.

Eighteen

Layla was much prettier than Celia remembered, even with pink hair and a nose ring. She was very much like her mother, only smaller boned, and her eyes were green rather than blue-grey.

It was around ten o'clock on Saturday morning and Celia guessed Layla hadn't been up long. Her hair, in two scruffy plaits, was unbrushed and there were make-up smudges around her eyes.

Even so, she looked sweet and young, with her oval face, small, dainty nose and big eyes. She was wearing a sleeveless black top tucked into flared jeans. She was slim, but there was a rounded softness to her limbs, and her pale skin was as smooth as cream.

'Come in,' she said, and Celia followed her up a flight of stairs to the first-floor flat.

It was part of an old Edwardian house, with high ceilings and decorative cornicing. Plenty of light flooded through the open sash windows, and the white walls lent a sense of airiness to what was, in reality, rather a small space.

'Have you ever been here before?' Layla asked, leading her aunt across the wooden landing to a compact, square sitting room at the front of the property.

The question wasn't meant to sound accusing, but it made Celia wince all the same.

'Yes,' she said, 'but not for a very long time. I think you'd just been born, actually.'

The room gave her an uncanny sense of déjà vu. It had changed since the last time, and yet it felt oddly familiar, too. She thought this was probably because it not only contained her sister's belongings, but also bore her unmistakable stamp.

Everything in it was stylish, a bit alternative, carefully chosen – and shabby. It had probably all come from some junk shop or other. The large sofa was an unusual shade of burned orange. The wooden coffee table, made from old railway sleepers, had watermarks, and it looked as if a cat had used the sisal rug as a scratching post.

The well-thumbed books on shelves on either side of the cast-iron fireplace reflected Sophie's eclectic tastes: travel, history of art, yoga, knitting, science fiction, spies and the Second World War.

'Who's that by?' Celia asked, pointing to an oil painting on the wall of a luscious, overflowing fruit bowl.

'Someone Mum met in Italy, I think,' Layla replied. 'Probably a lover.'

They both laughed, which helped to break the ice.

'Can I get you something? Tea or coffee?'

Layla vanished into the kitchen and came back with two mugs of Earl Grey. She sat on a tan leather pouffe opposite Celia, who had sunk so far into the orange sofa she feared she might never be able to get out.

'I'm sorry I didn't see much of you when you were growing up,' she said, looking at Layla and seeing a younger version of Sophie, which tugged at her heartstrings. 'I hope I can somehow make it up to you.'

Layla shrugged. 'It's OK. I know you're busy and your job's really full-on.'

Celia took a sip of tea. She was struck by the generosity of this statement. Layla had said it to make her aunt feel better. It was doubtful if Rupert or Rory would have been as kind, and Celia found herself thinking her sister hadn't done such a bad job after all.

With so many lost years, there was a lot to catch up on. She asked Layla about her life, her degree, her friends, her hobbies and interests, her waitressing job and her hopes for the future.

Layla was quite hard on herself and sounded down at times, but didn't seem annoyed by the questions. She answered each one fully, relieved, perhaps, to have the opportunity to open up and say how it really was.

She had a habit of twisting one or other of her plaits around her index finger while thinking, which Celia found endearing. To her surprise, she didn't even mind the gold nose ring, and wondered if she might actually grow to like it.

The only subject Layla wasn't keen to discuss was her mother.

'We haven't been getting on that well recently,' was all she would say.

Celia's guilt seemed to have morphed into a newfound concern and even affection and without thinking, she sprang to her sister's defence.

'She adores you and she absolutely does her best for you, you know. You've always been her number one priority.'

Layla frowned but didn't speak.

Later, they went for a walk in the park. It was a warmish day and lots of folk were out and about. Layla wasn't working until the evening and didn't seem in any rush for her aunt to leave. Celia wondered if she were a bit lonely, though she insisted she wasn't and certainly seemed quite capable of looking after herself.

They had sandwiches for lunch in a little café overlooking a pond, and then browsed in a few shops before returning to the flat.

'How about having Sunday lunch with us tomorrow?' Celia suggested. 'Or come midweek for an evening meal, if that works better. It's ages since you've seen Rory and Rupert. They'd love to meet you, and so would Neil.'

Layla's hand shot up, searching for her pink plait, which she wound around an index finger. Celia waited on tenterhooks, wondering if she were dreaming up a good enough excuse to say no.

After a few moments, though, Layla's face broke into a sweet, shy, ever so slightly goofy smile.

'I'd really like that. I've enjoyed talking to you today. Thank you for coming.'

★★★

'Are you really dating Terrell?'

Cilla the nail technician glanced up from the stool at Sophie's feet and gave her a funny look.

Sophie sat up straight, accidentally moving her right foot in the process, which made Cilla smudge the orange nail polish she was in the process of applying.

'No I'm not!' Sophie said hotly. 'Wherever did you hear that?'

Cilla shook her head and tutted. 'He's told everyone. Anyone who'll listen. He's an asshole. A long time ago, I went out with him a few times. Then I found out he had a different girlfriend for every day of the week. I told him where to go, but he kept on hassling me, phoning me and turning up at the salon. It was very embarrassing. He even tried to force my friend to persuade me to take him back. In the end, I had to ask Hung to have a word.'

She turned her head and nodded in the direction of a male colleague, sitting at reception. Hung was aged about thirty and very well built. You could see his beefy shoulders and muscly arms beneath his white overall top.

Sophie took a deep breath. 'I see.'

Afterwards, she bumped into Bunny and Wyatt, from the yoga class on the beach. Sophie had just left the nail salon, while the other two had met, by chance, in the grocery shop next door and were going for coffee.

They exchanged a few pleasantries, then Wyatt gave Sophie a wink.

'I hear you and Terrell have got together. He's a good-looking guy.'

He glanced at Bunny, who smiled back rather coolly.

'I'm not seeing him,' Sophie said with a frown. 'I don't know why he's giving everyone that impression. It's just not true.'

Wyatt appeared confused, while Bunny merely raised her eyebrows.

'Oh, he's full of nonsense,' she said dismissively. 'I don't pay any attention to what he says. He does love his yoga, though. I'll give him that.'

Having blocked Terrell's number, Sophie wouldn't know if he'd been trying to contact her or not. It was just as well she'd arranged to go out with Gigi later, though, in case he decided to turn up at her house anyway.

She wished with all her heart she'd never agreed to go out with him in the first place, but it was no use bemoaning her bad judgement. She'd learned her lesson, and the most important thing now was to freeze him off completely,

Gigi knocked on the door at five o'clock and her son, Eddie, gave the women a lift to the ferry terminal. They waited in a queue for about fifteen minutes, before boarding the sleek white vessel, along with several dozen other passengers heading, like them, for a night out in Manhattan.

Sitting on the open top deck, they watched as the ferry pulled away from the pier and started to skim across the glassy Atlantic Ocean.

They barrelled along Coney Island beach for a while, taking in the amusement park with its garish, retro rides. The famous Cyclone wooden roller coaster looked just as terrifying as Sophie recalled from her youth, though she seemed to remember it hadn't stopped her buying a ticket. She imagined she could smell French fries and candyfloss and hear the excited screams of children and adults but, in reality, they were too far away.

Soon after, they were passing under the Verrazano-Narrows Bridge, once the longest suspension bridge in the world. Sophie gazed up in wonder, awed by what was clearly a brilliant feat of engineering.

The wind was much stronger out here on the water and she'd tied back her hair to stop it blowing in her face. She was wearing her tie-dye dress, which would be perfect for tramping the city's hot streets, but was glad she'd brought a cardigan for the hour-long boat trip.

While they made a brief stop at Sunset Park, Brooklyn, she took a moment to check out the other passengers.

When the fourth or fifth person came into view, her guts turned to jelly as she recognised the tall, stooping figure of Joe. He glanced up, caught her eye and, for a moment, her heart stopped.

He gave a small smile, but there was no warmth in it, and his eyes were blank. Sophie's heart started beating again, but a heavy, sinking feeling lodged in her chest. She thought he was going to walk away without speaking to her, but when Gigi waved, he seemed to change his mind.

'How're you doing?' Gigi asked, giving Sophie a nudge. It wasn't clear if she was just being kind, or if the nudge was to make Sophie talk. In any case, she felt so miserable and tongue-tied that all she could do was keep her mouth firmly shut. She wouldn't know what to say anyway.

It seemed Joe was meeting his friend, Jared, for dinner in the Meatpacking District.

'I haven't been to the city in a while,' he explained, rubbing his chin.

He was wearing a clean, slightly creased, pale blue, short-sleeved shirt and tan chinos. He looked drop-dead gorgeous, which Sophie felt like a stab in the stomach; she'd never seen him in anything vaguely smart before and it really suited him.

Gigi mentioned she and Sophie were eating out, too, though they hadn't yet decided where. If she were hoping he'd invite them to join him for a drink at least, she was to be disappointed.

'Jared and I have known each other forever. We went to the same college. Since he married and had kids, we hardly see each other. We've got a whole lot to catch up on.'

Joe wasn't stupid and must have recognised Gigi's hint for what it was. This only made Sophie feel even bluer, and it was almost a relief when he excused himself and walked to the other side of the ferry.

It had been Gigi's suggestion to go into Manhattan and Sophie had leaped at the idea, but now she just wanted to curl up under a duvet and sleep.

Sensing her gloom, Gigi tried to cheer her up, pointing out that at least they had a name for her father, now. She avoided mentioning that the research they'd done earlier had also revealed there were a lot of men in the world called Billy Lightbody, and it could take a long time to find the right one.

'It was so lucky Yana kept that sketch,' Sophie agreed,

but without any enthusiasm. Seeing Joe again, and feeling the cold blast of his contempt, seemed to have sucked the joy out of everything.

She was distracted for a while by the sight of the gleaming tower of One World Trade Center, followed by the cheery promenade of Brooklyn Heights.

The gentle bounce of the ferry was soothing and really rather enjoyable, but still, she felt little pleasure when they reached New York Harbor and passed the Statue of Liberty. With those broken shackles at her feet and brandishing her iconic torch, to Sophie's jaded eyes she just appeared too green and rather tawdry.

Before long, lower Manhattan came into view with its higgledy-piggledy skyline of art deco spires, shimmering towers and dazzling office blocks. The ferry pulled in at Pier Eleven, Wall Street, and the passengers started to disembark.

'We'll go to South Street Seaport,' Gigi said, rising and picking up her handbag. 'It's not far and there's always stuff going on there. There are plenty of restaurants, too.'

It was after 6.30 p.m. but the heat hit them as soon as they stepped off the pier and onto the street. Sophie looked around for Joe but couldn't see him. After the relative peace and quiet of Rockaway, the noise of cars and the smell of hot dogs, fried onions and pretzels made her feel quite sick.

They started walking, and people seemed to be coming at them from all directions: men in dark trousers and rolled up shirtsleeves, the jackets of their suits slung over their shoulders; women in tight little dresses and trainers, striding towards the subway, their office heels stuffed into bags; workers in big boots and blue overalls spattered with paint and tourists in shorts and T-shirts, with cameras slung round their necks.

A drunk man with bright red cheeks and glassy eyes swerved into Sophie, almost knocking her over, and she let out a scream.

'Are you OK?' Gigi asked.

Sophie said she was, but bumping into Joe like that had really thrown her.

'I'm sorry I'm being such bad company.'

'Don't be silly,' Gigi replied. 'I'm enjoying myself.'

Once they entered the historic district of South Street Seaport, Sophie began to feel a little better. She was more at home in the cobblestone streets, amongst the early nineteenth-century townhouses, converted mercantile buildings and old-fashioned sailing ships anchoring the port.

The area was bustling with people, but no one seemed to be in a hurry. They were all here to enjoy the panoramic views of the harbour, and to shop, eat, drink and relax. Little by little, Sophie could feel the tension easing in her neck and shoulders and she managed to smile at Gigi for the first time in a while, hoping she could relax, too.

Gigi insisted they must check out Pier Seventeen, the most prominent shopping area, which had been damaged by Hurricane Sandy and rebuilt from scratch.

Most of the stores were open, and she treated herself to some silver earrings, shaped like starfish, while Sophie bought a scented candle for Layla and some home-made fudge for herself.

After that, they took their time choosing where to eat

and settled in the end on a seafood restaurant overlooking the harbour and Brooklyn Bridge.

It was quite late for dinner, by New York standards, and they were surprised and delighted to get the last free table on the patio, where they could listen to strolling musicians and enjoy unhampered views.

Sophie would have been anxious about the price of the food on the menu, having already insisted that she would pay. However, she was determined to show her gratitude to Gigi, and resolved not to worry until the credit card bill arrived.

She chose crispy calamari with a herb salad to start, while Gigi had a shrimp cocktail. They both wanted seared scallops as their main dish and also ordered a bottle of dry white wine and some sparkling water.

As the sun set slowly and majestically before their eyes, Sophie settled back in her seat, sipped her wine and tried to tell herself nothing would have come of her fledgling relationship with Joe anyway. Their lives were so different and they lived too far apart.

She'd be leaving Rockaway soon, most likely never to return. Before long, she'd be back in London, picking up the pieces of her old life, trying to help Layla find a better job and searching for one herself.

She didn't have room for romance; there was no bandwidth. And she'd rather stay single for the rest of her days than risk giving even just one small segment of her heart to a man, only for him to throw it right back at her.

'What'll you do about Joe?' Gigi asked, as if reading her mind. She cut a scallop in half before popping it, with some rice, into her mouth. 'I've never known him to be so standoffish.'

Sophie topped up her friend's glass and then her own. They weren't in a hurry and if necessary, they'd order another bottle.

'Nothing,' she replied, lifting the glass to her lips and taking a sip. 'Nada.'

Gigi made a noise, which sounded like a protest, but Sophie ignored it.

'He's obviously washed his hands of me and quite frankly, if he's so quick to judge and can't even be bothered to find out who I really am, he's not worth knowing anyway.'

'You sound very definite,' Gigi said, looking doubtful. 'Do you really mean it?'

Sophie paused, breathing in and out deeply. 'Yes, I do. For my sake, I have to.'

Nineteen

They took the train back to Rockaway and arranged an Uber to pick them up from the station. Sophie felt quite drunk in the car and regretted ordering the second bottle of wine, but Gigi, who'd consumed just as much booze, disagreed.

'Oh come on, you've got to let your hair down sometimes, gal.' She got louder and more American when tanked up and waved her arms around a lot. 'We had fun, didn't we? For chrissakes, we needed it. I know I did.'

They stopped outside Gigi's house and Sophie could hear gales of laughter as she stumbled home. It would be a miracle if her friend didn't wake up the whole street.

It took her a while to get the key in the lock and she tripped on the step and practically fell inside. Bending down to take off her shoes, she noticed a white envelope on the floor.

Turning it over, she saw her name written on the front in capitals: SOPHIE. So it wasn't a circular. Taking it into the kitchen, she poured herself a glass of water, swaying slightly and holding on to the edge of the sink as she drank it down. Then she carried the letter back into the front room and sat on the rocking chair while she ripped open the envelope.

Sophie, it began in childish block script. Impatient to find out who it was from, she scanned down to the bottom and her heart thumped when she recognised the name: *Terrell*.

She hurried to the door to secure the chain. There were no curtains on the windows now, and she peeked out to check for someone lurking outside. To her great relief the street was quiet, but still, she didn't feel entirely safe.

While she was with Gigi, she'd managed to put Terrell from her mind. Now, thoughts of him came rushing back. Retreating to the kitchen once more, where she couldn't be seen, she sat on the floor and again started reading the letter.

Sophie,

I'm gonna buy your house. My friends a millionaire. Hes gonna lend me the money. I'll knock it down and start again. You cant stop me coz you need the dough. My offers the only one your gonna get...

She swallowed. What did he mean by saying that she wouldn't get more offers? Was he threatening her? Her heart was hammering as she read on:

You shud not have sent me that text. You disrespected me and I dont like that.

I've made some enquiries and I'm not the only one

you tried to fool. Your not a nice person. Bad things happen to people like you. Its called karma.

You better watch out, Sophie. Get the hell outta Rockaway.

Terrell

Putting her hand over her mouth, she had to stifle a scream. She couldn't believe what she'd just read. That he was intending to destroy Piping Plover House was bad enough, but calling her a bad person and suggesting others thought so, too, was even worse.

Who had he been speaking to? Her mind started to race. She knew Cilla, for one, but Cilla said she hated him. The people at his yoga class? Yana? Gigi's kids? Joe? Complete strangers she'd passed in the street or sat next to on the beach? All of a sudden, she could sense danger and hostility everywhere, yet she hadn't done anything wrong.

She'd heard of jilted men wreaking terrible revenge on the women who'd supposedly scorned them. But they were only in news stories, they weren't real live people like her.

Terrell was probably just trying to frighten her, but as Cilla's experience showed, he had a track record of being a nuisance to women. These things could escalate.

Once again, Sophie found herself wishing to God that Celia were here and she wasn't alone in this big, rattling house with doors and windows that didn't close properly.

It crossed her mind to call the police, but she wasn't sure what help they could give right now. After all, Terrell hadn't actually made any overt threats. She had to hand it to him;

he'd been quite clever, even if he couldn't do joined-up handwriting.

Shock seemed to have cleared her head and she didn't feel drunk any more, but it was still a struggle to get up from the floor. Before leaving the kitchen, she checked the back door and all the windows were properly locked. Then she shoved the rocking chair up against the front door and left the downstairs lights blazing.

After getting undressed and climbing into bed, she lay still, clutching her mobile phone to her chest and listening out for every sound. The house often creaked a bit, as if turning in its sleep. This didn't normally trouble Sophie, but tonight, she was terrified.

Her mind started to play tricks, convincing her that Terrell was staring at her through the bedroom window, but it was only the branch of a tree, swaying in the salty wind rolling off the ocean. Then she thought she heard her door opening, but it was the overhead fan rattling and squeaking, as it did every now and again.

Sleep eluded her and at about 4 a.m. she started listening to an audio book. She soon gave that up, however, because she was afraid it would block out the noise of an intruder.

Instead, she waited for dawn to break, praying the light would banish her worst fears and bring hope of a new beginning.

As soon as the sun rose, she put on her bikini, grabbed a towel and went down to the beach. There wasn't a soul in sight and all along the shoreline, tiny piping plovers were doing their funny little dance: run, stop, peck, repeat. It was like watching a stage show and she could swear that they were performing it just for her.

The sky was a perfect sapphire blue and the sea looked like a vast strip of azure satin, which had been rolled out, leaving numerous lacy crinkles on the surface.

For a while, she strolled in bare feet close to the water, where the sand was cool and damp. Every now and then a wave would splash round her ankles and she was surprised how cold it felt. Wrapping the towel round her neck to stop it getting wet, she looked far out to sea, to the point where earth meets sky, and wondered about Pampy. Was she out there somewhere, watching her and caring what became of her, as she once had? And what about her real father? If he knew she existed, would he care, too?

A tiny grey crab scuttled backwards and burrowed into the sand while overhead, seagulls circled lazily or perched, motionless, on the breakwaters, looking like beady-eyed sentinels.

After no sleep, Sophie's body felt heavy and slow and her head ached, but her mind was as restless as the waves. She wished that the wind would whistle through her brain, catch her thoughts and carry them far away.

On she walked, past grand, beachfront houses into a less affluent area of tower blocks and bungalows. She could feel the sun getting hotter and regretted not bringing sunscreen and a cover up to protect her chest and shoulders.

Soon, she came to one of the wooden lifeguards' shacks. A group of young people in regulation orange shorts and vest tops were on the sand outside, doing their morning drill of burpees, press-ups and star jumps. Sophie felt weary just watching them.

One of them looked a little like Terrell, only younger. She was pretty sure that Terrell himself did his shifts a lot further up the beach, but his lookalike made her shiver.

During her sleepless night, she had pretty much made up her mind to put the house on the market as quickly as possible and leave Rockaway the minute this was done.

Now, despite her tiredness, she resolved to call the nearest estate agent as soon as she returned home. She'd try and book a visit from them this very afternoon and would accept whatever value they put on the property. If Terrell made an offer, which she'd refuse, at least she'd be out of the country by the time he got to hear of it. She wasn't proud of herself for allowing him to intimidate and effectively drive her from Rockaway, but honestly felt she had no other safe choice.

Deep in thought, she gradually became aware of a swimmer a little way away, quite far out in the ocean, and decided it was most likely a man, due to his powerful crawl.

Her heart started pumping. The man had left a pile of his things on the beach and she suddenly felt sure the tan shorts and sunhat belonged to Joe. When he stood up in the water, and his chest and shoulders emerged from the waves, she knew for certain.

She was about to turn tail before being spotted, but he glanced in her direction and it was too late. She could have scarpered anyway, assuming he wouldn't want to speak, but something in his body language told her not to.

As he continued to wade towards the shore, he slowed

down, as if deliberately giving her plenty of time to reach him. He wasn't exactly looking at her, but he wasn't looking away, either, and she formed the impression that perhaps he wasn't feeling quite as hostile towards her as he had been yesterday.

Her head was telling her to say a quick hello and move on, but a shred of hope had wormed its way into her heart and wouldn't budge.

As he emerged from the water, she couldn't help but notice his wide shoulders, strong chest, flat stomach and the thin line of light brown hair that began at his navel and trailed down to meet the top of his turquoise swimming shorts.

'Hi,' she said, when she was just a few feet away.

There was an awkward pause, when she feared the conversation was over before it had begun. He stepped onto dry sand and without thinking, she hurried over to his towel and jogged back to hand it to him.

'Thanks.' He shook it out and slung it round his shoulders, before peering oddly at her. 'You look terrible. What the hell have you been doing to yourself?'

Sophie was so taken aback she didn't know how to answer. Fortunately, he replied for her.

'Big night, last night, was it?' He gave a wry smile.

She lowered her eyes. 'I got carried away with the wine. I knew I'd regret it.'

'Tsk tsk.'

'And then I couldn't sleep at all. I'm absolutely knackered.'

They strolled over to his clothes, where he spread out his towel and indicated for her to sit down.

She sensed a reserve in him that hadn't been there before, but at least they were communicating again.

'Why couldn't you sleep?' he asked. 'Normally when I've been on the booze I sleep like a baby.'

She gathered a pinch of sand and idly rolled the grains around her palm with an index finger.

'I've got a lot on my mind. I'm going back to London as soon as the house is on the market, most likely in the next few days.'

'Why?' He seemed shocked. 'I thought you were planning to stay all summer, or most of it, anyway.'

She shook her head. She was still playing with the sand, which she found strangely therapeutic. 'Something's happened. I-I need to leave.'

'What's happened? Look at me.'

The urgency of his tone made her glance up, and she met his gaze. He seemed to be searching her face for clues, examining every fleeting expression, trying to analyse what it meant.

Under such scrutiny, it was impossible to pretend she was all right; he'd have clocked she was lying straight away.

'Terrell,' she began, and his face clouded over. 'No, it's not what you think. I went out with him once, he lunged at me, I pushed him off and said I didn't want to see him again. Now, he's threatening to make sure no one buys my house, so that he can. He wants to pull it down. He says his friend's going to lend him the money. He stuck a letter through my door, full of veiled threats. It was really nasty, really intimidating. It was waiting for me when I got back from the city last night. That's why I couldn't sleep. I was petrified he might do something. He said I should get the hell out of Rockaway, so that's what I'm doing.'

Joe made a noise like a high-pitched groan. 'I had no idea. You should have rung me. I would've come straight away.'

Sophie managed a small, sad smile. 'You weren't really speaking to me, remember? You'd decided I was a bitch.'

'That's not true—' he began, but clocking her expression of disbelief, he changed his tune. 'I suppose I did think you were a bitch, a bit of a one anyway. I'm sorry. I was shocked you even knew that dickhead or gave him the time of day. I could tell he was trouble the moment I saw him. And I did think—'

'I know you did,' Sophie said quickly. 'But it's not true, OK? That's exactly what he wanted you to think. I was never going to go out with him again. He wouldn't take no for an answer. Like you said, he's a dickhead.'

Joe placed one of his big hands on top of hers. It felt warm and delicious and she didn't want to move in case he took it away.

'I feel such an asshole,' he said quietly, staring out to sea. 'I'm sorry for jumping to conclusions. It was stupid.'

'It's OK, I understand.'

'It's not OK,' he insisted. 'I had no idea you were in trouble. I shouldn't have left so soon after we got back from Jamaica Bay. I should've stayed to make sure you were all right.'

'You weren't to know. I mean, I can see why he fooled you.'

Joe took his hand away.

'I don't believe he'll get the money together to buy your

house,' he said at last. 'I doubt this millionaire friend of his even exists. I reckon he's full of bullshit, but I agree, you can't take any risks. I'll ask around and find out all I can about him. I bet you anything you like, as soon as he knows I'm on to him, he'll back off. People like that are always cowards underneath. But in the meantime, you can't be on your own—'

She started to protest, but he wasn't listening.

'You can come and stay at my place for a while. In my spare room,' he added quickly. 'We'll go back to your house now, I've got the car. You grab your stuff and I'll take you to mine right away. It won't be for long, just until I sort this out.'

The offer was too good to resist. Relief spread through Sophie like a mug of hot chocolate on a cold day and all of a sudden, the world seemed to spring to life once more. She was no longer alone and with Joe's support, she felt sure that she could cope with anything.

Her eyes filled with tears but luckily, he was looking the other way. 'I'm so grateful. I really am. I appreciate it more than I can say.'

He dressed quickly and they walked to his car, which was parked in a nearby street. He waited outside Piping Plover House while she grabbed her bag and slung in her things, including the sewing box, wrapped in protective towels.

After loading her bag in his boot, she quickly texted Gigi: *I'm going to stay with a friend for a few days. I'll explain everything when we speak x*

It was only a ten-minute drive to Joe's place. Imagining

that he lived in an apartment, she was surprised when he drew up at what looked like a smallish, brand new house, clad in white cedar, in a residential area on the west side of the city.

'Home sweet home,' he said, parking in the drive and turning off the engine.

As soon as she saw the view, she gasped: 'Wow!'

The house, which was raised off the ground, sat directly on the white, sandy beach, with nothing between it and the ocean.

'Like it?' Joe said, behind her, and she nodded.

'It's beautiful.'

He explained that the original house was reduced to rubble by Hurricane Sandy and had been completely rebuilt. Strict flood safety regulations meant it had to be at least six feet off the ground.

There were houses on either side, but not so close as to be intrusive. Sophie imagined it would be fun to sit on the high deck surrounding the property, breathe in the sea air – and just be.

He carried her case up the wooden steps and she could soon see that inside was no less impressive. You walked straight into the main living room, which had cedar-clad ceilings and large sliding doors facing the sea. Light seemed to fill every corner.

Glancing around, she could tell this wasn't a show home; it was clearly lived in. Papers were scattered across the grey sofa and wooden coffee table, and there were various empty mugs and glasses lying around. It seemed clean, though, and very comfortable.

From the main room, you walked into a big, light kitchen, which was all straight lines, white surfaces and bang up-to-date, silver-grey appliances.

Joe strolled over to the stainless steel fridge and opened the door.

'Help yourself to anything you want,' he said, pointing to a row of cold drinks on the top shelf.

Further down, Sophie spotted bread, butter, cheese, cold meats, milk and yoghurt and, in the bottom drawers, a selection of fruit and salads.

'Glasses are here, mugs there, plates there and cutlery in here,' he went on, opening cupboards and drawers one by one. 'The utility room is next door. Don't worry about doing any washing, though. My housekeeper cleans and takes care of all the laundry.'

Sophie was astonished.

'Remember my father left me some money when he died?' Joe said, as if he could see into her mind. 'It enabled me to buy this place and continue with my painting and poetry. I'm very fortunate.'

Next, he took her upstairs to her bedroom, which had its own corner balcony, plus an en suite shower room with white furniture and coppery brown tiles.

'I hope it's OK?' he said, putting her bag down on the wooden floor.

She almost laughed because by any standards this was fabulous, and compared with Piping Plover House, it was a palace.

'It's gorgeous,' she replied warmly. 'I don't think I've ever stayed anywhere nicer.'

'Good, I'm glad. Why don't you unpack? I'll give you a shout later, when lunch is ready.'

So much had happened already this morning that Sophie had completely forgotten about food, and had no idea of the time, either.

She was surprised when she found out it was midday, and remembered she'd eaten nothing since last night.

It didn't take long to hang the majority of her clothes in the white wooden wardrobe and tidy the rest away in the empty chest of drawers against the wall.

Her king size bed, with its crisp white duvet and pillowcases, looked incredibly tempting, but she didn't dare lie on it in case she nodded off. She was certain that she'd sleep well tonight. She felt safe here, where Terrell wouldn't find her, and with Joe for company.

After about half an hour, Joe tapped on her door and invited her down for lunch. They ate tuna niçoise outside on the deck, under a giant umbrella.

A middle-aged couple came out of the house next door, wearing brightly coloured bathing suits and carrying paddleboards.

'Hi, Joe, how are you doing?' the woman said. 'I need to talk to you sometime about that portrait. I think my daughter might come home in a couple of weeks.'

'Sure,' Joe replied. 'Just let me know and we'll fix a time to start.'

When she and her husband left, Joe explained to Sophie that the woman had asked him to paint her daughter and grandson. They were a good family, but a little over-friendly, like some of the other neighbours.

'I can't even go for a swim here without someone coming down and inviting me for breakfast, lunch or dinner. Maybe they think I'm lonely. I guess I sound anti-social. I shouldn't complain, but I value my peace and quiet. That's why I tend to swim elsewhere.

'I'd like to paint you sometime,' he added, with a smile. 'If you'll let me.'

She suddenly remembered the sketch of Yana done all those years ago by her real father. She'd only eaten a couple of mouthfuls of salad, but started to push back her chair.

'Can I show you something?' she said and hurried upstairs to fetch the drawing from the pocket of her suitcase.

Back down again, she spread the sketch out on the table.

'It's good, really good,' he commented, 'especially when you consider how young he was at the time. You can see he's got a sense of humour and he's very observant. Look at the eyes. They're perfect. There's a lot of detail in the places where it matters.'

Hearing Joe speak about her father's work in this way made Sophie all the more keen to track him down. She pointed out his name, which had been so well disguised.

'Unfortunately, it turns out there are literally scores of Billy Lightbodys all over the world. Who knew? I imagined it was quite an unusual surname when I first heard it.'

Joe put a forkful of tuna and lettuce in his mouth and chewed thoughtfully.

'I'd be surprised if he didn't use his talent in some way, in his career, I mean. Did you Google *Billy Lightbody Artist*, or *Billy Lightbody Cartoonist*?'

Sophie picked up a big black olive and nibbled on

the edge. 'I tried that, but nothing came up. I tried *artist, cartoonist, sketches, drawings, paintings*, anything I could think of, but I drew a complete blank.'

'Do you think he was always known as Billy?' Joe was talking as much to himself as to her. 'Maybe he became William later on, when he was older. I considered using my real name, Joseph, when I started selling my paintings, but changed my mind. Nobody ever calls me that.'

The idea hadn't occurred to Sophie.

'Do you mind?' she asked, picking up her mobile and starting to scroll.

'Go ahead. Don't forget to eat, though. It might go cold.'

On opening up the search engine, Sophie's heart started to race again. 'What shall I put – *William Lightbody Artist*?'

Thinking she might finally be on to something, she tapped in the words without waiting for Joe's approval. It seemed to be an age before anything happened, then, all of a sudden, a name and photograph flashed up onscreen: *William Lightbody, Irish cartoonist and illustrator.*

Her fingers started to tremble when she found his page on Wikipedia.

William Boyd Lightbody (b. 1954) is a Northern Irish cartoonist and illustrator, living and working near Belfast. He had worked as an editorial cartoonist for the Belfast Daily Telegraph and the Irish Times. He has illustrated over 200 children's books, including 17 written by Sara McIlhenny, which are among his most popular works.

Spouse: Jennifer Plant (m. 1986)

Children: 2

There was a lot more information about his background, education and career, and he had his own website, too. Sophie pulled up a series of photos of him, poring over them almost forensically.

He looked like a fairly typical, late middle-aged man, with a friendly, intelligent face, glasses and thinning, grey-white hair.

'Can you see any resemblance?' she asked Joe, suspecting she knew what the answer would be.

'Not really, to be honest. See if you can find one of him when he was younger.'

Scrolling down, she eventually discovered a few grainy snaps from the seventies and eighties. They weren't very good, but at least they were in colour and one thing was clear – this William, or Billy Lightbody, used to have a shock of dark red curly hair.

'Oh my God!' she said, with a gasp. 'Look!'

Joe glanced at the shot and his eyes widened. 'Jesus! Do you think that's him? Your father?'

Sophie felt lightheaded and took a sip of water to try to calm down.

'I don't know, but it seems a bit of a coincidence. He's got red hair, he's the right sort of age, he's from Belfast and he's a good artist.'

'Here, wait a moment, let me check something out.' Joe took his own mobile from his pocket and searched for images of William Lightbody's cartoons and illustrations. He concluded that they certainly bore some stylistic resemblance to the Yana sketch, but he couldn't say for sure if William and Billy were one and the same artist.

Refusing to give up, he continued to scroll until he came to some of William Lightbody's earliest work. Pinching on one particular image to make it bigger, he stared hard for a moment and sipped on some water.

'Hey, look what I've found!'

'What? I can't see anything.'

'Look at the bark on the tree.'

Squinting, she scrutinised the trunk all the way from the roots to the topmost branches.

'Still nothing,' she said with a shrug.

'Look at it sideways,' Joe commanded. 'Really look.'

Frustrated, she grabbed his phone and turned it sideways. Now, as clearly as could be, she saw the words 'William Lightbody' written in small, scratchy letters, made to look like cracks and crevices in the tree's thick, gnarly surface.

For a few moments, she was unable to speak. She just stared at the signature in incredulity.

'He could just have copied the idea?' she asked at last, unwilling to set aside her disbelief.

'Highly unlikely,' said Joe. 'It's a very distinctive signature, his artist's trope, if you like. If you look really closely, you can see the letters are the same shape, too. I'd say it's definitely been done by the same hand.'

They sat in silence for several minutes while Sophie gazed out at the ocean.

'I'm going to email him,' she said at last. 'I won't tell him I'm his daughter; it might be too much of a shock. I'll say I have some information about my mother that he might want to know. If he doesn't reply, at least I'll have tried.'

Twenty

Staying with Joe was so relaxing and enjoyable that Sophie felt as if she were on holiday, rather than in hiding.

For several days, while he was making enquiries about Terrell, she barely left the house, only popping down to the beach every now and again to swim.

The neighbours were very friendly, just as Joe had described. In other circumstances, she would have loved to get to know them. Until her situation was resolved, however, she tried to avoid getting into any conversations and scuttled home as soon as possible after leaving the water.

Not going out much or speaking to people wasn't really a hardship, though, because Joe's place was so comfortable and it was filled with books and music.

He rented a small studio in town, where he often went for a few hours to paint, but he was always back in time for supper, which Sophie made. She enjoyed cooking in his kitchen and besides, she felt it was the least she could do to thank him for his kindness.

As she didn't have a laptop with her, Joe let her use his. One morning, after he left, she sat at the kitchen table, a mug of coffee at her side, and composed an email to William Lightbody.

In it, she explained she was the daughter of Teresa Walsh, née O'Brien, and Teresa had died some time ago after a short illness. That while going through her grandmother's things in Rockaway, New York, Sophie had discovered a letter to her mother, never sent.

I believe you made friends with my mother in Rockaway one summer, when you were teenagers, and that I've found a letter which concerns you. If you'd like to know more, please get in touch. I live in London but am currently in Rockaway, disposing of my grandmother's house, which she left to me and my sister in her will.

She sent the message to the email address on William's website, and tried not to raise her hopes. She allowed herself to check her inbox every morning and evening, but never in between, and resisted the urge to do any stalking on social media.

Five days into her stay, Joe turned up in the middle of the afternoon with some news. He'd heard on the grapevine that Terrell had been seen hanging around Piping Plover House, ringing the bell and asking neighbours if they knew where Sophie was.

Joe hadn't told her, because he didn't want to worry her, but he'd been sufficiently concerned to speak to the police. As it turned out, Terrell was well known to them and had been before the courts several times. He was currently on probation for issuing a bad cheque. If found guilty of a new offence of stalking or intimidation, he'd most certainly go to jail.

It was highly unlikely he'd give Sophie any more trouble and if he did, the police would be on to him straight away.

Sophie was delighted the matter seemed to have been sorted, but she also realised it meant she'd have to leave Joe.

'I guess I should go and pack my things,' she said. 'You'll be pleased to have the place back to yourself.'

'Stay tonight,' he insisted. 'We'll have one more supper together. I'll drive you home in the morning, if you want, or later if you prefer. As far as I'm concerned, there's no hurry. I like having you here.'

His words warmed her, and she realised how pleased she was they'd cleared up their misunderstanding and made friends again. But still, the shadow of their inevitable parting hung over her and she couldn't feel happy for long.

'What shall we eat?' she asked, fake-cheerfully. 'Do you fancy steak, if we can get hold of some? I'll cook it on the barbecue.'

'Sounds great.'

He looked a bit sad, too, but it might have been tiredness. While he went off in the car to buy steak, she made salsa verde, potato salad and easy melon ice cream, which she put in the freezer. By the time she'd finished, it was past five o'clock and she decided that, just this once, she'd allow herself to check her mailbox early.

There was something from her bank, and the usual spam, but one particular name jumped off the screen and made her knees go weak: **William Lightbody.**

Dear Sophie,

Thank you for your email. I did, indeed, know your mother, and I'm so sorry for your loss.

We met one summer in Rockaway when we were both about seventeen. She was a lovely person and I'm sure you miss her very much.

I'm interested to hear about the letter and would like to know more. Why don't we do a zoom call in the next day or two? Can you make tomorrow at 2 p.m. your time? If so, I'll send you a link.

I look forward to hearing back from you.

Yours,

William

She sat for quite some time, absorbing what she'd read. He sounded friendly and polite, if understandably cautious. More importantly, he wanted to know about the letter. He'd also suggested talking face to face, so he must be keen to see her, too.

Wasting no time, she wrote back there and then and

agreed with his suggestion of a chat tomorrow. He replied almost as quickly, sending her the promised link.

When Joe returned, she was in such a state of excitement and nerves that he made her sit on the deck and take some deep breaths, while he went inside to pour her a glass of wine.

'What shall I say? Do I tell him I'm his daughter? He might hang up.'

'Just be yourself,' Joe advised. 'Tell him what you know and see what he has to say. If he reacts badly, that's his fault, not yours, and there's nothing you can do.'

The steak was delicious, especially washed down with the bottle of Cabernet Sauvignon, picked up at the supermarket. When it got dark, he told her the names of the stars that were visible from where they sat. She had to promise that when she spotted one of them back in London, she'd think of him and send him a 'mind message'.

'Do you think it'll work?' she said with a smile.

'I don't know, but we can try.'

They spoke a bit about Layla, and he mentioned a friend who made wildlife documentaries for American TV.

'He might be able to give her some work experience. I can put her in touch with him if she'd like that.'

'That's really kind. I'm sure she'd love it. Did you never want children?' Sophie added, and he thought about this for a moment before answering.

'I guess it was never a burning desire, but if I'd been with someone who really wanted them, for their sake, I wouldn't have said no.'

'There's still time.'

He glanced at her and pulled a face. 'No way. She'd have to be much younger than me. I'm not into cradle snatching.'

The bottle of wine was almost finished, and he poured what was left into her glass before suggesting they go inside.

'We haven't had any ice cream yet,' she said, and they agreed to eat it in front of the TV. When they'd finished, he lay propped up on a cushion at one end of the sofa, resting his bare feet in her lap. An old movie was on in the background, but they weren't paying much attention.

His feet felt a little cold, and she began to rub them tentatively between her hands, massaging the soles and in between the toes. She liked his feet. They were strong, with toes that had clean, square, trimmed nails. Stroking them was surprisingly sensuous. It also felt so natural that she hardly realised what she was doing, until he groaned with pleasure.

'Mm, that's gorgeous. You don't mind, do you?'

She looked at him and smiled. 'Not at all.'

'I'll do yours in a minute – if you want me to.'

Gradually, his feet started to warm up and she ran her hands over his ankles, feeling the knobbly bones on either side, and up to his shins. Here, she pushed gently into the muscles and tendons around the bone, applying more pressure where she thought it was needed.

The blond hairs felt soft beneath her fingers and his skin was taut and tanned. On she went, over his knees and up his thighs to the hem of his shorts. Every now and again, she checked his face for signs of discomfort or boredom, but he was blissed out, with eyes closed, head resting on his bent arms and a small, serene smile playing on his lips.

After a while, her hands stole up his shorts a little way; she wanted to know how the flesh felt there. It was smooth, soft and ever so slightly furry. He sighed and a low moan rose up from her belly to her throat. Her desire to go further made her feel quite sick, but she wasn't sure if it was what he wanted, too.

She stayed still for a moment. The next minute, he sat up, put his feet on the floor and in one quick movement, he was by her side.

'Sophie?'

She looked into his eyes. Now she knew. Moving even closer, she raised her chin and soon his mouth was on hers, his hands around her head, cradling her gently, as if she were a precious vase that could easily fall from his grasp and break.

Her tongue slipped between his teeth. It was just a small, hesitant movement, a sort of reconnaissance mission. Straight away, his tongue responded by seeking out hers, and for a moment they seemed to entwine, like clematis round a tree. When they unwound, she slid her tongue in front of his teeth, exploring their smooth surface, hard edges and the gaps in between.

She found one space, wider than the rest, and poked in her tongue, making him laugh.

'Shall we go upstairs?' he said in a low voice, when she finally drew away.

Her stomach fluttered, but when she checked his eyes

again, his strong, steady gaze was enough to convince her she was doing the right thing.

She nodded and he took her hand while leading her to his room, only letting go when she was standing right by the bed. Without any warning, he gave one push and all of a sudden she was flat on her back.

'Sorry, I couldn't resist,' he said with a grin. 'I'll take a shower. Stay where you are.'

While he was next door, she quickly removed everything, except her knickers, and jumped under the bedclothes. She felt too shy for him to see her all at once; she'd rather he did it bit by bit.

There was nothing prudish about him, though. He emerged, still damp and naked from the bathroom, and stood in front of her, legs wide, hands on hips.

'This is me,' he said with a grin. 'Hope you like it!'

'I do!'

Laughing, he threw off the bedclothes and they both went quiet, taking each other in.

'You're gorgeous,' he whispered, kneeling beside her while his hands started to roam over her breasts, gently pinching her nipples and rolling them between his fingers.

Gradually, they moved down to her lower abdomen. He didn't seem to mind any of the bits that she worried about, like her tummy fat and flabby thighs. He took his time, looking, touching, squeezing, and all the while planting hot kisses on her neck, her mouth and her shoulders. His breath was deep and heavy. He seemed to approve of all of her, which made her relax.

She made no protest when he pulled down her white lacy knickers and dropped them on the floor.

'Let me see you,' he said, shuffling to the other end of the bed, where he knelt up again and swiftly parted her legs like a V.

Shyness would have enveloped her once more, but his gaze was intense, admiring even a little grateful.

Bending down, his tongue flicked this way and that while she made little moans. Now his fingers pushed inside her, his thumb circling and pressing until the strength of what was building was so great, she felt on the brink of an explosion. It was almost too much, but not quite...

When he stopped, Sophie opened her eyes to find him by her side again, kneeling up high. He was asking for her to pleasure him now, he was *begging* her. She was more than happy to oblige.

'Wait,' he said suddenly, gently pushing her away before he came.

He lay flat on the bed and looked at her with a smile that seemed to penetrate deep into her guts. She wanted him so badly, it hurt.

'Hop on,' he said, helping as she wriggled eagerly up his warm body. Then he raised his hands above his head while she reached forwards. Instinctively, their fingers interlaced as their movements synchronised. Heat curled deep in her belly and she bit her lip.

'I won't last long,' he said hoarsely, perhaps giving her the chance to pause, but she'd tipped over the edge herself and couldn't stop if she wanted to.

She came with a shocked cry, and he a groan of disbelief.

'That was incredible,' he said, catching his breath. 'I've never known anything like it.'

'Me neither.'

They both laughed.

His arm wound round her back as she snuggled into his side, pressing her nose into his chest and breathing in his warm, salty smell.

'I feel so lucky,' she whispered. 'I didn't think I'd meet anyone I liked ever again.'

'Me neither.'

She started to fall asleep, but his voice cut through the darkness.

'Don't go back to London,' he said quietly. 'Stay here – with me.'

Her arm snaked even more tightly around his waist, her leg around his thigh. They couldn't be much closer if they tried.

'I won't,' she replied. 'Not yet, I promise. How could I, now I've found you?'

She was woken the following morning by the sound of his voice behind her.

'I've brought you some tea.'

Rolling over, she opened her eyes to find him standing close by, with a blue and white striped mug.

He was wearing a pair of baggy, pale blue cotton pyjama bottoms and nothing else.

'Last night was so dreamy,' she said with a sigh.

He sat on the edge of the bed and she stroked his tanned back, drawing circles and figures of eight with her fingertips.

'Want to do it again?' He turned to her with a cheeky grin.

'What, now?' She was still half asleep, basking in the afterglow of yesterday.

'Why not?'

He had a point. It was just that she wasn't used to so much pleasure. Somewhere along the line, self-criticism and self-denial had worked their way into her psyche.

'What's the time?' She looked for her mobile but must have left it downstairs.

'It's around eight. We've got all the time in the world.'

Before she knew it, his pyjama bottoms were off and so were the bedcovers.

'I've got morning breath,' she squealed, when he bent down to kiss her on the mouth.

'I don't care.'

Today, he was like a man possessed and their lovemaking was quick, fierce, intense and beautiful. He must have been thinking about it since he woke up, probably planning it, too.

'I wasn't expecting that,' she said afterwards, lying back on the pillow and taking some deep breaths, feeling her heart rate start to slow.

'I bet you were,' he replied with a grin.

Stretching out her arms and legs, she realised she'd never felt so happy, and told him so.

'Will it last?' she asked anxiously.

He reached out and took her in his arms, squeezing so tightly he made her gasp.

'It will if you want it to, Mary Poppins.'

She was aware she'd have to go back to Piping Plover House sometime, to pack up the last of her things and get the place on the market. However, the prospect didn't seem nearly as bad now Terrell had been warned off, and she and Joe didn't have to part.

Even so, she didn't fancy being alone after speaking to William Lightbody, and she needed to use Joe's laptop, too.

He urged her to stay at least one more night and have a morning swim to calm her nerves. He also offered to remain at home if she liked, but she said no. With him being around, even in a different room, she might find speaking to her father more difficult. She wanted him there for the post-mortem, though.

After the last conversation with Layla, she'd received a couple of reassuring texts. It sounded as if Layla were feeling a little more positive. She'd applied for an internship, though she didn't say where, and was also planning a long weekend in Paris in the autumn, though she didn't say with whom.

Another message arrived while Sophie and Joe were having breakfast, and Sophie wondered how her daughter would react when she found out about him.

Hi Mum, hope ur well. All good here. Luv ya xx

It was short but sweet, and thankfully, very different in tone from some of their previous communications. The news about Joe could wait, Sophie decided. She didn't want to rock the boat now.

He left at about half past ten to start a painting and decorating job for a friend. He was giving mate's rates, so he wouldn't earn much money, but said he found the work therapeutic.

'It's less stressful than being an artist. I'm never completely satisfied with my poems or paintings, but I can feel proud of transforming someone's house.'

Once he'd gone, the minutes seemed to tick by painfully slowly. Sophie went to the beach in her bikini and had a short swim, but her head was full of chatter and she couldn't seem to turn the volume down.

Later, she had a shower, washed her hair and put on some make-up for the first time in a while. Gazing at herself in the mirror, with her wet hair reaching down to just below her shoulders, she thought she looked quite different, as if she'd stolen someone else's identity.

Her complexion was smooth and clear and her blue-grey eyes sparkled. A light tan all over gave her a healthy glow, and the lines on her forehead and around her eyes were less pronounced.

She looked *happy*, that was it, despite being on tenterhooks right now. Realising how strange and unfamiliar the emotion felt, she almost laughed. Some people were happy a lot, but she seemed to have forgotten how to be joyful or even content. She made up her mind not to let this happen again.

Unable to eat any lunch, she walked around the streets for a little while, but soon felt too hot. By 1.45 p.m. her stomach was churning and her chest felt tight. Opening the laptop, she stared at her father's email, hovering her mouse over the link. Her head swam with the knowledge that he was just a few clicks away, and she felt quite faint.

Finally, unable to stand it any longer, she pressed on the mouse and the link opened. She was five minutes early and would have to wait some more.

Fetching a glass of water from the kitchen killed a few moments, and she sipped it, facing away from the screen, hoping the time would go more quickly.

When someone spoke while her back was turned, she was so startled she nearly dropped her glass.

'Sophie, is that you?'

Swivelling round, she saw the same late middle-aged man's face that she'd studied a few days earlier, searching for clues.

'Hello,' he said, with a cautious smile. 'I'm William Lightbody. It's nice to meet you.'

For a moment, Sophie couldn't speak. Seeing him, albeit virtually, gave her goosebumps and she didn't know where to begin. The longer the silence went on, the more it seemed to crush her, and she began to think she might have to end the call without having so much as opened her mouth.

'You have a letter?' he asked at last, no doubt sensing her nervousness and wanting to help out.

It was just the nudge she needed.

'Oh yes,' she replied quickly, picking it up from the table.

'Thank you for agreeing to talk to me. I-I really am very grateful.'

He had a kind, intelligent countenance. He looked, to Sophie, like someone who lived a good life and who was content with his lot.

He was clean-shaven and wearing a smart, brown and white, open-necked checked shirt. The desk he was sitting at looked polished and rather distinguished. To his left was an old-fashioned brass lamp and behind him, a bookcase, which seemed to cover the entire wall.

Sophie glanced down at the letter before raising her eyes again. 'Shall I-I read it to you?' she stammered, feeling foolish and as if she were falling to pieces. This wasn't the way she'd wanted to present herself to him at all.

'No, wait, don't read it yet. Tell me about yourself and your mother,' he said gently, in a noticeable Northern Irish accent. 'When I left Rockaway, I wrote your mum dozens of letters but she never replied. At the time I couldn't understand it. Then, out of the blue, she got in touch. That was, ooh, over thirty years ago now. We corresponded for a little while but then she stopped again. I often wondered why.'

His voice was pleasantly low, with an upward inflection that made almost everything sound like a question. The significance of what he'd just said made Sophie's head spin. Without realising it, he could just have solved the mystery of why her grandfather, Donal, wrote the letter to her mother, and why she and the rest of the family, including Sophie, never went to Rockaway again.

The dates coincided and what's more, if Donal had found

out Teresa and Billy, or William, were back in touch, it would certainly have made him mad with fury.

'Did she, did she tell you why she didn't reply to your letters after you first met, when you were teenagers?' Sophie wanted to know. His answer surprised her.

'She never received them,' he replied, deadpan. 'Her father – your grandfather – intercepted them and tore them up.'

The cruelty of this made Sophie gasp. If her grandfather hadn't interfered, her mother and Billy might have stayed together, or at least remained in touch. In this scenario, she might not have been deprived of having a relationship with her real father for all these years.

'Did my mother say anything else – when she got back in touch, I mean?'

'You mean, that we had a child?'

All at once, it seemed as if her heart stopped and the world ceased to turn. Even the particles of air surrounding her stood still. Frozen to her seat, her heart pumping wildly, she stared at him, dumb and disbelieving. He *knew*?

Her silence was as loud as gunfire, as startling as thunder.

'Are you that child, Sophie?' he asked at last. His tone was so full of unexpected compassion that it made her well up.

'Yes,' she replied, as her bottom lip quivered and the tears started to trickle down her cheeks. 'Yes I am.'

The protective barrier she'd tried to build around herself before the meeting crumbled instantly. Without any kind of force field, she felt naked and oh so vulnerable. She was a hot mess of anxiety and fear.

Rarely had she seen a man cry, so it was a shock when

William's eyes filled up, too, and he wiped them with the back of a sleeve.

'Dear God,' he said, spluttering through his words. 'I've waited, hoping for this moment for so long. I didn't dare come and find you. Teresa cut off all contact with me that second time, after her husband and father got to hear of it. I assumed she'd never told you who your real father was. I couldn't risk messing up your life; I thought it wouldn't be fair.'

Sometimes life has a way of exceeding all expectations. It can bring your wildest dreams to life and make them even better than you could have imagined. These rare, golden moments can only be fully treasured after some degree of suffering, struggle and pain. Only after you've lost someone can finding them be truly appreciated.

Through her tears, Sophie managed to tell William she'd only recently learned the truth about him from her sister, and she'd been looking for him ever since.

'When I found you, I didn't know if you'd be angry and deny you were my father, or if you'd even be willing to speak. I was terrified of rejection, but I had to give it a go. Thank God I did.'

It wasn't possible for them to tell each other everything about their lives all at once. However, Sophie was curious to know about her two half-siblings.

'Do they look like me?' she asked. 'Can I see a picture?'

William seemed puzzled.

'They? My wife and I only have one child – our daughter, Maria.'

It was Sophie's turn to frown. 'But it says on your website and in Wikipedia that you've got two.'

'That's right, I do.'

As the penny dropped, Sophie experienced a tingling feeling, which spread right through her body before settling somewhere in the centre of her core, where it radiated warmth. She'd never felt anything quite like it before. It reminded her a bit of how she used to feel when she arrived at Piping Plover House and saw Pampy again. It was like coming home, but different. It was like finding a new home and realising it was better than the old one. It was an enormous and fulfilling sensation of being whole.

He smiled and nodded, sensing her joy.

'You're always in my thoughts. You have been from the moment your mother told me about you. She even sent me a photograph. Look!'

After rummaging in his jacket, which was hanging on the back of the chair, he pulled out a brown leather wallet. Inside were several pocket-sized snaps, which he flicked through before locating the one he wanted.

Sophie gazed at it in amazement. It was a school photo, the one she used to dislike because of her round face and freckles.

'And here's one of Maria at about the same age,' he said, holding up another snap. 'And one of her now. See how alike you are.'

It was true. The woman before Sophie was younger, plumper and her nose was a different shape, but she, too, had pale skin, strawberry-blonde hair and a slightly quirky, alternative look.

'Wow!' said Sophie, her eyes glittering with disbelief and exhilaration. 'I'd love to meet her one day.'

'You will.'

They hadn't discussed the letter in Pampy's sewing box and when Sophie read it out, William welled up again.

'How could he do that to his own daughter? Poor Teresa. It's beyond belief.'

It seemed unlikely William would have any idea why the letter ended up where it did, but to Sophie's surprise, he told her that he, too, had something she might find interesting.

'I got a letter from Orla about eighteen months ago.'

Sophie's ears pricked.

'I've kept it because it meant a lot to me. Would you like to see it?'

Crouching down out of sight, he rootled in a drawer of the desk, before reappearing with a faded white envelope.

Sophie listened in silence while he read the contents to her.

The more she heard, the greater the depth and height of her sorrow and delight. She hadn't realised the two could coexist so intensely in just one heart.

Orla, or Pampy, told William, or Billy, that Terry had passed away and thought he had a right to know. Orla said she'd been appalled by her husband's behaviour towards him and her daughter all those years ago. She said it was wrong of Donal to destroy Billy's letters and force the couple apart.

I told him it was wrong to lie about who Sophie's father really was, too, but he wouldn't listen. I'm sorry to say I was weak and in the end, I gave in.

When Donal discovered, via Teresa's husband, that

she'd been in touch with you again, I asked him to leave well alone. I said it was none of his business or mine and we should let husband and wife sort things out between them.

Donal got very angry with me, very abusive, not physically, but verbally and emotionally. I'm afraid I couldn't stand up to him then, either. I knew I should leave him – I should have left years ago – but I was scared. I had no money of my own and nowhere wto go.

Women nowadays are braver. They won't suffer bullying husbands, and quite right too, but my generation was taught to put up and shut up. Everybody suffered as a result, including the children.

She had, however, done one brave thing. After offering to post Donal's savage letter to their daughter, Pampy had folded it up and stuck it in her sewing box, where it wouldn't be discovered.

After that, it was down to her to break the news to Teresa that she couldn't return to Rockaway.

It was a horrible thing to have to do, a dreadful task, but at least I could tell her as kindly as possible. Of course Teresa was terribly upset and blamed me for not supporting her against her father. I wasn't surprised, but it hurt so much not to see her or my granddaughters, not even after Donal died.

Why Pampy hadn't destroyed Donal's nasty missive was

anyone's guess. Sophie decided she must have wanted to keep it as a reminder to herself of how mean her husband was. This way, after he died, she'd never fall into the trap of looking back with rose-tinted spectacles at the long life that they'd shared together.

William was almost at the end of the letter, when he paused for a moment, and looked at Sophie.

'This is the bit I think you're going to love.'

I've decided to leave my home, Piping Plover House, to my two beloved granddaughters, Sophie and Celia. Some may find this surprising, as they never much liked one another.

I can't reverse the harm Sophie and her mother suffered, and I contributed to in no small part. However, I hope my gift will bring happiness to the sisters, who loved the place so much. I also hope it will help them find a way through their differences. They need each other; we all do.

She signed off as simply, 'Orla'. She'd written the letter just a few months before her death.

'What do you think?' William asked, when Sophie continued to sit in silence.

'It sounds like a swansong, the last words of a dying woman. I think it was a brave thing to do. She doesn't try to downplay her part in the lies and deception, it's all there in black and white. She was obviously full of guilt and regret and it must have been very hard to admit it. It's so sad she never saw her daughter, or Celia and me, ever again.'

For some reason, William seemed slightly frustrated by Sophie's response. Scratching his head, he rocked back and forth in his chair.

'Of course it's sad, desperately so,' he said impatiently. 'But what about the house? Don't you think by leaving it to you both that she was trying to tell you something?'

Sophie pulled a face. 'She wanted Celia and me to reconcile, for sure, but there's no way that'll ever happen. We can barely be in the same room together. Celia's determined to sell the house and once it's gone, I doubt we'll ever cross paths again.'

They'd been talking for well over two hours and Sophie suddenly realised she was exhausted. She was on such a mental and emotional high, however, she wondered if she'd ever be able to sleep again.

William looked tired, too, but she didn't want to let him go for fear of losing him once more.

'This is just the beginning, Sophie,' he said, reassuringly. It was as if he knew what she was thinking and wanted to calm her fears. 'I'd like you to meet my wife, Jennifer, and Maria too, of course. Come to Belfast. I can pay your fare if necessary. In the meantime, let's schedule another Zoom call.'

It really did seem like a fairy tale come true, and as they said goodbye, both had tears in their eyes again. When Joe arrived home about an hour later, Sophie had so much to say that she didn't know where to begin. Her story came out in a muddle and he had to stop her several times to ask for clarification. Even then, several aspects of the tale remained a mystery to him.

The main thing, he said, when she finally fell silent, was that she and her father had made contact, liked each other and wanted to meet in person. The conversation had also cleared up for her an enormous number of doubts, resentments and question marks.

'Before we spoke, I thought I'd want to have a go at him for shagging my mum, then leaving her in the lurch. But the minute I saw him, I knew there was more to it than that. For some reason, I really trust him. I can hardly believe it, but he seems like a genuinely nice man.'

'We do exist,' Joe said drily.

The hole in her soul that had been aching to find its missing piece had been filled. If her heart were any more jam-packed, it would surely burst.

'Thanks for listening. I love you, Joe. I know it's early days, but I really think I do.'

'Me too,' he replied, kissing her on the mouth. 'I'm so glad for you, Mary P.'

Twenty-One

It was a sad moment for Sophie when the real estate people turned up. Soon, they were nosing around the property, opening cupboards, asking about the central heating and air conditioning and talking about the type of buyer they'd expect.

'I can imagine a youngish couple wanting this as a doer-upper,' said one man, who was aged about thirty and wearing tight grey trousers and pointed brown brogues.

'There should be plenty of buzz. This house hasn't been on the market for so many years,' said another, older chap, who was dressed almost identically.

To them, of course, the house presented a money-making opportunity. It was their job, and Sophie didn't blame them. For her, however, the prospect of handing over the keys to a complete stranger was horribly painful. It didn't matter how long Celia had been saying the place had to go, she still couldn't make peace with the idea.

Before the 'For Sale' sign was to be put up, she invited

Joe, plus Gigi, her children and assorted boyfriends and girlfriends for takeaway pizza.

Sophie was surprised when Gigi announced her husband, Mario, would be coming, too, as she'd been beginning to think he existed only in his family's imagination.

Because of the strange hours he worked at the fire station, it seemed he was always asleep when Sophie was up and vice-versa, so they'd never actually met.

From what she'd heard about him, though, she wasn't particularly keen to put that right. Convinced he was a bad-tempered, macho, Godfather-like figure, she was certain they wouldn't gel. She could hardly ban him, though. He was Gigi's other half, after all.

As there were next to no chairs left in Piping Plover House, Nino brought some plastic fold-up ones from home. Sophie lit a citrus candle and they sat in a circle, with their plates on their laps, sipping Coke, wine or beer, while they ploughed their way through large pizza slices laden with cheese, pepperoni, olives, prosciutto and tomatoes.

It soon became clear Mario was nothing like the image that Sophie had formed of him. Far from being large, loud and domineering, he was, in fact, quite small and rather quiet, as well as affable and unassuming. Wearing a stripy polo shirt, navy shorts and red espadrilles, he had a sizeable potbelly, a bushy grey-black beard and moustache and unusually hairy arms and legs. He reminded Sophie of a well-fed badger.

Unlike his wife, he seemed to have few opinions of his own, or ones he wished to share, anyway. Hiding behind his beard and moustache, he seemed positively alarmed when Joe asked what he thought of proposals for a new housing development nearby. The plans had just gone up online. It wasn't a particularly controversial question, but Sophie noticed Mario catch Gigi's eye, pleading for guidance.

Gigi was more than happy to oblige, being a right old chatterbox.

'It's a terrible idea,' she announced dramatically. 'The houses look like rabbit hutches and there's not enough space for residents' parking. It'll cause chaos in the surrounding streets.'

She'd obviously been to the hairdresser recently, because her purplish-red hair was shiny and bouffant. She was wearing lots of gold costume jewellery and very high black heels with golden bows on the toes.

Nino sneaked a can of beer and poured the drink in a glass, hoping no one would notice. Of course beady-eyed Gigi spotted it immediately and confiscated the glass. Mario, on the other hand, merely raised his beetling eyebrows and shook his head disconsolately.

Sophie decided his fierceness was just wishful thinking on Gigi's part, a ruse to try to frighten the kids. No wonder Gigi got so stressed, with no one to back her up. On the other hand, the children were turning out all right.

When they'd finished eating, the teens took Joe to their place to play table tennis, leaving Gigi, Mario and Sophie alone for a while. Gigi was thrilled Sophie and Joe had got it together and naturally wanted the lowdown.

'He's a keeper, Sophie, I'll tell you that for nothing.'

Sophie smiled. 'He's gorgeous. I adore him.'

She would have mentioned his bedroom prowess, too, but with Mario present, decided to hold her tongue.

When she recounted her Zoom call with William, both Gigi and Mario were agog.

'I'm so happy for you,' Gigi enthused, and even Mario was sufficiently moved to speak.

'That's quite a tale,' he said sombrely, smoothing down his moustache. 'You couldn't make it up.'

A car door slammed in the street close by and Sophie turned to look, forgetting her view was obscured by large shrubs.

'Thank you!' someone said, in an accent that sounded peculiarly English. There were other, quieter, voices too, and the sounds of bags being wheeled across the road.

'Are you expecting anyone?' Gigi asked, and Sophie shook her head.

Unable to contain her curiosity, Gigi stood up, rising on tiptoe to peek through the bushes.

'Oh my God!' She spun around, goggling at Sophie in disbelief. 'Your sister's here!'

Sophie thought she was joking.

'Don't be—' she started to say, but before she could finish, footsteps clattered on the wooden steps and who should appear but Celia, dragging her suitcase behind her.

Sophie was so shocked that for a moment all she could do was stare, while Celia gave a small, nervous smile. Soon after, two more people appeared.

'Layla! And Neil?' Sophie ignored her sister, running past to her daughter, and flinging her arms around her neck.

'What on earth… what are you doing here?' she managed to say.

They all started to speak at once, but fortunately, Gigi stepped in.

'Why don't you come and sit down? I'll fetch some drinks and you can talk about it, one at a time.'

Layla was tired and pale, but then she'd had a long flight and, unlike her mother, hadn't been by the beach. Also, the pink in her hair had started to grow out, leaving a rather odd, gingery parting.

None of this detracted from her loveliness, though. Sophie wanted to feed her, kiss her and spoil her rotten.

'I've missed you. It's so good to see you,' she said, taking her daughter's hand and giving it a squeeze.

'You too,' Layla replied. 'I only found out I was coming yesterday!'

Now she'd recovered from the initial excitement, Sophie had a million questions she was itching to ask.

'Why are you here? I thought you said you couldn't come because of work? Whose idea was it? Is everything OK?'

Layla appeared slightly shifty. 'I— Celia will explain.'

Sophie glanced at her sister, who was wearing a prim, white, broderie anglaise summer frock with puffed sleeves. She looked surprisingly meek, with her hands in her lap and one bare ankle crossed neatly over the other, but Sophie wasn't fooled for a moment.

The joyfulness she'd felt on reuniting with Layla rapidly switched to apprehension. It was obvious something was going on, but whether that something was good or bad, she couldn't tell.

Even Neil was acting strangely. When she glanced at him, his gaze quickly slid away.

'You'd better tell me what's happened.' Her voice sounded raspy and she swallowed a few times to clear the frog in her throat.

Neil reached out to put a reassuring hand on Celia's knee, and she smiled back gratefully. This only served to increase Sophie's unease.

Having witnessed her sister's embarrassing flirtation with Joe, she'd rather assumed her marriage was on the rocks. Now, Celia and Neil were acting like lovebirds. It was all very confusing.

Gigi returned with another bottle of wine, some cans of lager and a few extra glasses from home.

After setting them on the floor in the middle of the group, she sat down without a word and pretended to examine her long, pink fingernails.

Celia cleared her throat. It felt a bit like being in church, waiting for the vicar to begin the service.

'Since I got back to London I've been doing a lot of thinking,' she said at last, looking directly at Sophie. There was a rapt silence; you could have heard a pin drop. 'I've realised we're both victims of our family's secrets and lies.'

Sophie, who felt she had far more right to be called victim, frowned in annoyance, but Celia raised her hand. 'Let me finish, please. Hear me out.

'I think growing up in our unhappy family affected us both badly, in different ways,' she went on. 'Instead of being there for each other, it drove a wedge between us. You understandably hated me, because I was the favourite, and I was jealous because you had more freedom. I totally failed to give you any support.

'I wish I hadn't told you about your real father in the way I did. It was a horrible thing to do, and I'm sorry. I really want to try and make it up to you.'

At this, Sophie couldn't help snorting. She pulled a sceptical face, but Celia ploughed on.

'Neil and I have decided we don't want to sell Piping Plover House after all, we want to keep it and we'd like you to run it and manage it however you want.'

Sophie was momentarily lost for words. But then her eyes narrowed suspiciously. 'Is this some sort of sick joke?'

It was Layla who piped up next. 'It's true, Mum. Celia came to see me. She told me all about your father and everything. I'm really sorry. It must have been a huge shock.'

Mario had a minor coughing fit and swigged some beer to soothe his throat. No one seemed to notice, though.

'Celia thinks you should turn the house into a writers' retreat, or a yoga studio, or whatever you want,' Layla continued, with shining eyes. 'You've always loved this place. It seems only fair you should be allowed to fulfil your dream and keep it in the family.'

Celia went on: 'I won't interfere with any of your plans. The place is yours to enjoy. All I ask is that I can come and visit sometimes, maybe with Neil or the boys. I might do some yoga classes, if you have any, or join a creative writing course, or take up tai chi,' she added with a smile.

Neil put up his hand, like a schoolboy. 'Can I say something?'

'Go ahead,' said Celia.

'We're right behind you, Sophie,' he promised. 'I know we haven't been before, but we are now.'

His words seemed to come from the heart and his expression looked genuine, too. At last, Sophie's distrust began to melt.

'I'm shocked and amazed,' she said, looking at each one of them in turn. 'I don't know what to say. I never thought in a million years anything like this would happen.'

Her eyes glimmered with hope and she smiled, tentatively, for the first time since her unexpected visitors had arrived.

Seizing the moment, Gigi raised her glass. 'This definitely calls for a celebration. Mario, can you fetch that magnum of Champagne from the refrigerator in the garage? And ask Joe and the kids to come join us. Oh, and bring some nuts and pretzels. And Champagne glasses,' she cried after him, as he set off up the street.

Before long, there was a whole crowd of them on the porch, talking and laughing and sipping Champagne. Layla was taken aback to meet Joe and discover he was Sophie's new partner. She was so caught up in the general excitement, however, that she didn't bother to reproach her mother.

If Celia were taken aback, too, she didn't show it. In fact she spoke only a little to Joe. She wasn't in any way rude or standoffish, but didn't bat her eyelashes and flirt with him either.

Eddie was with one of his girlfriends, Diana. Tallish, blonde, and wearing a short, black miniskirt, Sophie recognised her as the one he'd been snogging in his driveway when Nino was fixing the bikes.

All the same, she noticed Eddie still managed to have eyes for Layla. It seemed he just couldn't help himself. Sophie knew Layla too well to imagine she would be beguiled by Eddie, captivating as he was.

Mariella's boyfriend, Danny, on the other hand, didn't leave his girlfriend's side. He must have been proud of his many tattoos, because he was showing them off in a citrus vest top with an unusually low neck. Sophie shuddered on seeing the ghastly, forked-tongued serpent again, slithering from his navel right up to his jawline.

Surrounded by so many adults, Nino might have been bored. He sat for a while, playing a game on his phone, until Neil went over to join him. Quite what they found to talk about was anyone's guess, but they chatted for a long time and Neil even had a go at Nino's game. Once or twice he gave a shout – 'Yesss!' – and Sophie saw him punch the air like a kid. She glanced at Celia, who raised her eyebrows.

It was past midnight when Gigi and family left. Everyone was a bit drunk and Mario hung on to his wife as they staggered down the stairs.

Sophie and Joe watched them from the bottom step, to make sure they arrived home safely. When they'd gone inside, Sophie, who hadn't given any thought to tonight's sleeping arrangements up to now, suddenly remembered there was only one bed.

'What are we going to do?' she asked Joe, with a frown. 'We can't all fit in my bed. Some of us will have to sleep on the floor.'

Joe was in no fit state to drive, but offered to call for a

taxi and put everyone up at his house. However, Celia soon joined them and explained she'd already booked herself, Neil and Layla into a hotel.

'I knew you'd got rid of practically everything. You've done an amazing job, by the way.'

'Thanks,' said Sophie, taken aback.

Celia touched Sophie's arm.

'Shall we have a quick look at the ocean?'

Again, Sophie was surprised, but it was a beautiful, balmy night so she agreed.

'Coming?' she asked Joe, but he shook his head.

'I'll leave you two to talk. You must have loads to discuss.'

As soon as they were alone, Sophie felt awkward and uncomfortable, just as she'd known she would. After all, almost any conversation with Celia led to a row. Even after Celia's unexpected offer on Piping Plover House, it would require a big leap of faith to believe she'd truly changed and wanted to be friends. Was Sophie prepared to take that leap?

She pondered this for a moment. She had tried for so long to convince herself she didn't care about Celia, but she'd always known it wasn't really true. She'd hated her sister, yet somewhere deep down inside she'd wanted her love, too.

At the entrance to the beach, Celia took off her white sandals. Sophie's feet were already bare. There was no one about and the contrast of pale sand and black, velvety, star-studded sky was ethereal and beautiful.

In silence, they made their way across the sand to the water's edge. Some lights, probably from fishing boats, twinkled in the distance, and the waves made a swishing sound as they lapped around their toes.

After taking a deep breath, Sophie decided to try to put aside her fears and misgivings for now. She mentioned she'd tracked down and spoken to her real father, and she'd found him warm and lovely.

Celia's response was instant and heartfelt.

'I'm thrilled and amazed,' she said with feeling. 'I never thought something so good could come from something so bad. I hope you meet him soon and start to form a bond. It sounds as if he's really keen to get to know you properly, which is a fantastic beginning.'

They were standing quite close together. Slowly and tentatively, Celia reached out to find Sophie's pinkie finger, and linked it with her own.

Sophie didn't move. In fact she hardly dared breathe. To her, this one small gesture meant more than anything in the world. It was the hope of reaching a new place of understanding and growth.

Of course, Celia didn't know about the letter Pampy had sent to William not long before she died. But it was late, Sophie was emotionally exhausted and she decided it could wait.

Just before they turned around, however, she thought about Pampy's words, and shivered.

I've decided to leave my home, Piping Plover House, to my two beloved granddaughters, Sophie and Celia. Some may find this surprising, as they never much liked one another.

I can't reverse the harm Sophie and her mother suffered… However, I hope my gift will bring happiness to the sisters, who loved the place so much. I also hope it will help them find a way through their differences. They need each other; we all do.

Sophie didn't believe in ghosts, omens or prophecies. And until recently, she would have scoffed at anyone who suggested the dead could send messages to loved ones from the grave.

Now, though, standing on Rockaway Beach beside her sister, gazing far out to sea while the others waited for them at home, she could swear Pampy was up there somewhere, looking down on them and smiling.

'Thank you,' Sophie whispered silently to the stars. 'You didn't forget me after all.'

Acknowledgements

A great big thank you to my sister, Sarah Arikian, her husband, Steve, and their expanding family. I've spent countless happy summers with them at their gorgeous Rockaway beach house, which of course provided inspiration for this book.

Thanks also to my fabulous agent, Heather Holden-Brown, and all at hhb agency ltd, and to my brilliant editor, Rosie de Courcy, along with the super talented team at Aria/Head of Zeus. I swear Rosie has the gift of being able to turn straw into gold!

Finally thanks to you, my readers, who have stayed with me on this journey. Your cheery messages give me more pleasure than you can possibly imagine. Please keep them coming!

About the Author

EMMA BURSTALL was a national newspaper and magazine journalist before becoming a full-time author. *Tremarnock*, the first novel in her series set in a delightful Cornish village, was published in 2015 and became a top-ten bestseller. Find her online at emmaburstall.com, or on Twitter @EmmaBurstall.